TAC LEADER

#1

What Honor Requires

Other Books by Bob Anderson

Sarge, What Now?
Grandfather Speaks
Anderson's Rules

TAC Leader Series

#1: What Honor Requires
#2: Night Hawks
#3: Retribution

By Jerry Ahern & Sharon Ahern
and
Bob Anderson

The Survivalist Series

#30: The Inheritors of Earth
#31: Earth Shine

For more exciting
E-Books, Audiobooks and MP3 downloads visit us at
www.speakingvolumes.us

TAC LEADER

#1

What Honor Requires

Bob Anderson

SPEAKING VOLUMES, LLC
NAPLES, FLORIDA
2013

#1 What Honor Requires

Editing assistance by Pamela Anderson and Kim Kuri

ISBN 978-1-61232-939-0

Question: "What do you call people who when faced with a fearful situation, do nothing?"

Answer: "Civilized?"

— Dialogue between Charles Bronson's character and his son-in-law from the movie *Death Wish*. This was following a vicious attack on his wife and daughter, that left the wife dead and the daughter terribly injured.

First Memory—
Year 1998

Doc heard them talking; hearing seemed to be the only sense he had that still functioned.

"Okay Nurse, what have we got?" the doctor asked.

Nurse – "Fifty-year-old, white male, with multiple bullet wounds, abrasions, and lacerations."

Doctor – "Have we typed and cross-matched?"

Nurse – "Yes."

Doctor – "Well, he got himself pretty well shot up, didn't he?"

Nurse – "Yes, but, as they say, you should have seen the other guy."

Doctor – "Okay, let's get started; put him all the way under."

'Doc' Roberts couldn't tell if his eyes were open or closed. He knew he was returning to the deep sleep from which he had just awakened. He knew his name, even if he couldn't remember it at the moment. He knew where he was, even if he couldn't remember it either at the moment.

The mask settled over his mouth and nose, and he decided he would take a nap and "think about it tomorrow." He was out.

Later, the doctor, still standing at the operating table, stopped and thought, *Four hours working on this guy. Man, I haven't seen a mess like this since I was an intern on the Lower East Side. I'm getting too old for this crap.*

Blood spurted onto his face shield, "More suction! Damn it, we're going to lose him if we're not careful."

While the nurse wiped away the blood, the doctor thought, *Buddy, if I'm too old to do what I'm doing, you sure as hell are too old for what you've been doing. You made 50, but I'm not sure you'll see 51. It would help if we were in a hospital. I need a damn x-ray machine. I'm digging around in you like it's 1880, and I'm a Dodge City saw bones digging a bullet out of the town marshal. You know fella, that's not a bad analogy. Who the hell did you think you were, Wyatt Earp?*

An hour later, Dr. Michael Fortuno told his assistant to "close him up." He had to get some coffee. His eyes hurt; the lighting was bad. His back hurt; the operating table was too low. He smelled bad; there were no air conditioners, just fans.

He stripped off the gloves, mask, and finally the surgical gown. He threw the entire bundle into the biohazard container. *The conditions might be 1880,* he thought, *but the precautions are still 1998.*

"Okay." He said, as he pulled a chair to the folding table set up in what passed as the doctor's lounge. "I dug enough lead out of that guy to sink the Bismarck."

Jean Bracken, the Nightingale, bagged her scrubs, mask, and gloves, pouring a mug of what passed for coffee.

"Thank you Mike," she said. "I owe you big time and so does he," she said, as she pointed to the man they'd just worked on for nearly six hours.

"You know," Dr. Fortuno admitted, "I don't know if he's going to make it or not. These conditions are primitive. I wish we would've had a more sterile environment. This guy might croak because some bugs got in while we were digging the lead out."

"Mike," she asked in all seriousness, "did you do your best?"

"Hell girl," he said flashing a grin, "I did better than my best. I thought we lost him on the table twice. Yeah, I did my best, the best I've done in 15 years. Kinda nice to know I still have 'it,' you know?"

"Yeah, I know," she said, as her dark eyes filled with tears. "Win, lose or draw, you have my thanks and his too."

"Jean," Fortuno said, as he leaned closer toward her. "You asked me to come, and I did. You asked for my help, and I gave it; but, I have some questions. Tell me more about this guy."

"Mike," she said, with both a smile and a tear, "like I said, he's a friend. His name is Marv Roberts, but everyone calls him 'Doc.' If he were conscious, the two of you would talk about what it is like to 'still have it.' "

"If he makes it, I can guarantee you one thing. He'll buy you a Jack Daniels and the best cigar you've ever smoked. If he doesn't, I'll buy it for him. You and I will get drunk, toast absent friends, and I'll cry a lot."

Part One
The Treasure Hunt

Chapter One

"RRRRrrrrring!" "RRRRrrrrring!"

Doc picked up on the second ring, "Hello."

"Good Morning," said the voice from the other end. Doc recognized the voice as Harry Devlin, better known as Hank, but he also had many other monikers and AKAs.

"Hey, Hank." Doc said. "What's going on?"

"Well," Hank began, "are you up for a mission?"

Oh God, what has he come up with this time? Doc thought. "Just what kind of 'mission' are you talking about?" He asked.

Basically, Hank's plan was simple. Three weeks from today, he wanted them to enter Mexico and go to an isolated region near the mountains of northern Mexico. Hank claimed to have it on "good report" that there was a deposit of undiscovered and "easily found" gold.

This had to be project number 2,097 in a seemingly unending line of projects Doc had heard Hank talk about over the years; but, for some reason, this one appealed to Doc. Normally, Doc would not have been interested in a project like this; but, the more he thought about it, he decided this might be exactly what he needed.

Doc was tired, more than tired. He'd become disgusted with the world and disgusted with himself. He'd all but quit running and hadn't worked out in karate in over a year. He started back on cigars after 18 smoke-free-years; he was putting on a spare tire, finding less hair on his head, and was now wearing bifocals. Worst of all, he just turned 50 in January.

He felt bad. He was bored. He was frustrated. He sure as hell was not where he figured he'd be at 50. Oh, he had his share of successes; some being pretty substantial. He enjoyed a decorated military career as an active duty Air Force cop and was now a First Sergeant in the Air Force Reserves.

He had two great kids, two wonderful grandkids, and a good-looking wife. Pam was Doc's third wife. He always said, "Third time's the charm."

Fifty or 50, however Doc said it, 50 was the hill, and he felt like he was over it. Five decades or half of a century, either way, there was definitely more time behind him than ahead of him. What did he have to show for 50 years of living?

The last 12 months had been difficult, the hardest for him in a long time. He had a business venture fail, he lost time, he lost money, he lost sleep, and he lost a friend; it was not a good year in his book.

He knew he needed to get focused and regain control of his life. He had made the decision to go back to school and finish a combined Master's and PhD program he'd been piddling with for three years. He also got refocused on his military career and made the decision to complete some too long delayed professional military education. Doc and Pam now had a second grandchild. This reminded him of how old he was getting.

Going back to school, though positive, seemed to be taking a toll on him. He was ready for a break. He needed to clear out his head. He knew if he didn't get his head screwed back on correctly, it would start damaging his relationship with Pam. Pam was the best thing that ever happened to him. She knew him and understood him.

So, for the first time in many years, he listened with real interest as Hank described project 2,097. Doc didn't expect they would really find gold; but right now, two weeks in the wild sounded exactly like what he needed. Hank was optimistic, as he said, "Maybe heaven will smile on us."

Hank, in addition to having an incredibly adaptive and analytical mind, probably was a borderline genius. In any event, Hank had one of the best minds Doc had ever come across, and he was also one of the three best bow, rifle, and pistol shots Doc knew.

Doc knew Hank's motivation was simple: self-satisfaction. It didn't matter if they found any gold; it was only important that they might, if there was actually any there.

When Doc explained the "mission" to Pam, she understood. Most of the time, she went out of her way to understand him and he the same. Over the next few days, Hank and Doc worked out the details of the trip.

Hank suggested they start the trip from his house in Presidio, Texas; this made sense, Presidio was on the Mexican border. He would allow two days to get there; a day to get to Rancho Dela Vega, then a day to get the campsite on horseback. Then ten days on site, and two days coming back, 14 days total.

It would be the perfect male getaway. They would camp in the field, ride horses, spit, and scratch, tell lies, and other essential male things done best without the censor of their loved ones.

They decided on the responsibilities each would have to properly prepare. Hank was over the technical gear and transportation to Rancho Dela Vega, a working ranch he'd located. He would make arrangements with them to obtain two horses and two pack mules for 12 days. Once there, they'd transfer the field and technical gear to the mules then head up to the mountains.

Hank would bring two small two-way radios, which he'd charge in the vehicle on the drive up. Most importantly, he'd bring the gold finder. According to Hank it was a "mineral analyzer" he'd been developing over the last couple of years and was the reason for this mission.

Doc planned to drive to Hank's house a few days before they started the trip. They would travel to Rancho Dela Vega in Hank's Ford F-250 pickup with extended cab. Doc was in charge of the camping supplies and field gear. He grabbed a pencil and paper and started planning for the adventure.

They would eat on the road driving from Hank's house to Rancho Dela Vega. The next day, they'd plan to get some food 'to go' from the ranch, something easy to munch on while riding the horses to the site.

After that, they'd eat a combination of freeze-dried camp food, military M.R.E.s, and lots of beans. When they returned to Rancho Dela Vega, they would enjoy real food again. On the trip back to Hank's house, they'd eat on the road.

Water would be their biggest concern. They would be up in the high mountains. Fortunately, since it was the fall season, it shouldn't be exceptionally hot during the day, but they would still have to strictly ration their water.

Doc began researching the known watering holes in the area they would be at. He would contact the people at Rancho Dela Vega; he was sure they could supply him with this information, especially since their animals would need watering. Any water retrieved from the watering holes for human consumption would have to be filtered. He'd bring water filtration kits for each of them.

Doc began staging the necessary items for their trip in the spare bedroom. Both he and Hank would need a small, single man tent with a floor and a medium weight sleeping bag. He knew it would be cold at night in the high mountains of Mexico. They would each need two Mag Lites, one six Cell C, and a Mini Mag Lite. He knew the Mini Mag Lite would come in handy and could be easily carried in their pockets.

He and Pam had invested in some good camping equipment. As he went through it, he set aside the items thought appropriate for this trip. His pile included bug repellent, a collapsible grill, coffeepot, two cups, one frying pan, one cooking pot, griddle, camp shovel, saw, and camp axe.

He would also carry his camera. He loved photography and thought it would be a good opportunity for some good picture taking. With the other items he'd staged for the trip, he placed his cased 35mm Nikon with one close up lens and an 85 to 210mm zoom telephoto lens.

Lastly, he located his repelling equipment to bring as well. He'd bring two 115' lengths of military gold line, two harnesses, and an assortment of hardware. He didn't know if they'd need it, but he thought it better to be safe than sorry.

They decided on simple and practical clothing. He and Hank would wear jeans with long sleeve denim shirts, denim jackets, and cowboy boots with riding heels. In addition, they would wear gloves, bandanas, and Western straw hats. He knew the sun would not show mercy.

They would both carry binoculars. In addition, they'd carry a fixed blade sheath knife and a sheathed folder knife on their belt. In their pockets, they'd carry a Swiss Army knife.

The next day, Doc called Hank. He updated him on the supplies and equipment he'd gathered and discussed what armament they would carry. Hank reminded him that the Mexican government restricted firearms possession and highly enforced it. Guns were not allowed on this trip. This made Doc very uncomfortable. "Well, they don't have restrictions on bows and arrows," Doc said to Hank, as he hung up the phone.

He walked into his "war room" and reached for his two P.S.I. compound bows, one for each of them. He set them both for an 80 lb. draw and packed an over-the-shoulder quiver for each. These included 18 broad heads and six field points. In addition, each had six broad heads in their bow mounted quivers.

The pouch on the over-the-shoulder quiver held two extra strings, a stringer, extra points, a sharpener, and a pair of wire cutters. He felt the bows would give some degree of protection against the wild beasties in the Mexican mountains, be they two-legged or four.

He looked over the pile of equipment and supplies. It seemed to be a reasonable and comfortable load for two pack mules and horses. He knew Pam would be pleased when he realized very little would need to be purchased. He and Hank had the majority of what was needed. If everything worked as planned, the entire two weeks would cost no more than $300 apiece. *Not a bad price for a working vacation to get one's head straightened out,* Doc thought.

He went back through his list again and realized that working out the mission requirements and logistics was actually kinda' fun. It was decided it would be best if he could arrive at Hank's a few days early, so they could go over the equipment, plans and details of the trip together.

When it was time for Doc to head to Presidio, he packed his gear in the back of his pickup truck, kissed Pam good-bye, and headed out of Houston on Interstate 10. It took Doc a little less than 10 hours to get there, but he decided it was worth it when he pulled into Hank's driveway. Hank and his wife Denise had a beautiful place, which consisted of 10 acres. The front three acres included their home site and an open field they used as a 100-yard rifle range.

The back acres were an absolute paradise. Deer and other wildlife roamed freely; wild turkeys came in from the neighboring lands and across the Mexican Border. It was heavily wooded with cane, chinaberry, and oak trees. The little creek, which marked the Mexican border, was a magical sight. It made beautiful gurgling sounds as it rushed across the rock and sand bottom. It was a place that Pam and Doc spent lots of time on previous visits.

Presidio stands on the Rio Grande on the opposite side of the U.S./Mexico border from Ojinaga, Chihuahua, about 240 miles south of El Paso. The junction of the Conchos and Rio Grande rivers at Presidio was settled thousands of years ago by hunting and gathering Indians. By 1200 AD, the local Indians had adopted agriculture and lived in small, closely knit settlements, which the Spaniards later called pueblos.

The first Spaniards came to Presidio in 1535, when Álvar Núñez Cabeza de Vaca and some companions stopped at the Indian pueblo. They placed a cross on the mountainside and called the village *La Junta de las Cruces*. Later, a penal colony and military garrison of 60 men were established near Presidio in 1760.

American settlers started coming to Presidio in 1848 after the Mexican War. They assimilated into the Hispanic population, and their descendants are primarily Spanish speakers today. During the Mexican Revolution, General Poncho Villa often used Ojinaga as his headquarters for operations and visited Presidio on numerous occasions.

Doc was glad he had agreed to arrive early. He knew it was important, so they could shake down the equipment, run a couple of function checks, and make sure everything fit the way it was supposed to. He learned a long time ago to double and triple-check everything; and then, check it again. Once they were in the field, they were stuck with what they had or without what they thought they did have.

He believed everything should have its place and be in its place. He knew most people had a tendency to pack either too much or too little. Hitting the groove of knowing exactly what is necessary is wisdom gained only from experience.

A long time ago, he learned that a personal "go-to-war" bag could mean the difference between comfort and discomfort, between life and death. A "go-to-war" bag was designed to carry little essentials that folks often forgot about. His was a waterproof Swiss Engineer's shoulder bag.

As they were going through the equipment, Doc said, "Did you know since the days of Roman legions, more soldiers and campers have died due to personal neglect than to any enemy or animal?"

Hank looked surprised, "Really?"

"Yep," Doc said, "most often due to a lack of foot and teeth care. That's why my 'go-to-war' bag contains mole skin, heavy duty toenail clippers, dry socks, extra eye glasses, a small first aid kit, toothbrush and other essential stuff. I also keep it separate from the rest of my gear."

"Good thinking Bubba," Hank replied.

They continued loading and unloading the equipment until they were both comfortable with what they had, where it was and how to get to it. As expected, some equipment was duplicated and could be left behind. There were just a few items they needed to pick up on the way out of town.

They were pleased with the process of staging the equipment and were confident they had what they needed. They had plenty of time to practice with the bows, try to out-lie each other, and visit with an old friend, Mr. Jack Daniels.

Doc told Hank there were several reasons he agreed to this mission. He said, "First, I just need to get away from my world for a while. Dr. John Gray, the guy who wrote the book *Men are from Mars* and *Women are from Venus* would call it 'needing to be in my cave for a while,' and he'd be right. Second, it gave me just the reason I needed to get back into shape."

Over the last year, Doc had practically well stopped running. He used to run three to five miles a day; he would use it as a stress reducer. On weekends, he would stretch his runs out from five to ten miles, which gave him the opportunity to lose himself in the rhythm of running.

He liked feeling his body in motion, moving. It was a feeling he knew most humans easily forgot, as they go through the day-to-day nonsense of making a living instead of living their lives.

Physical activity gave him a way to exercise, control weight, clear his mind, heal his heart, and test himself against himself. Karate was also very important to Doc. It gave him a way to address his physical capabilities as well as his spiritual and intellectual capabilities.

As a student of martial arts, he studied an Okinawan style called *Sho Rin Ryu Karate Do*. Through his studies, he learned how much there was to remember. As a sensei himself, a teacher of the martial arts, he found the more he learned, the more there was to learn.

His Sensei, Joel David, told him many years ago, "Do not learn Karate; become Karate!" Joel was one of the most influential people in Doc's life. Doc held his black belt for more than 22 years; however, he still encountered lessons Joel taught him long ago that he was just now ready to experience.

Doc found that one of the curses of having an education, either academic or experiential, is that simply 'knowing' does not prevent stupidity, pettiness, or laziness. But, one of the advantages of an education is that when you are ready to find your way back from the darkness, you know how to do it. Doc knew he was in one of the darkest holes he'd ever been in. But he was ready to climb out and knew he had the tools to do it.

The day Hank called about the mission, Doc threw away the cigars, cut back on the junk food, reduced his intake of 'Jack,' hit the streets running, and started working out again.

He knew his body well enough to know he needed to start reasonably with the running and was pleased with how he was doing. The first day, he ran one mile. On the second day, he ran two miles and stayed there for a few days. He knew this routine would allow his knees and quad ligaments to tighten back up. Plus, it would let his breathing abilities catch up with his mind.

He knew from experience that, after just a short period of successful running, he would have a tendency to push either too far or too fast. He knew this was not smart at 50, so he held back. For once in his life, he was intelligent about this process.

He knew he'd have the same tendency with weight training. His focus was to build up the chest, arms, and shoulders. He figured the sit-ups and crunches would take care of the waist. The running and karate would be sufficient for strengthening his legs and reducing the spare tire.

He didn't cut himself much slack. He started the process of running and weights at the same time. He held back on distance and weight for the first two weeks. By doing this, it would let everything "settle into place" and let his body get used to the new demands he was making on it.

By the morning of the third day, he was hurtin'. His chest hurt when he moved, breathed, or touched it. He knew that when his muscles hurt due to use, as opposed to abuse, he'd hurt until his muscles got used to the strain and were able to repair themselves. So, when he started hurting, he backed off of the weight, increased the repetition, but did not quit.

It was working. His daily running was getting significantly easier, substantially faster, and measurably longer. The pain was now gone from his chest and arms, beginning to feel substantially better.

He began working on his Katas. He explained to his neighbor who asked him what he was doing that "Katas are choreographed martial arts movements used to teach balance and technique combinations. They help prepare you for real life situations and opponents." His Katas improved to about the green belt level. He was still a ways from performing at the black belt level; but all in all, he was pleased with how he felt about his physical, spiritual, and mental progress.

Doc and Hank knocked off a few four-mile runs together. It was obvious to Doc that Hank had also been getting into shape. They practiced rigorously with the 80 lb. compound bows and were pleased it did not create shoulder problems for either of them. This was a major improvement.

They spent their last day in Presidio on final packing, final equipment checks, and a final run through the plans, maps, and other essential mission information.

Denise made a marvelous cucumber salad to go with the mouth-watering steaks Hank cooked on the grill. After dinner, they sat outside watching the sunset. Doc couldn't help but think, *Damn, it just doesn't get any better than this.*

Chapter Two

At 0530 hours, they started for the border in the dark. Hank felt they should take his F250 since it was larger than Doc's Dakota Sport. The F250 rode well, and they were comfortable with the gear stowed in the flat top shell that covered the truck bed.

Hank had a good radio, but Doc was glad he brought the Eagles on cassette because most of the local stations were in Spanish and he didn't speak Spanish. Hank insisted on calling this a mission. Doc didn't argue with him, even though he knew it was more of a quest than anything. During the drive, Doc learned that Hank was about as burned out as he was.

This was no great surprise. Although they lived their lives differently, the two were more alike than either of them would admit to. Their lives had always taken similar paths.

Although they were both respected in their professional activities, neither was where they wanted to be nor doing what they wanted to be doing. Interestingly, neither of them had a real good idea of what it is they wanted to be doing.

As Doc said, paraphrasing Sir Arthur Conan Doyle's hero Sherlock Holmes, "They had taken whatever was impossible and discarded that in favor of whatever was left. However improbable, it was possible."

Both Hank and Doc were making their livings doing the 'possible.' Doc found by doing the 'possible,' he was left with a dehydrated view of passion. He always believed that 'gain potential' was the better option. Gain potential is the possibility of gaining that which is sought, coupled with the possibility of losing that which is had.

Without the gain potential, without stretching, life can become rather vanilla, and for Doc and Hank, it had been vanilla. They both had succumbed to failures put on them by "lesser men and circumstances," but there was one thing they could not be faulted for. They both prided themselves for living by "The Code."

Years ago, it wasn't necessary to define "The Code." It was something that "men" in generations past just knew. No definition or explanation was necessary. In those days, when you used the term "man," it brought up images of strength and security; and, loving husbands and dads. Unfortunately, they found this was not so true today.

Doc still resisted defining "The Code." In his opinion, if you didn't know what it was, then you probably wouldn't understand his definition anyway. Doc was fond of saying, "Too often today, men get the blame for the males in the world. Being male is easy, trust me, I know. Being a man is much more difficult; trust me, this I know also."

So, there they were, two over-the-hill gringos headed for old Mexico, singing "Witchy Woman" along with the Eagles. They were headed for a quest they could not expect, to a place neither had been, and having the time of their lives.

Once they passed Customs and got out of town, it was easy to let the mood of the trip settle in. Going through Customs was pretty simple; the Mexican government favored tourism and with the exception of weapons, weren't too picky about letting people into Mexico.

The reverse would be true when returning into the United States from Mexico. Drug traffic is the biggest concern for Custom inspectors when people return from Mexico.

There were two simple facts Doc found to be true in his professional experience. The first is that more money can be made selling drugs to Americans than to Mexicans; and secondly, more money can be made selling guns to Mexicans than to Americans. *What a wonderful concept, thanks to NAFTA,* Doc thought.

Doc and Hank had neither guns nor drugs, so their plan was to simply drive across the international bridge, disappear, and return in about 12 days.

It took only a minute to get across the international bridge. Soon, they were out of the hubbub of the town and out of civilization. After driving only 15 minutes, it seemed they had traveled 150 years back in time.

Doc always believed that regardless of where you travel, once you get out of town and into the country, people are pretty much the same all over the world. It's only in those "civilized centers" of trade and commerce that the negative aspects of profit and abuse are found.

During his tour at Clark Air Base in the Philippines, he was amazed to learn the Negritos, the Philippine aborigine, did not have a written language until after World War II. They had to develop one for dealing with "civilized man" because they found that he would lie and could not be trusted. They existed for centuries with transactions based on individual honor and speaking of the truth.

The Negritos he met were generally barefoot, about five feet tall, gentle, hard-working, while they never complained and personified honor and truth. They did this in a manner he'd never found in corporate America or politics and only once in organized religion. He often wondered if the terms "savages" and "civilized" were not backwards.

About midday, they stopped to top off the gas tanks. Hank had auxiliary fuel tanks in the Ford, but they figured it would not hurt to top off, stretch a while, and take a break. The gas station had one pump and seemed to be older than Doc, but it worked.

Inside, what stateside would be called the service area, stood the oldest tire changing machine Doc had ever seen and a broken bubble tire balance machine.

In the next "bay" was a concrete pit area that a car would drive over to allow the worker to make repairs, change the oil, etc. The concrete had absorbed sufficient grease and oil that it now ranged from dark brown to totally black in color.

A stack of unsalvageable tires ringed the "driveway" rick-racked in the tight woven pattern that only a master tire man was capable of. Doc knew this; his dad had been one. This "tire fence" would still be standing long after the building had rotted away, which in this case appeared would happen in about two weeks.

Outside, a variety of fragrances swirled in the breezes, cooking smells, animal smells, and flowers of a dozen different types. They were so strong that when Doc closed his eyes, his mind could see everything by their individual smells.

The place was neat and functional but certainly not modern and fancy. The one concession to modern times was a sparkling new Coca-Cola machine standing in what appeared to be the office and living quarters for the owner.

Doc noticed only two electrical outlets in the entire place. One went to the Coke machine and the other to a vintage Zenith television with a black and white screen about the size of a saucer.

Hank nodded toward the TV and said, "How in the world do they still get tubes for something that old in this neighborhood?"

"Well," Doc said, "from the look of that picture, there's not enough current to burn a tube out. What is that, about a 1955 model?"

"Your guess is as good as mine," Hank said, "but I'll tell you one thing; when we come back through, I'm going to try to buy it off of him. I know a collector in El Paso that would pay a fortune for that relic."

They roamed around "downtown," while the owner, Jesús, serviced the vehicle. Jesús, unlike most American service station attendants, knew how to service a vehicle. He topped off both gas tanks, checked the belts, and checked the fluid levels. He then checked the tire pressure and had every window, headlight, and taillight spotless when they returned.

"Señor," Jesús motioned for Hank to examine one of the belts under the hood. "I would suggest changing this belt as soon as possible."

Hank agreed and asked if he had one in stock.

"No, Señor," Jesús lamented, "there are not many vehicles such as yours around here. But my cousin has a larger station in the next town, and I am sure he can help you. It's only 20 kilometers further on this same road."

Jesús gave Hank directions to his cousin's store and collected his money from Hank. He smiled when Hank paid him in U.S. dollars and, in short order, Doc and Hank were on the road again.

Exactly 20 kilometers later, they reached the station. Hank pulled in and explained to Jesús' cousin, whose name was also Jesús, what was needed.

Jesús #2 smiled and confirmed, "Si Señor, no problem. I will have you on your way in 30 minutes."

While they waited, they watched the local kids playing a Mexican version of stickball in the street. Thirty minutes later, true to his word, Jesús #2 waved for them to come back to the truck.

"Are you sure these guys aren't ripping us off?" Doc asked as they walked back.

"No, I forgot to change the damn belt. I knew it was bad," Hank said, "but with everything else going on, I just forgot. Besides, I checked the replacement and it's top-of-the-line and still cheaper than the Chevron in Presidio."

Jesús #2 waved as they drove off, and Doc realized he was really touched with these people and their lifestyle. Their life was totally uncomplicated by all of the inane bullshit that fills the average American's day. Sure, they were lacking in some of the luxuries, but they were also lacking in some of the complications and confusion.

They knew what their day would be like and took simple pleasure from simple things. At no place along the trip did Doc see excesses nor did Doc see the debilitating poverty common in the inner cities of their own country.

Yes, these people were poor by American standards, but they were not poor by their own. They were willing to work hard to have a better life. They only asked for a fair shot at that better life.

"You know what really ticks me off?" Hank said after about 30 minutes of silence and with a force he didn't usually use.

"No, Hank, what is it that really ticks you off?"

"You know my place butts up to the Mexican border, right?" Hank started.

"Yeah, I know that," Doc said.

"Well," Hank said, "every day and most nights you can hear the choppers fly over my place, and occasionally, you'll see the Border Patrol vehicles come down my road looking for these people."

Hank thought for a moment and added, "I don't know what makes me angrier, that they would illegally enter our country or that they would feel it necessary to illegally enter our country to survive. They fall prey to the 'Coyotes,' the S.O.B.s who agree to guide them illegally across the border. Half the time they either rip off their own people or kill them."

Doc knew what Hank was talking about. Just two days before, CNN had reported on a party of 28 illegals that had been found in a train car on a rail siding in Amarillo. All but two had died in the stifling heat and filth of that train car, and those two probably would not survive.

"Unfortunately, it is a pretty common story and an ongoing problem," Doc said, not knowing what else to say.

"Yeah, I know," Hank whispered, "but that doesn't make it right." Doc could hear his frustration gradually building. "These folks have dignity and are just doing what you and I would do if faced with the same economic factors."

"I agree," Doc said. He didn't understand the mindset of some people faced with famine, disease, or war. Why do they stay in a place where they are at the mercy of these conditions? Over the years, he'd met a lot of legal and illegal Mexican immigrants.

Sure, there is a criminal element among those who deal drugs, steal, rob, and even commit murder. But over the years, Doc had also determined that every society had this element. It is like the Chinese symbol Yin-Yang. In every light, there is some dark; and, in every dark, there is some light. Doc continued to think about this.

On occasion, a group or society might exist for a period of time without the criminal element, which is the case of some closed religious communities. But, these are like-minded people who have withdrawn from general society and isolated themselves from the rest of society. This isolation could be philosophical or geographical and was proven to work for a while.

When that element does not exist, the group or society develops the tendency to lose its "combative" edge. He'd studied groups that became too emotionally weak to withstand the criminal onslaught; the criminals discovered them as "easy pickings."

Doc related this to an old saying, "When there is a broad line of demarcation between thinking men and fighting men, you find your thinking done by cowards, and your fighting done by fools."

Doc knew most people didn't understand criminal behavior. Why should they? Criminal behavior is the aberrant behavior of a selected few who have for a variety of motives elected to breaking the rules. Most of the time, criminal behavior is as a result of a lack of ethics, personal values, or the individual strengths that encourage the majority of us to do the right thing.

Criminal acts, on the other hand, do not necessarily indicate criminal behavior. A moment of misjudgment or lack of responsibility can result in a criminal act that destroys lives, families, and careers forever.

Doc had found that not all criminal acts are committed by criminals. He subdivided criminal behavior into four categories: minor crime, serious crime, deadly crime, and evil crime. When the offender becomes repetitive or serial, a new dimension is added that is so diabolical it will strain the imagination.

These serial criminals, such as serial rapists, child molesters, and serial killers transcend conventional wrong-doing by adding horror and fear on a community level. These are truly urban terrorists.

In the past several years, Doc knew there was a movement growing in the United States to seek explanation or find justifications for acts that make no sense to anyone. How can a seemingly normal, loving, young mother strap her two sons in their car seats and drown them? Doc just could not understand this.

How can a Harvard graduate and teacher mail bombs to people for 18 years? How can a seemingly normal man murder, dismember, and eat his victims, right in the middle of a downtown apartment building?

How can a successful, bright, and engaging law student stalk and murder women in a five-state area? How can a respected businessman seduce, murder, and bury 27 young men and boys under his suburban home?

Doc tried to clear his mind of these wicked thoughts and focus on the adventure ahead.

Chapter Three

They arrived at Rancho Dela Vega at 1630 hours. They were glad to be off the road after driving for almost 12 hours. It was a beautiful place. It had an adobe main house and out buildings, a mountain backdrop, and a cactus and rock landscape.

It was a working ranch that also catered to the occasional gringo guest who was around for hunting, adventure, or a totally secluded amorous interlude.

Manuel Gutierrez, the manager, met them in the drive and arranged for their gear to be taken to the staging area near the corral. He escorted them into the main house and showed them to their rooms. The place was a mansion by any standards.

The cathedral ceiling of the great room was at least 20 feet high. The adobe motif was extended to the interior of the house with arching doorways and heavy exposed beam construction. Fresh flowers filled the room with the scent of a garden.

The furnishings were a beautiful, yet functional blend of black cast iron and dark, heavy woods covered with both tanned leathers and native weavings. The fireplace in the great room covered the entire wall. The mantel was a massive 6-inch thick mahogany slab that was 12 feet in length and polished to a mirror finish.

The firebox was equally large, well able to handle 5 or 6-foot logs. It was capable of heating the entire house by means of interconnected vents and ducts that went to each room from the central chimney.

They were anxious to check out the animals out at the corral, but decided a quick shower would do them some good. They not only smelled better, but were in much better moods. The original excitement of the trip was returning, since they were off the road and clean. Now, they could focus on the next leg of their trip.

After a quick tour and a fast snack, they were back at the corral to examine the animals and equipment they would be relying on for the next 11 days.

"Are you sure these guys are big enough?" Doc asked as he pointed to the size of the animals.

"Si, Señor," Señor Gutierrez was quick to answer. "I have reviewed your equipment specifications and weight allowances. I assure you these animals will be more than sufficient for your needs."

They checked the pack frames, lead ropes, saddles, blankets, cinches, bridles, bits, and saddlebags. It was obvious the equipment was not new. Yet, everything was in excellent condition, revealing that well broken in look of quality leather that has been used for hard work—used, but apparently taken care of properly with constant attention. They checked everything one last time and staged it all for final loading on the pack animals in the morning.

"I figure it will take about an hour to pack up in the morning," Hank said. "We have a full day of riding tomorrow before we get to the site. I want to leave a little before daybreak. That will get us a good start and allow us to make some distance before the sun is overhead. Hopefully, we'll get there before dark."

"I agree. It'll also give us some time to settle the animals and equipment in before we hit those foot hills," Doc added. "They'll be more used to us after a couple of hours and it should make for a more pleasant ride."

After supper, they watched the sun slowly set behind the mountains and suddenly discovered 10 billion stars in the night sky. Doc was putting the final touches on the primary edge of his Jack Crain Life Support System X with a Randall Norton stone and sipping Black Label Jack Daniels.

Doc was leaning back in his chair with his feet propped on the rail when Hank commented, "I know you favor big knives but damn! Where did you get that monster? Let me see that thing."

Doc passed the Crain over to him and said, "Years ago, I started reading a series called *The Survivalist*."

"Yeah, you told me about it, written by your friend, Jerry Ahern, right?" Hank asked.

"Uh huh," Doc said. "At the time I started reading it, I didn't even know Jerry. Anyway, I really enjoyed the series and the hero, John Thomas Rourke, who carried a Crain Life Support System X."

"Well, to make a long story short, Jerry and I eventually met, and I really liked him. A few months ago, we were discussing knives, and I asked him if he had one of the knives that Rourke carried in the book. He said he did and might be willing to sell it."

"I told Pam that Jerry had one of the Crain knives and that I really wanted it. I convinced her it would be a good 'investment' based on all I had read about it and the fact that it was the knife Rourke carried in the series."

"So, she goes behind my back and buys the thing from Jerry for my Christmas present. She kept it in my gun safe for three weeks, gift wrapped, before she finally broke down and gave it to me."

"Neat Lady," Hank said.

"You know it! Check this out," Doc said pointing at the etching on the blade.

"Damn, Life Support System X, Proto Type 01!" Hank read out loud.

"Yeah, although Rourke is fictional, I can truly say I carry his knife." Doc beamed.

"So, you're going to carry that monster into the field?"

"Sure," Doc said. "This is a twelve inches long, two inches wide, and a quarter of an inch thick blade, with an additional three-inch long cutting edge on top and made by one of the best knife smiths in the world."

"The double quillon guard is two inches long, a quarter of an inch thick, three quarters of an inch wide, and has a screwdriver point on each end. The eight-inch hollow handle is wrapped with silk cord, carrying a compass and enough stuff for a man to survive off of in the wild."

"The knife is virtually indestructible and the saw teeth will do everything from pop barbed wire to cut bone or wood. Besides," Doc said grinning, "it never let Rourke down."

Chapter Four

They rode for several hours. The morning was beautiful. Earlier, the breeze had been nice but was it was gone now.

Their shirts were just beginning to stick to their skins. They had taken off their denim jackets, rolled them up, and tied them to the saddles with the latico straps at the base of the cantle. Doc knew he would soon be thankful for the straw cowboy hats and bandanas they wore.

With a silent apology to Roy Rogers, Gabby Hayes, and Lash LaRue, Doc applied another handful of the SPF-40 sunscreen. He pitched it to Hank who also screened up before throwing it back.

They didn't talk much today. Part of the reason was that they had been together for three days now and had pretty well covered all of the subjects they had stored up since the last meeting, which was about nine months ago.

However, the bigger reason was that they were in awe of this country and its stark beauty; but for some reason, they were both feeling a bit uneasy. For the last two hours or so, Doc could have sworn he "felt eyes" on him; but as far as he knew, they were the only people on this plateau.

Hank didn't say anything, but Doc could tell he felt it too. With a nod of agreement, they moved further apart. They had fallen back on an old military patrol technique called spacing. Slowly, with about 10 yards between them, they continued to move across the plateau.

Under the guise of picture taking, Doc scanned the area with the telephoto lens, faking a shot every now and then. Hank appeared to follow an eagle with his binoculars, but it was not the bird he was looking for. The only sounds were those of the hoofs of the horses and burros clip clopping along on the hard ground.

The hair on the back of Doc's neck was standing straight up. This always happened when he felt uncomfortable in a place. To make things worse, his butt was really starting to hurt.

Hank guided his horse next to a stand of mesquite and dismounted. Doc moved next to him, dismounted, and did an exaggerated stretch that he hoped identified him as an out of shape gringo with a sore butt and no idea he was being watched. Doc moved closer to Hank.

Hank picked up his horse's right front hoof and appeared to be digging out a rock. There was no rock. When Doc was close enough, Hank said, "Do you see them yet?"

"Not yet. Why do you think there's more than one?" Doc asked.

"I can feel them on at least two sides," Hank said. "They are good enough not to be spotted, but they forgot something. A hunter never looks directly at his target; there is something extrasensory that happens when he does."

"The target can feel you watching." Hank explained. "Remember when you were in school or in a crowd and you felt someone looking at you? Eight times out of ten you found the person staring at you. The rest of the time you were simply too slow—they had already looked off." He kept fiddling with the horse's hoof, while he scanned the area in front of him.

Doc had positioned himself to face the area behind Hank and appeared to be taking an incredibly long drink from his canteen. He kept the mouthpiece covered by his hand so no one could see the screw cap was still in place.

"Nothing to see on this side either," Doc advised.

"Well, I guess we'll find out who it is when they are ready to show themselves." Hank grunted, "Sure wish I had my pistol."

"Yeah, I'd feel a lot better with the Widow Maker, myself." Doc commented, longing for his custom 45-auto loader. "Oh, what the hell, if you're going to wish, wish big. Give me a Mini-14 and three 30-round magazines." He laughed as they mounted back up and moved out.

Hank kept peeking around, but neither of them saw anything or anybody. An hour or so before dark, they topped a rise of a large hill and saw IT. The structure was more than a house or building. IT rose out of the ground like a small walled castle.

"Whoa," Doc said, "where the hell did that come from?"

"Wherever it came from, it hasn't been here long," Hank said. "It looks too new. It's quite a place. Do we go up or not?"

"No, I don't think so," Doc said. "It's almost dark. And while I'm not thrilled with the aspect of camping out on the hard ground, I'm less thrilled with the prospect of walking into a place that should not even be here, after a day of being watched by someone who doesn't feel like showing their face."

"What do you say we back off a mile or so, pitch camp, and check it out after daylight? We can at least see what is happening, if and when something does happen."

"Okay," Hank agreed. "I noticed a good camp site about a mile back. We'll get a good supper, and I'll take the first watch."

Before the night had settled over them, the burros were unloaded, a small fire had been built, and Hank had his tent set up. Doc finished stacking the gear, dug out the small cooking pot, and stirred up some Mountain Home freeze-dried spaghetti and meat sauce.

"You think you're going to need that tent?" Doc asked as he passed Hank a plate.

"Nah, I figure we'll stand separate watches and wrap up in our serapes and snooze," he answered. "I thought it would be a good distraction for whoever is watching us.

They finished chow, cleaned the pots and plates with sand, stowed the cooking utensils, and settled in for the evening. Doc found a comfortable and secluded spot that allowed him a good view of camp. The surrounding high desert also allowed him to keep an eye on his partner.

Hank found a similar position on the opposite side of camp about 50 yards away. With hand signals, Doc told Hank he was going to crash for three hours, that he had the duty, and to wake him if there was a problem. Hank acknowledged, and Doc settled down, wrapped in his serape with the big Crain LSX securely in his grip.

Close to midnight, Doc's mental alarm clock went off. He was awake and instantly aware of where he was and what was going on. Slowly, he rose up and spotted Hank. Hank nodded, signaled he was going to sleep and that Doc now had duty. Doc acknowledged and slipped downward out of sight, closely watching his surroundings.

The night was incredible; there must have been 10 million stars out, each trying to outshine the other. By 0300 hours, Doc had counted 24 minor shooting stars and six real humdingers. He had spotted two coyotes, a transient family of javelina, a monster owl, and an assortment of snakes and two horny toad lizards.

Still no bad guys, Doc thought. He opened the tactical cover on his wristwatch, an IndiGlo Iron Man, and read the time. He looked to Hank's position, and right on time, he saw his head come up.

They nodded to each other, and both stretched to warm up cold muscles cramped by long hours of inactivity. They settled in as they waited for morning. When the rose glow of morning started to show over the eastern mountains, they moved back to the campfire, and Hank put the coffee on.

"Well, what do you think?" Hank finally asked. "Where were the bad guys?"

"I don't know," Doc admitted, "but I know they weren't out here with us."

"That's a fact," Hank said. "I heard a small plane landing last night over in the direction of the castle. It was about 0400 hours. Nothing else though. Let's get a cup of coffee, break camp, mosey down to the castle and find out what's going on."

"I'll tell you one thing," Doc said, slipping into a scraggly old Hollywood voice he often imitated of the great cowboy character sidekick George "Gabby" Hayes. "It's like I told Lash LaRue, 'Lash, ain't none of us likely to get outta here alive.' " He snickered in a faithful representation of the old cowboy's laugh. "Well, Pilgrim. Let's get to it, we're burning daylight," he said, shifting into his imitation of the "Duke."

So, they mounted up and, after a short ride, came up to the structure they had seen the evening before. Even in the early morning light, it looked remarkably like a small castle. There was an eight-foot wall surrounding the house, garage, and yard.

Two gates, one for vehicles and one obviously for personnel stood along the front perimeter. The personnel gate opened onto a concrete walkway that led to the front entrance, which was a massive feature with heavy, double doors at least 10 feet tall.

The house, or castle, was two stories tall with what looked like battlements along the roofline. It was made of stone, a dark almost blood red rock that was not native to this area. Within the compound, which appeared to cover over three acres, was a satellite dish, an Olympic-size pool, a covered corral and tack room, a pump house and an electrical relay station connected to the 25 windmills located at the rear of the property. In front of the connected double garage, there stood a red convertible Mercedes Sportster.

They looked quizzically at each other and then simply rode up to the front gate and rang the bell. A voice intercom mounted in the wall spoke in English, "Yes, may I help you?"

"You're American?" Hank asked with surprise. The voice held no trace of accent.

"Yes, may I help you?"

"Well, no, I don't guess so," Hank said as he winked at Doc. They had decided to play it innocent as a naïve tourist. "We're just two Americans out for a relaxing vacation, and we thought we'd say hello."

The box remained quiet for several minutes before the voice returned. "I'm sorry; I do not get many guests out here. Please give me a moment to straighten up, and I'll buzz you in. Really, I am glad you're here."

About 10 minutes passed before the buzzer sounded to the vehicle gate.

They pushed the gate open and then led the horses and burros through to the covered corral. "Please, drop your gear and come inside; my man will take care of the animals," the voice said from another intercom station. The voice still offered no identification.

A vaquero appeared from the tack room and took the reins and lead ropes. He gestured toward the pathway to the house. Doc got the distinct impression that he did not speak because he could not. Of course, if he had spoken, it would have been in Spanish which would have done Doc absolutely no good anyway.

They approached the door to the manor, castle, or mansion—they couldn't decide what to call this place. The front door opened slowly, and a lovely Mexican girl dressed in conventional maid or servant's attire greeted them. She took their hats and guided them into the great room. It was even larger than Rancho Dela Vega.

If Rancho Dela Vega had been opulent, this place was grandiose. Where Dela Vega had been traditional, this place was modern, all glass and chrome.

Where Dela Vega had carried the sense of the Southwest and the Mexican culture, this place had a flavor all its own and Doc was not sure what that flavor was.

They waited for about 15 minutes for the Lord of the Manor to make his appearance. Down he came from the second floor, each step a study of movement in itself. Nothing was hurried, and nothing was rushed. Obviously, this was a man who prided himself on being in control, to whom power was essential.

"Good morning," he said finally. "I am Val, Val Richards." Doc and Hank recognized his voice as the one who had answered the intercom. Val moved to shake hands with both of them.

His handshake was firm and dry; Doc had expected an effeminate limp wrist, damp mackerel handshake. However, it wasn't the way he shook their hands that got Doc's attention the most.

As they shook hands, his eyes were intensely focused on Doc's. Doc noticed the same thing when Val shook Hank's hand. He gave the impression he was genuinely happy to meet them, but there was something more; Doc just couldn't put his finger on it yet.

He guided them toward the great room to be seated. Brunch was prepared and served. As they ate and visited, Doc evaluated their host.

Val Richards was about five foot ten and powerfully built. His wide shoulders and large arms belied his almost feminine mannerisms. His clothes, a tailored jogging suit, were casual but clearly expensive.

Doc realized that Val's running shoes would have cost over $200 at the outlet mall, where Doc had bought his.

The suit top was open, and since he wore no undershirt, a virtual mat of red and gray chest hair escaped. From around his neck, a heavy chain of beaten gold supported some kind of symbol.

His blonde hair was longish yet perfectly styled. Everything about him spoke of money, intelligence, breeding, and power. What the hell was he doing in the middle of the Mexican mountains?

They spent the next several hours in animated conversation with this most unusual man. He kept them stocked with Crown and Coke and some of the best cigars Doc had ever tried.

Val was very open with his history. His family was from back east, but he had moved to Texas several years ago where he earned his MBA. He made a comfortable fortune handling the financial dealings of several medium-sized corporations before he decided to go independent.

That was about three years ago, and he had done extremely well, which was obvious by the size and condition of this place. He said that this was in fact one of three "retreats" he owned. His business required that he travel a lot, so he simply maintained a complete domicile in each of his primary areas.

When he spoke, he dominated the conversation. When he listened, he did so with an intensity Doc had never seen before. It was as though Val was recording everything that was said, every movement that was made, even the nuances of speech, gestures, and inflections. He did not just communicate; he absorbed whatever was going on around him.

If you were the subject of his attention, you were the focus of all of his attention. When he changed focus to the other person speaking, the shift was complete. It was as though the non-speaker did not exist until Val Richards acknowledged that person with his attention.

Through it all, he was articulate, glib, intelligent, and well-versed on virtually any topic that came up. In fact, he was totally engaging, and the time passed quickly.

Val Richards glanced at the Rolex President on his left wrist. "Gentlemen, the time has flown. I have thoroughly enjoyed our visit, and I insist you stay the night. Let me show you to the guestrooms where you can shower and clean up."

"We are extremely casual here; there are jogging suits and slippers in each room that should fit you comfortably. Please, indulge me. I assure you that a pleasant meal and good night's sleep indoors will be appreciated when you continue your journey in the morning."

"Sounds good to me," Hank began. "What do you think?"

"Why not," Doc answered as they climbed to the second floor. "I have to agree that I look forward to at least one more night in a bed before camping out among the cactus again."

The guestrooms, each with its own bath, were tastefully appointed. The view from the double windows was impressive. Disposable razors and toothbrushes, along with a variety of deodorants and shaving lotions, indicated that Val Richards was in the habit of entertaining. Doc found that interesting since Val had claimed to not have many guests.

A quick shave, a relaxing few moments on the throne, a hot shower and Doc felt rested, clean, and ready to tackle the evening. The jogging suits fit, and the slippers felt like heaven after wearing boots for three days.

Maria, the maid, collected their dirty clothes and assured Doc they would be cleaned and pressed by the time they returned from the evening meal.

Doc met Hank at the head of the stairs. Their jogging suits matched; they looked better and certainly smelled better.

"Almost like uniforms aren't they?" Hank asked indicating the matching suits.

"Yeah, I was thinking the same thing; what the hell is this thing?" Doc pointed to the embroidered symbol above the left breast pocket.

"I don't know," Hank answered, "but it appears to be the same symbol Val Richards wears around his neck which looks like solid gold. Probably a family crest or business logo, but it is far too complicated for my taste."

Supper was excellent, consisting of a marvelous salad, a steak grilled to perfection, and a twice baked potato. The fare rivaled the best restaurants. The food was not simply served; it was presented. and it tasted as good as it looked.

The wine selection was excellent, according to Hank who knew about such things. He and Val Richards discussed the bouquet, color, etc. Doc, with somewhat simpler tastes, asked for another Tecate, a popular Mexican beer.

"So, tell me about the project that brings you here," Val Richards directed.

Doc nodded at Hank, since it was really his idea and Doc was just along for the fun of it.

"Well," Hank began by looking off into the distance to gather his thoughts "without going into a lot of technical detail . . ."

"Oh, that's okay Hank," Val interrupted, "I am sure I can keep up with you."

Hank smiled; he did love a challenge. "Okay, about a year ago, I began development on a device that locates specific metals, raw and refined," he began.

"Really?" Richards said, "Magnetic, I presume."

Hank smiled. "Not really, actually it is based on harmonics." Hank was in his element and launched into a 45 minute dissertation on metallic resonance, harmonic reflection and absorption resulting from a variety of mediums, such as air, water, dirt, and rock.

Doc had not understood it the first six times Hank explained it to him and was sure he wouldn't understand it this time either. So, he decided to excuse himself. No one seemed to notice however, so while Val Richards sat apparently enthralled by Hank's explanation, Doc took another Tecate and one of those great cigars and headed out back to the veranda.

"A good cigar is like a good woman, hard to find and requires a lot of attention," he quoted as he struck the match and held the fire to the tip. While you don't have to inhale to enjoy a cigar, Doc had always thought "If you're going to smoke, smoke." He inhaled a lung full, let it out slowly, and took a sip of Tecate.

Doc was amazed how quickly the day had gone by. The evening was again beautiful; the night perfumes were moving on the breeze. Hank had found someone who would listen to him. The Tecate was cold, the cigar was excellent, and his butt didn't hurt. Doc whispered, "It just did not get much better than this."

His eyes were adjusting to the darkness when he saw something. About halfway between the covered corral and the electrical relay station was a small concrete structure that protruded out of the ground about a foot. It was surrounded by a large, round garden of cacti. Doc only saw it because of the angle of his view. With Tecate in hand and cigar in mouth, Doc strolled off the veranda and toward the, whatever "it" was.

Moving along the path, he could tell it was the entrance to something. The door looked almost like the tornado shelters common in Texas and Oklahoma, except that everything but the doors was totally underground on this one.

Doc wondered, *Why have an underground structure in your backyard that can only be accessed by walking through a garden of cactus plants?*

"Curiosity killed the cat," Doc mumbled as he neared the structure. He was purposely walking as though he'd had too much to drink.

His attention was deliberately unfocused on anything, yet he was able to coast, stumble, and amble along closer and closer to the concrete enigma. Standing with his legs spread comfortably, he tugged down the front of the jogging suit pants and took a leak on the cactus garden.

"A man needs a place he can piss off the back porch if he wants too," Doc quoted his son, silently taking mental measurements of the doors, frame, and concrete support structure. This, like the house, was brand new and was equally well-constructed.

This was not the door to a seldom-used tornado shelter or root cellar. They don't even have tornadoes in this part of Mexico. Even the walkway to the semi-hidden door was eloquent. Patio blocks that floated on the gravel would have worked just as well.

This was a damn sidewalk, and it did not just lead to the door; it wound up at the door after several turns. That was why Doc had almost missed it; the door and the walkway were camouflaged.

Who the hell camouflages the entrance to a root cellar in his own backyard in the middle of the Mexican mountains? "Only a very careful man trying to hide something," Doc said softly.

Part Two
The Devil's Den

Chapter Five

Doc heard a muffled footstep behind him and made an exaggerated motion of upping the front of his pants and exclaiming with obvious satisfaction, "Oh yeah, that's better!" before turning around.

Leaning against the covered corral wall was a whip-thin man in western cut clothes. Continuing his act, Doc whistled and stumbled back toward the veranda, showing no indication he'd seen the man.

"Lovely night, eh?" the visitor said almost in a whisper. Doc jumped as though he had been startled.

"Hell's bells! I didn't see you there," Doc lied. "Hope you don't mind me watering the cactus, but you gotta go when you gotta go." Doc laughed and stumbled toward him.

"Howdy, I'm 'Doc' Roberts, didn't see you around earlier." Doc wiped his hand on his bandana and sized the man up before shaking hands.

"I just got back," the man explained in an unnervingly soft voice that had the inflections all wrong. It was almost as though he was singing softly rather than speaking quietly.

Doc figured his accent was New England, Vermont or New Hampshire. His speech patterns also indicated an Eastern background; he identified himself as Jamie, just Jamie. He explained he was a "friend" of Val Richards and was also staying over.

"I didn't hear you drive up," Doc told him.

"Oh," Jamie whispered, "I was out horseback riding and came in the back gate; it's at the other end of the corral."

Doc looked and could see a horse tied at the back gate. That meant Jamie had seen Doc at the cactus garden, dismounted, and quietly moved up to watch him. Something was definitely weird, and weird in Doc's book usually meant something's wrong.

"Well, come on Jamie," Doc said wrapping his arm around Jamie's shoulders and pulling him toward the house. "Let's get back and get another beer, I'm buying!" Doc laughed good-naturedly, drunkenly, and he hoped convincingly.

"Sure thing, Sweets," Jamie whispered. Doc definitely did not like this guy. He did not like his aftershave, he did not like his accent; and Doc especially didn't like the fact that Jamie was wearing a shoulder holster under his western cut shirt.

Doc had suspected as much because Jamie was standing with his shirt unbuttoned to mid-chest and his right thumb hooked nonchalantly at the belt. Doc confirmed it without reacting when he wrapped his arm around Jamie's shoulder and both started moving toward the house.

Jamie and Doc walked in the house like old buddies, but Doc shot one glance at Hank, reading his eyes instantly. Jamie was introduced to Hank, but Val Richards clearly knew Jamie and was visibly excited to see him. He asked, with that now irritating intensity, "Jamie, everything go all right?"

"Sure, Val, no problems at all. I'll tell you about it later," Jamie whispered. "Right now who wants to party?" He pulled a mirrored serving tray from the wet bar and wiped it clean.

Doc suspected what was coming next. "Not me man, I'm wasted," he said quickly without taking overt notice of what he was doing. "I'm crashing, early day tomorrow. Thanks, Val. It's really nice of you to entertain two strangers like this. The food was great, the liquor wonderful, and those cigars are sinful!" Doc laughed and shook Val's hand.

"Anytime fellas," Val graciously gestured toward the kitchen, "Maria will have breakfast ready at about 5:30, and you can't hit the trail hungry." He laughed, they laughed, and Doc nodded toward Hank. "Help me upstairs partner. I think I've had too much Tecate or Crown or something."

"You never could hold your booze," Hank laughed and grabbed Doc under the arm helping him to stand. "See y'all at breakfast, if this dead beat wakes up."

Hank laughed some more, and they moved up the landing. "What the hell is going on?" he whispered. "I've never seen you drunk; what gives?"

"I'm not drunk, you asshole," Doc whispered back. "We have to talk now, and this seemed a good way to get you in my room without anyone paying particular notice." Doc purposely stumbled, and Hank almost dropped him.

"Hang on, Cowboy," Hank said loudly and looked over his shoulder, winking at Jamie and Val Richards and mouthing S-O-R-R-Y. Jamie just stared; Val Richards flashed his hyper-white smile and waved, always the gracious host.

Before they entered Doc's room, Hank put an index finger to his lips and then pointed to his ear, his eye, and then door. He was signaling that he felt as though whatever they said in the room could or would be overheard and even seen by someone else. Doc nodded that he understood, and with a smile, began conversation for other ears to hear as he pushed the door open.

"Man, I'm sorry, but I feel like hell." Doc winked and nodded toward the bathroom.

"Okay," Hank said smiling, "before this gets any worse, I'm going to put you where you can't make a mess."

They headed toward the john, and once inside, Hank turned the shower faucet to hot and let the room fill with steam and the sound of running water.

"There," he whispered into Doc's ear, "that should take care of any microphones and camera lens, provided no one is tacky enough to bug the crapper."

"Yeah, it should," Doc said keeping his voice low. "What do you think is going on here?"

"I don't know man. This guy Richards is as out of place here as a turd in a punch bowl," Hank said as he scratched his head. "He has too much money, and he's in the middle of nowhere. His story is either total bullshit, or this guy makes more money doing what he claims to do than anyone I've ever heard of."

"I agree. Something is way outta kilter here." Doc leaned over to give a couple of healthy heaves and gags for the hidden mikes. He made sure to be loud enough to be heard over the running shower.

"I found something out back that makes no sense either." Doc told him about the door and the concrete entrance camouflaged in the garden.

"Luckily, I was play acting because our boy Jamie spotted me by the garden, parked his horse at the back gate, and tried to sneak up on me."

"You said 'tried,' so I assume you were able to cover yourself?" Hank asked hopefully.

"Oh sure, I was taking a leak. He may be suspicious, but it's all suspicion at this point," Doc assured Hank.

Hank began, "Okay, we're a good 40 miles from anywhere, in a place that can only be reached by one road, horseback, or air drop. We are in a castle, inside a compound. The house staff alone consists of at least three people, not counting the chef."

"Add Val Richards, his guest Jamie, the ranch hands necessary to cover what Val Richards says is the extent of his spread, and we're up to 12 maybe 15 people. But so far, I've only seen the maid, the vaquero that took our animals when we arrived. We know there's a chef, but we haven't seen him."

"I figure that totals up way less than half the folks we should be seeing here. Combine that with a tornado shelter supreme in a non-tornado region, and disguised at that." Doc said, "Plus, the stealth approach of our boy Jamie, and oh by the way, he's packing."

"Yeah," Hank said smiling, "a Glock, probably a Model 17 under his left arm. I spotted the butt when he reached for that glass of White Zinfandel downstairs."

"What's your best guess?" Doc asked already figuring drug runners. "Well, the way our boy Jamie was preparing the serving tray," he answered, "I suspect our boys downstairs are enjoying some coke and I don't mean 'The real thing.' "

"Yeah, that was my guess. Let's get a goodnight's sleep and get the hell out of here tomorrow. The hair on the back of my neck hasn't lain flat since we got here," Doc complained as he rubbed the back of his neck.

"Sounds like a plan to me. Sleep with one eye open and that butcher knife of yours close by," Hank said winking as they prepared to leave the bathroom.

Doc washed his face and moistened his hair, remembering to splash water on the front of the jogging suit. He opened the door and stood face-to-face with Jamie.

Jamie had brought Doc's clothes, which he laid out on the bed. They had been cleaned and pressed. Even the boots had been cleaned and shined and the spurs properly reattached.

"Peaceful dreams, Sweets," Jamie purred.

Out of spite, Doc blew him a kiss—Jamie frowned. Doc smiled; Hank shook his head and went back to his own room. Doc locked the door, wound and set his West Bend Travel Clock for 0430 hours, then slipped out of the jogging suit and back into his own clean underwear. Before going to sleep, he positioned his clothes and boots where he could find and slip them on in a hurry if need be. *Always plan ahead,* he thought.

He went to the bathroom and turned the sink faucet on for a drink of water. On the way to the bed, he drank the glass of water and set it on the nightstand. Next, he turned the light out, pulled the Crain from its sheath, slid it under the blanket, and silently prayed he didn't roll over on it during the night.

Chapter Six

Downstairs, Jamie's face was purple with rage. "What do you think you are doing?" he hissed.

"Jamie, Jamie," Val Richards said and flashed his best smile. "Don't get excited, I was just having a little fun. This is the first time we've had *unexpected* guests. I wanted to test our security, and so far, I am extremely pleased. Besides, you watched them for most of the day yesterday. You told me yourself that they were just sportsmen out for a camping trip."

"I told you that's what they looked like to me. But, I can't be sure. I know they are not as naïve as you apparently want to make them," Jamie whispered, his face still livid. "I don't like the idea of 'testing' security. No one should even be here that we didn't bring!"

Val Richards prided himself on being in control. Hell, he was control. "Jamie, right now, two strangers are sleeping upstairs. We did not bring them; it was by sheer luck that we knew they were coming."

He walked slowly around the couch, his voice remained calm and his gaze remained detached. He picked up a crystal ashtray from the end table and closed the distance to Jamie. "I believe," Val continued, "that shows the potential for unexpected guests to arrive even in the middle of the wilderness." He smiled benevolently, set down the ashtray, and smashed his fist into Jamie's unprotected gut.

Jamie, with his breath gone and his gut wrenching, collapsed on his knees. After a moment, the first attempts to obtain oxygen were rewarded.

Val Richards sat on the edge of the couch and stroked Jamie's hair back into place. "Jamie," Val said looking directly into Jamie's red and tearing eyes. "Never, ever use that tone of voice with me again."

He spoke quietly, his voice controlled with just a hint of danger. He knew that made him all the more dangerous in Jamie's mind.

"Besides," Val laughed gregariously, "tomorrow they leave, none the wiser, and we have a wonderful weekend planned. Remember?" He licked his lips in anticipation.

Jamie regained his footing and his ability to breathe. He nodded, smiled, and started for his own room. *Yeah, they'll leave in the morning,* he thought, *but now someone knows where you are, you arrogant asshole, even if they don't know who you are or what you're doing here.*

Chapter Seven

Doc was awake before the alarm went off but just laid in bed listening. He had not set his mental alarm, and the West Bend had not gone off yet. That meant something had awakened him, but he didn't know what.

The Crain was where he had stashed it, and he pulled it close. Still feigning sleep, he tossed and turned over so he could see the face of the travel clock. It was 0350, and his senses were on full alert; but, there was nothing he could see.

The house, though he thought of it as a castle, was quiet and dark as a tomb. Outside, a full moon and the same 10 billion stars as the other night lighted the area almost as brightly as daylight.

Keeping out of the light from the window, he crept slowly toward it. As dark as it was, any camera operating in the room now would have to have infrared to see anything. Sound was his biggest concern.

Wearing nothing but his jockey shorts and the Crain, he slowly drew back the hidden edge of a curtain. Looking between the curtain and the window frame, he examined the grounds between the house and the covered corral.

He watched for about 10 minutes and was starting to head back to bed and write off the eerie feeling as his own imagination when something caught his eye. One of the cacti in the little garden was beginning to glow. Doc looked closer and realized that it was not glowing; rather it was being illuminated by the light coming from the doors to the "tornado shelter" secreted in the middle of the garden. The double door was opened from below, and he watched as someone quietly laid the doors fully open against the concrete frame.

Jamie's head poked out of the entrance and turned slowly; his eyes devoured the grounds for a sign of anything or anyone out of place. He stopped.

Remembering what Hank had said, Doc shifted his gaze to a spot about a foot from Jamie. Jamie turned and looked slowly up toward Doc's window. Doc let his mind go blank and refused to look directly at Jamie.

Jamie shrugged and went back downstairs. After a slow count of 10, he reappeared. Working quietly, but with practiced skill, he hoisted what looked like the world's largest garbage bag out of the hole and onto a little cart a few feet away.

As Jamie pulled the cart with its load toward the covered corral, there was a squeak as the rollers moved on the uneven surface.

That must have been what woke me up, Doc thought.

Jamie moved toward the corral and disappeared. A few minutes later, Doc saw the back gate open and watched as a Jeep Cherokee with its headlights off quietly exited the compound.

Hell of a time to be emptying the trash, Doc thought and went back to the bed and just lay there, thinking.

At 0430 hours, the alarm went off; Doc flipped the lights on and made a big production of standing in the window stretching and scratching. The gate was still open.

Okay, he thought, *Jamie's not back from the trash run.*

Doc jumped in the shower for a quick wake up, toweled off, shaved, and brushed his teeth at the sink. As he passed the window, he noticed the Jeep Cherokee pulling into the compound. Its lights were still out. The total elapsed time was 45 minutes.

Interesting, Doc thought. He slipped into his freshly washed denims and freshly polished boots. Collecting his pocket trash from the nightstand, he buckled on the Iron Man.

The previous evening he had removed the Crain and wrapped it in his denim jacket before they entered the house. It just seemed like a good idea, more polite.

Most folks don't care for someone walking around the house with a short sword strapped on. Besides, if he needed it, he wanted it to be a surprise.

However, he was not in a good mood this morning, so he ran his belt through the loop and buckled the Crain to his left side. He knew he was making a statement, and he didn't really care.

He met Hank at the landing to the stairway. Both were carrying their personal gear.

"Sleep well?" Hank asked. "Like a dead man," Doc lied.

"Me too," Hank lied.

It was 0515 hours when they hit the kitchen. The coffee was on, the bacon was frying, and the eggs were cooking. The biscuits were already baked. Doc snagged one that was already buttered and sat down with the coffee mug.

"How far is the site from here?" Doc asked Hank.

Hank glanced at his watch and replied, "We should be there shortly after noon."

Val Richards walked in with that too-white smile and too-happy demeanor. "Good morning, fellas. You ready to hit the road?" he asked.

"Yep," Hank answered, "as soon as we stock up on some of these vittles. Man, if it tastes half as good as it smells, it will be great." It did, and it was.

By 0610 hours, they were loaded, saddled, and ready to go. As they rode slowly out of the castle grounds, Val Richards waved; they returned the wave, and the horse Hank was riding broke wind. Jamie was not to be seen.

They said nothing until they were well out of site of the castle and out of the pickup range of even the most sophisticated listening equipment. Hank pulled up next to an outcropping and dismounted.

"Okay," he said, "time to compare notes and figure out what the hell is going on back there."

Doc squatted next to him and told him about waking up, Jamie's movements, and the garbage run.

"How long was he gone?" Hank asked.

"I timed 45 minutes, exactly," Doc answered.

"How big was the garbage bag?" Hank asked. "How much would you say it weighed?"

"I would guess the weight at about 100-125 pounds. The bag was long and cylindrical and it appeared to be completely full. I would guess about 6-feet by 2-feet."

"What color?" Hank asked.

"Couldn't tell for sure," Doc said. "It appeared black, but it could have been a dark blue, dark green or very dark brown."

"You know what you're describing?" Hank frowned.

"Yeah, that's what it reminded me of also; a body bag," Doc admitted.

Doc was familiar with body bags. They had been around since the Vietnam War. Tough, durable material with lateral zippers and carry handles; body bags were considered the "glad bags of coffins." Most of the time, body fluids did not leak out, and the smell of decomposition was held inside until the zipper was moved.

Originally they were designed to move the dead from the battlefield, now police departments, EMTs and fire departments used them as well as rescue and recovery units across the country. Civilians could even order them out of a few catalogs.

"Okay, hold on," Hank winced. "We just spent the night in a mansion with some of the best food, liquor, and cigars I've had in a long time. Our host was 100 percent appropriate, though a bit different I will admit."

"Nothing was really out of order, nothing that could have been construed as being negative. Hell, he invited us to stop in on our way back. Now, you say you saw his other houseguest hauling out the garbage at 0400 hours, in what we think was a body bag. Is it just me, or does this sound just a little nuts?"

"I know it sounds crazy!" Doc said frustrated as well. "Okay, answer me this. Why does a guy empty the trash at four in the morning when he has to haul it off to some other place that is at least 20 minutes away and makes the trip with the vehicle lights off? Riddle me this!" Doc quoted as he remounted his horse and continued off in the direction they had been traveling. "Riddle me that!"

Hank rode in silence for the next two hours. Occasionally, he would turn back to look at Doc. He would stare for a moment and then shake his head.

By 1330 hours, they had reached the campsite. They reined in, dropped the supplies, and made a remuda by tying off one of the ropes between two trees and tying the two horses and two burros to the rope. They set up camp without much conversation. Doc built a small fire, and Hank broke out the beans and cooking pots.

Finally he said, "Okay, so what do you figure is going on, drugs?"

"At least that, for sure," Doc answered, "but I think there's a lot more going on in that castle. Val Richards is too smart and too sophisticated for just drugs. Hell, he's just too damn 'too.' "

"He is smooth," Hank agreed.

"He reminds me of a guy I used to work for," Doc said thinking out loud. "He could be amiable, articulate, and one of the most charming men you have ever met. He had a degree in counseling and a MBA like Val Richards, and like Val, he was really different."

"How so?" Hank asked.

"Well, looking back on it," Doc began, "I sincerely believe the guy was a sociopath. What's more, I know he had a professional psychological background. In my book, that simply confirms the fears he had about himself. I have never known anyone who studied psychology that was not at least a little afraid of their own selves. I think Val Richards is in the same boat but even more twisted. He may even be a psychopath!"

"Well, Dr. Roberts," Hank began pompously, "how did you arrive at this diagnosis?"

"First of all," Doc countered, "it is not a diagnosis; it's a hunch."

"Well of course," Hank said smirking, "I am familiar with that highly technical psychological term."

"Let me finish, wise ass," Doc said as he pitched a rock at him. "First of all, there was not a single picture or photograph on display in the castle. Did you notice that?"

Hank nodded in agreement.

"Second of all, every room in the house had at least two mirrors," Doc continued, "except the dining room, which only had one and it is directly in front of where Val Richards sits at the table. Third, Val Richards is obviously someone who prides himself on always being in control."

"I'll bet the man rarely loses his cool, and when he does, it is for special reasons and circumstances. Fourth, not much by itself, but did you notice he never told us the name of his company?"

"Fifth," he said ready to conclude, "there are no signs of normal socialization inside that house; none from Val Richards, none from Jamie, and none from the other employees."

"I have seen Holiday Inns with more personality and lived-in quality. Plus, remember what Val said about not usually having visitors?"

"Yes," Hank said. "So what?"

"Well," Doc responded, "I counted 22 rooms in that damn castle, not counting bathrooms. Drop Val's room, Jamie's room, Maria's room, and one for the chef, the kitchen, the great room, and the exceedingly large utility room; that's 15 rooms unaccounted for—a bit much don't you agree?"

"It leaves me thinking we have a compulsive, power-oriented, narcissistic, avoidant personality type with too much money, weird friends, weird habits, a tornado shelter where there are no tornadoes, too many empty rooms, and 'a partridge in a pear tree.' "

"Did you ever figure out what that medallion was Val had around his neck?" Hank queried.

"No, some kind of symbol," Doc answered. "We can run some checks when we get back to the States. I would also like to run some checks on our boy Jamie as well as Val."

"I suspect that Val Richards has no record, or at least not under that name. However, our boy Jamie is wound too tightly; he is too intense. I'll bet money your computer program can find a rap sheet on that boy."

"You know what this means?" Hank asked shaking his head.

"Of course I do. We have to go back for evidence," Doc answered. "Pass the jalapeños."

Chapter Eight

After supper Doc asked, "Hank, have you ever walked into a situation and sensed something so strong that you could almost touch the sensation? No evidence, nothing you could pick up and look at, just an incredibly strong feeling that came from so deep inside yourself you could feel it."

"Yeah," Hank said, "so what?"

"There is a lot about Val Richards that bothers me," Doc said. "Call it a gut hunch, a feeling, or even a superstition, but this guy is evil. Evil is something you can't describe. It is something that if you've ever encountered it, you recognize it in all of its different guises, shapes, and sizes."

"The first time I saw it was in a 13-year-old boy. I was stationed in the Philippines, and this kid, an American dependent, had taken another kid into the jungle, choked him into unconsciousness, and stolen his watch."

"This child criminal showed absolutely no remorse. His eyes were like those of a doll. They had color, they had animation, but they had no life. He moved, walked, and talked like the rest of us, but he was dead on the inside. I could sense the same kind of evil at work here."

Doc continued, "After my tour in the Philippines, I returned to school to finish my Bachelor's degree. I had switched majors from journalism to psychology. This was when I began learning about deviant and aberrant behavior, as well as avoidant, narcissistic, sadistic and masochistic personalities and tendencies."

"Over the years, I met more dangerous people by way of the counselor's couch than I ever did as a cop on the street."

"Later, I began to study the more severe forms of aberration—rapists, pedophiles, and serial killers. As a cop, I had intervened when emotions, desperation, or drugs sent someone spiraling into hell; now, I studied cold-blooded, premeditated predators."

"These 'dark-siders,' as I called them, were unbelievable. I started with a morbid curiosity about what I thought was a rare and unusual social phenomenon; it became a study of evil."

"I found that serial criminals ran up incredible scores in their particular areas of perversion. For example, the average pedophile assaults about 73 victims before charges are ever filed. I found that serial killers had established several national body dumping grounds across America."

"I learned that, until very recently, departmental communications and intelligence gathering procedures had handcuffed the efforts of law enforcement and victim's groups to locate, identify, and even recover the bodies of victims kidnapped in one location and dumped in another part of the country."

"There had been little, if any, way of sharing departmental information and intelligence in a meaningful way with other departments across the country."

"It's interesting that you mention this," Hank said. "I've been working on a computer database that would upgrade department and agency intelligence gathering and data sharing."

"I remember," Doc said. He knew Hank had started working on this about the same time an animal named Henry Lee Lucas was arrested. Lucas, a cockeyed drifter with a taste for violence, sex, and violent sex was apprehended; and, a new dimension to the horror was added. He had told of a national underground band of killers. Lucas claimed the members of this group were organized, mobile, and had been kidnapping, torturing, raping, and murdering victims from one end of the country to the other, undetected and even unsuspected for many years.

Lucas spread his story that a person would be kidnapped by a member of the group in Texas, moved across the country, and a dead naked body would be found in a location several states away from the kidnap site. With no ID, there was no way to establish a pattern of criminal behavior because the different law enforcement agencies never realized they were working on the same cases.

For months, Lucas pandered his story and confessed to murder after murder, then tens of murders and finally hundreds of murders; each new confession initiated action on the part of law enforcement agencies. As investigations were either initiated or re-opened, it appeared more and more delays would necessarily keep Lucas from his appointment with the Grim Reaper, a legal execution.

Finally, law enforcement agencies began to accept that Lucas' wild stories were just that, wild stories. There was no malevolent band of sickies patrolling the country's highways, truck stops, and towns. Lucas was simply telling people what they wanted to hear. The longer he talked, the more murders he confessed to, and the longer he stayed alive. Law enforcement agencies eventually stopped listening.

It is possible that many unsolved murders may have been resolved by Henry Lee Lucas. It was again decided the criminal was using the system and the blood of victims to escape punishment. The stir created by Lucas' story of an underground ring of murderers and perverts traversing the country kidnapping and killing people began to subside.

"I believe that anyone can kill," Doc said. "A normal person would have to be pushed far enough, hurt bad enough, and become angry enough. Their need to protect either themselves or someone else, usually a loved one is the reason. I sincerely believe anyone can kill. People kill by accident, by neglect, or when they are impaired."

"Soldiers and policemen may be called upon to kill to protect this nation or the people they are sworn to protect. People can even kill out of love or sometimes because of it. Evil kills because it can and because it enjoys killing."

"It's Val Richards' eyes that caught my attention. They were the same kind of eyes I had seen in the 13-year-old suspect years ago. They were the same ones I had seen when I interviewed a father accused of raping his own daughter. He looked at me with those cold, doll eyes and said, 'Well, you tell me what is wrong with raising your own partners?' "

"My investigation confirmed that incest, brutality, and domestic violence had been an integral part of this man's family history for five generations. What he had done was learned behavior. Even worse, it was behavior that had been taught to him in a sick and sinister way—it had become 'normal' in that family."

Doc continued, "Remember Jeffrey Dahmer and Richard Ramirez, the Night Stalker. These were men with their own demons. They were demons. Their insatiable appetites were to be slaked no matter what bizarre and despicable acts the process involved. While they demonstrate one level of evil, it was only one level."

"They had acted alone and in secret. While in no way do I excuse or condone what they did, they were very much victims themselves. They did what they did because in some twisted, diabolical, insane twist of reality they had too. Whatever made them 'different' also made them into a predator that would feed on the rest of mankind until caught or killed."

"There is no rehabilitation of creatures such as them. Our society today is not comfortable with that type of statement. Our liberalized concepts of right and wrong say nothing is indefensibly wrong, therefore nothing is indisputably right."

"This allows and even requires the exercises of justification attempts for what cannot and should not be justified, including the rationalization of the totally irrational behavior of mad men such as these."

"In all honesty, I believe these people scare us. We want to find out why something happened in the hopes that it will also explain how it happened. In my opinion, society is made up of people who have agreed formally or tacitly to live together in groups that we call family, towns, cities, etc."

"Society must have both rules and laws to govern its members and to maintain order. There must also be a belief system or mores to protect the collective psyches of those groupings."

"Victor Frankl, I believe is one of the greatest psychotherapists of our time. He was the author of *Man's Search for Meaning* and was a Jew who lived during World War II. He survived the death camps, lost his family, and endured unspeakable physical, mental, and emotional deprivation. He is often quoted out of context by the liberal thinkers behind such movements as Stop Capital Punishment."

"One of his most famous quotes, 'When a man has a WHY he can deal with any HOW' speaks to man's ability to survive. It does not mean to accept the behavior of the Nazis or excuse it or to justify it or to explain it, only to survive it."

"When Frankl is misquoted, it can seem as though with an explanation comes an excuse. By learning WHY, can we escape accountability for our actions?"

"Charles Whitman," Doc continued, "had a walnut-sized brain tumor when he climbed to the top of the Tower at the University of Texas and began killing passers-by with a high-powered rifle and telescopic sight."

"That did not matter to his victims or their families, but there is in fact another breed of predator. This predator hunts and destroys not because he must but because he can."

"And, that my friend is what I saw in the eyes of Val Richards. This man will do anything he wants to, because he can. People are evil because they choose to be. In reproductive terms, they are asexual—they are their own creators, their own Gods."

"Ted Bundy was a student of the law. He studied the law and tried to use it as a tool for his murder spree across America. He was intelligent, entertaining, and articulate; he entertained the media and flirted with fame."

"Hell, he married a woman in the middle of his murder trial, and like Henry Lee Lucas, he tried to delay death by recounting the murders he had committed or for which he wanted credit."

"Jim Jones was supposed to be a man of God, a student of God's word. He studied that word and used it as a tool for the seduction, torture, imprisonment, and eventual death of his own flock. He too was intelligent, entertaining, and articulate."

"He had wealth, power, and control beyond the imaginings of most people. He made only one mistake. He violated what I call 'The Rule of Ego,' which simply says never believe your own bullshit. Val Richards strikes me as the kind of man to believe his own bullshit," Doc said.

"Hank," Doc concluded, "my gut tells me we have stumbled on to some kind of predatory evil, the same kind of predatory evil I have studied all of these years."

Hank was silent for a long while. Then, he nodded and said, "Man, I hope you're wrong because if you're right —damn, that's some sick shit."

Chapter Nine

Doc and Hank finished their meal and tidied up. For all intents and purposes, it was the camp of a couple of weekend prospectors with visions of Montezuma's treasure in their eyes; but under the shade of the awning they had erected, much planning was taking place.

"All right," Hank started, "I estimate we are about 18 miles from the castle. It should be located just about here," he said placing a mark on the map. "Jamie was gone for 45 minutes on his 'trash run,' right?"

"Almost exactly," Doc confirmed. "Now remember, I never saw a headlight; but the moon was full and he would've had no problem driving as long he kept at a speed reasonable for the terrain."

"Okay, let's say top speed of 20 miles per hour," Hank continued to figure. "Furthermore, let's say that Jamie drove straight there, turned around, and drove straight back, call it a 22-minute trip one way."

"That means it would take three minutes to go each mile at that speed. Divide the 22-minute, one-way trip by three minutes per mile; the max distance he would have traveled would be 7.4 miles. Let's fudge a little and call it 10 miles."

He marked off the distance and then drew a circle with the castle at the center. Scratching his head, he wondered aloud, "Now where the hell did you go, Jamie, and what the hell did you do?"

They both examined the circle looking for something that would indicate the location of Jamie's midnight trash run.

"Let's focus in this area," Hank pointed to the northern half of the circle. "If he had gone in any other direction, you would have known by his return route."

"Agreed," Doc said, "but there are no towns or settlements marked on the map in that direction. There's nothing but open desert extending away from the castle in all directions, nothing. I don't see any place for him to go to in the area he would have traveled."

"I agree," Hank said smiling. "So if he was not going to someplace, what was he doing? You joked about him 'taking out the trash' I suspect that was exactly what he was doing. Where do you take trash?"

"To the dump," Doc said.

"Exactly," Hank agreed, "so let's go over this area again and see if we can find a dump."

"I doubt it will be marked," Doc said.

"No, it wouldn't be marked," Hank answered, "but now that we have an idea of what we're looking for, that should help. Bingo!" He smiled and pointed at the map.

Roughly five miles northeast of the castle and a few yards north of the line indicating the road Jamie would have taken was an area called Arroyos del Hermanos, translated in English as the Brothers' Arroyos.

It was a system of interconnected gullies that paralleled the road for about a mile before connecting to a river that eventually empties into the Gulf. From what they had seen so far, the gullies would be dry this time of year.

"How far is this from where we are right now?" Doc asked.

Hank looked at the map, consulted his compass, and said, "About a four-hour ride. Any idea what we may be looking for?"

"I'm not sure," Doc admitted. "I hope I'm wrong about this whole situation, but I suspect if I am right, we'll know it when we see it. That brings up the next question. What do we do about it?"

They readied the small amount of equipment they would take for their little excursion. Hank found a natural depression next to the cliff face and secreted the more valuable parts of their gear.

Once covered and camouflaged, it would be safe until they returned. They left the camp looking as though they were still there. A casual observer should be fooled. It might be a needless precaution but "better safe than sorry," Doc quoted.

Hank had been adamant about not carrying firearms on this mission. "Look, I don't like it either, but I have no intention of spending time in a Mexican jail. Besides, they won't be needed," he had assured Doc.

As Doc sat, adjusting the 80-lb compound bow and making final checks of the pulleys, strings, and arrows, he was pleased to see Hank doing the same.

Hank looked up and caught Doc smiling. "Okay, next time we'll smuggle a gun in," he said.

"Why, Hank," Doc said full of self-righteous indignation, "I never said a word."

Always succinct Hank simply said, "Bite me."

Both reached into their packs for a few other pieces of "essential equipment" they thought might come in handy.

When they saddled up, they were packed light for the journey. Doc's Crain knife was buckled on the left side of his belt. His Randall Model 1 Fighter was mounted horizontally in the middle of his back, facing left next to his Gerber Multiplier tool knife.

He had a double-edged A.G. Russell Sting inside his denim jacket in a special sheath sewn in the left armpit. He had the shoulder quiver fully loaded, hanging from the saddle horn on the left side.

A bow-mounted quiver carried six extra arrows attached to the bow that rested across the pommel of the saddle.

Hank was outfitted similarly. A Cold Steel combat Tanto knife was secured to his left side. Its Carbon V blade was the finest steel in any commercial knife on the market.

Tough and durable, Carbon V would rust if neglected and could stain if you weren't careful. Hank had carried this knife for years, and although the sheath told of hard use, the knife still looked new.

Hank had his Leatherman and his Schrade sharpening steel hung on the right side of his belt. His hunting knife, a Puma White Hunter, was in the knife sheath of his over-the-shoulder quiver, which also hung from the saddle horn.

Their saddlebags contained a day's supply of rations, binoculars, a first aid kit and a pair of two-way radios. They topped off their canteens and headed the horses in the direction of . . . who knew where.

Hank started to whistle, and then Doc recognized the tune. It was the theme from *The Magnificent Seven*.

Doc smiled and said, "We're about five people short."

"I know," Hank said without a smile, "I know."

Chapter Ten

Jamie walked slowly to the Jeep Cherokee. His belly still hurt where Val Richards had struck him.

The son of a bitch, Jamie thought. *He knows better than to treat me like that. What the hell was the matter with him? We've been together too long and have been through too much together for that kind of crap! Who the hell does he think he is? He'll regret it. He'll be sorry! He'll be damn sorry!*

Jamie slid carefully into the seat of the Cherokee. Painfully, he leaned forward, inserted the key and cranked the four-wheel-drive vehicle.

I wonder if he broke something inside me, Jamie idly thought. *This hurts like hell. If he has hurt my insides, I'll kill that arrogant bastard.*

He pulled the Cherokee out of the castle's compound and headed north. He had a date. He smiled at the thought, a date with delight. *I need some delight after the last 24 hours I have had.*

Things had started off so nicely, he thought. *The pickup had gone off without a hitch, and the delivery went just as well.*

Oh, he licked his lips, *the delivery. The delivery had been exquisite, simply exquisite.* He felt himself getting hard with the memory; he always got hard with the memory. He rubbed himself and shuddered.

Chapter Eleven

Doc and Hank had pushed the animals a little, but they had made it to the Hermanos Arroyos just before dark. The weather was cooler now and the horses seemed to enjoy the exercise. The moon was now full, and it was almost like daylight on the desert floor.

A couple of times, they had to ride down into some gullies and arroyos. Once out of the moon's glow, there was absolutely no light. They dropped the saddles and made the animals comfortable in a little draw. It kept them quiet and out of sight, and it would be cooler there during the next day.

They took down the compound bows and quivers of arrows, wishing they were rifles with 30 shot magazines. They grabbed their bedrolls and found a good spot for a cold camp.

While they were both competent with bows, Doc originally thought they would only be carried as a precaution. Now, they had possibly become indispensable. To no one in particular, Doc quoted John Thomas Rourke, "Plan ahead."

They hunkered down to grab some sleep before searching the area in daylight. Doing it at night was a sure way to break a leg or get snakebite.

The sun was just coming up when Hank nudged Doc awake. Quietly, they looked around for signs of visitors during the night, two-legged or four. Seeing nothing, Hank simply nodded and adjusted his quiver over his shoulder.

Doc's was already in place, and they left the draw in different directions with a plan to establish an over-watch of the area, ensuring they were alone before they began to explore.

Twenty minutes later, they were in position on opposite sides of the bluff overlooking the Hermanos Arroyos, hidden from sight but not from each other. They checked the areas immediately adjacent to each other's position and hand signaled each other, "Clear."

Next, they turned to the arroyos. It was a beautiful sight but stark at the same time. A system of small canyons and draws had been cut into one section of the dry riverbed.

For about three miles in each direction, these canyons and draws cut the surface of the desert floor, often to depths of 40 to 50 feet. The sides were steep with a crumbling mixture of loose rocks and sand.

A man or animal in the bottom of one of these would have to walk out along the natural bed of the canyon. There was no way to climb out without ropes and gear. Even then, it would be a chore. Doc heard a short call like a crow and looked at Hank who was pointing.

There was a cloud of dust being raised to the south. They watched patiently as it grew. Fifteen minutes later, Doc heard the crow again. Hank was confirming what Doc already knew.

It was the Jeep Cherokee from the castle, and Doc was willing to bet all his money in the bank that, Jamie was at the wheel.

He was right. They settled back to watch; this was the part they both hated, the waiting.

It took almost 10 more minutes before the Jeep Cherokee slammed on its brakes. When the cloud of dust had passed, the driver's door opened and he, Master Jamie, stepped out.

He looked around slowly, checking the area. Then, he opened the rear door of the Cherokee and climbed up to stand on the floor of the cargo area. Standing upright and supporting himself on the roof and door of the Cherokee, he had an unrestricted view of the desert floor for miles.

Again, he checked to be sure he was alone. Once satisfied, he walked away from the vehicle toward the arroyo. As he walked, he took his bearings from a group of scrubs at the edge of the arroyo and moved along the edge.

At one point, he stopped, looking around again. Doc froze and looked away but, it wasn't Doc Jamie sensed. He stood for a long time, watching the outcropping which Hank was sitting behind.

He must have stood there for 10 minutes, never moving—looking, listening, sensing. Finally, he began moving again. He made several visual sweeps of the area before he descended into the arroyo.

He had been doing something with his hands, but Doc was too far off and at the wrong angle to see. Once he dropped below the rim of the canyon, Doc caught a beam of reflected light in his eyes; Hank had signaled with his mirror.

It meant that no radio gear or visible antennae were observed, and with their short-range line of sight portables, they would have no fear of being picked up by larger sets. They had decided on colors for call signs before setting out on the mission.

"Blue, over," Hank's voice whispered in Doc's earphone.

"Red, over," Doc responded equally quiet.

"He is by himself, and if he is armed, it's probably that shoulder rig under his shirt. Nothing else visible, over," he advised Doc.

"Roger that, what was he doing with his hands? Over," Doc asked.

"Are you ready for this?" Hank said with hardness in his voice. "He was jacking off, over."

"Hmmm, over," was the only response Doc could think of.

"Blue moving, over," Hank said shifting position, Doc covering him. When he was in position, he radioed, "Blue set, over."

"Red moving, over." It was Doc's turn to move and Hank's turn to cover. "Red set, over."

They kept this dance up for about ten minutes, watching the rim of the canyon where Jamie had gone in and keeping a watch on the neighboring area.

One would leap frog from a position of cover and concealment to another, while the other covered the movement. Then, the other would repeat the movement. Finally, they were at the edge, concealed by low scrub brush.

They turned off the radios and removed the earpieces. It was very quiet on the desert floor. From opposite directions, they crawled as close to the edge as they could without disrupting loose soil.

They could see nothing. Doc turned, but Hank was already up and moving to the spot where Jamie had entered the arroyo. Doc silently cursed then moved into a position where he could offer some cover for Hank if need be.

Chapter Twelve

Hank moved quietly but quickly down the path that Jamie had used. He recognized it as a game trail out of the arroyo. From rim to floor, it took him almost five minutes even though it was only about 25 feet. His only concern was being quiet—he was successful.

He would take a step and listen; take two steps and listen; take a step and listen; take three steps and listen. He did this all the way to the floor of the tiny canyon.

I know I should be nervous or something, Hank thought, *but all I feel right now is alive. My senses are incredibly sharp, the colors are so vibrant; the smells—what is that smell?*

Closer and closer to the canyon floor he moved. Finally, he reached it and sat for a moment, reading the trail Jamie had left behind.

He went right here; he is following the floor. Hank's thoughts were keeping him company now. *The signs were obvious. Slowly, slowly, don't get in a rush; you remember how to do it. Take one step at a time, look where you are going to step; and, watch for twigs or loose gravel.*

Now, check around you, look back—and then step. Each time, don't change. That's it; you still have it boy. I'm proud of you—stay focused. Freeze, senses on alert—what is it? What changed?

Slowly, he realized a soft breeze had touched his face and cooled the sweat that covered it. The cowboy hat had been left topside, his bandana wrapped around his forehead like a sweat band. It kept the droplets from rolling into his eyes. He stood there frozen, digesting the sensations and images his brain was painting from the stimulations his nerves were providing.

On the breeze, he caught two things—sound and that same smell. He tried to make some sense of the sensations, but they didn't make any sense. The smell was foul, and the sound was like a small child's private laughter, tiny almost fragile—there were cooing sounds.

All right, he said to himself, *I don't know what you have found, but you've damn sure found something.*

Quietly, he slipped one of the arrows from the bow-mounted quiver. It had three razor edges, injector razor inserts, and could cut a hole nearly three-quarters of an inch across. The penetration was excellent, and blood loss of the target would be massive.

God, I hope I don't have to use this damn thing, he thought, and then he stepped around the edge of the wall, straight into hell. He stopped dead still. He didn't make a sound, but he wanted to—he wanted to scream.

Chapter Thirteen

The sound was coming from Jamie. He whimpered and cried as he moved. He was in total rapture. His eyes were closed, and his mouth was opened, sucking air in short gasping breaths.

He saw nothing and heard nothing except his own noises. They pleased him; they excited him. He paced himself with his breathing.

Hank had never seen anything like what he was looking at. Jamie stood next to a large boulder, and the body of a young boy lay face down on the boulder, naked and dead. The boy had been dead for hours, possibly a day from what Hank could see.

Jamie stood with his pants down behind the boy thrusting, whimpering, and cooing. Hank stood there for what seemed an eternity.

First, he tried to make sense of what he was seeing. Then, he tried to make that sense go away and then just stared.

"You sick, perverted piece of shit," Hank finally said slowly through clenched teeth. "Pull your damn pants up and back away from that boy's body. Keep your hands where I can see them, and do not turn around."

The fury in his voice was thick but cold and somehow more menacing than if he had shouted the words.

Jamie froze in mid-stroke. Instantly, he was totally aware of where he was, what he was doing, and who had caught him at it. He immediately recognized Hank's voice.

He appeared calm on the outside, even detached; but inside, his heart raced, and the synapses of his nerves and senses were firing like never before. He realized he had been caught, again. He realized he would have to kill again, and the thought excited him.

Slowly and carefully, he withdrew. Bending with his hands out and away from his body, he stooped and with his left hand tugged his pants back into position. Then, he waited.

Slowly, he pulled great breaths of air into his lungs and let them out of his pursed lips. It calmed him, focused him, and prepared him.

Hank moved to the center of the narrow arroyo. He was now about 20 feet from Jamie.

"Hello Sweets," Jamie said, "I thought we would meet again. Did you come around for a go at my 'honey' here? He's sweet I'll tell you. Would you like me to show you?" He stepped back from the body and moved to one side.

Hank's voice was hard as nails "Jamie, I'll tell you one last time. Do not move unless I tell you to. When I tell you to move, do exactly what I say and exactly the way I say to do it. If you deviate, I will kill you. Do you understand me?"

"Sure thing love," Jamie's voice showed no fear and, no concern, only contempt.

Who does this piece of work think he is? Jamie thought. *Does he really believe he has trapped me? Doesn't he realize that he is the one that's about to die? Do you have any idea the joyous things I will do to you as you're dying? Or even better, the things I will do to you after you're DEAD?*

As his mind screamed that final word, his body was already in motion. His body started to spin, as his right hand slid inside his opened shirtfront. His thumb broke the quick release snap, and his claw-like hand snatched the Glock Model 17 from his left armpit. He was as quick as lightening as he pivoted on the ball of his left foot.

When his right foot slammed into the ground, about a shoulder's width from his left foot, he was in a ready shooting position. Jamie had been fast, and he knew that his opponent didn't have the chance to move.

He was confident he had totally surprised his opponent, this Hank asshole who had interrupted his date. Jamie thought, *No matter, now I have two to enjoy. Double your pleasure, double your fun.*

Jamie believed Hank had no way to know which way he would spin and no way of knowing he had a gun. And he would have no way to know killing was a pleasure to him and that he could and would do it, without hesitation.

But, Hank did know; he knew it all. He also knew the gun could only be under Jamie's shirt. Hank knew he did not have enough room to spin the other direction and that Jamie was a cold-blooded sickness who would not hesitate to kill him.

Jamie had already decided, *No games with this asshole. Just bop, bop, and you're bleeding, Love.* When he stopped spinning, he was right. Jamie's opponent had not moved, but something was wrong.

Jamie's mind asked, *Where's his fucking gun? What the hell is he doing standing like that?*

Jamie had just an instant of hesitation, just an instant, and then he fired. This slight hesitation was what Hank counted on. He hesitated because Hank was not in a conventional shooting position for a gun, and he had not moved at all in reaction to Jamie's movement.

Hank was in the classic shooting stance of a standing bowman, left foot in front, right foot behind, left arm straight out holding the bow, right arm pulling back the string with the notched arrow.

His middle three fingers on the right hand were used to pull the string back, the arrow resting between the index and middle fingers. The right thumb pointed straight up to contact the anchor point at the base of the right ear.

It was a rock solid stance; one Hank had practiced many times. Hank had not moved because he had no reason to. He had assumed this stance before he had spoken the first word.

While the draw weight on the compound was 80 pounds, the holding weight was only about 25. Hank could hold that all day. He was already aligned on where he knew Jamie's body would be when the spin was complete. Hank saw the hesitation, the surprise, heard the gun, and in that instant loosed the arrow.

Jamie screamed, but nothing came out. His chest hurt! He looked down and saw something sticking out of his chest and blood soaking through his shirt.

That doesn't make sense, he thought. The only sound he could hear was the faltering and interrupted beat of his own heart. *That doesn't make sense.*

He had time to wonder. *Two arrows, how could there be two arrows.* He decided it did not make sense. Then, he died.

Chapter Fourteen

By the time Doc got to the bottom of the gully and hiked to the death scene, Hank was sitting on a boulder about 12 feet from the body. He had Jamie's Glock and had already gone through his pockets.

"You okay?" Doc asked. Hank had not said a word or even looked up at Doc's approach.

"Yeah, fine. Thanks." Hank kept spinning the Glock on his finger, like a cowboy would spin his Colt .45. "By the way, nice shot."

"Yours too," Doc acknowledged. "I think we both knew what he was going to do, and we both knew what we would have to do. I just wish there had been a way to avoid it."

"Me too," Hank agreed. "But if ever a son of a bitch deserved to die, there he lies."

"Find anything on him?" Doc asked.

"Wallet, keys, pocket notebook, and this," he said brandishing the Glock. "I was right; it is a Glock model 17."

Doc said, "Never doubted it for a minute; any ID on the boy?"

"No," Hank said. "He was naked when he was put in that bag. The good news is he was dead at the time also. There's nothing else is in the bag, nothing. I haven't checked the wallet or the notebook; I was waiting on you to get here."

"Those things will wait. Let's take a break before we start." Doc suggested, as he handed Hank his pocket flask. Hank took a swig and then read the inscription on the flask. It was an old military toast. It said "To us and those like us, damn few left."

"Hoo Rah," Hank whispered and handed it back.

"Hoo Rah," Doc said as he took a swig. Doc fired up one of Val Richards' expensive and wonderful cigars, and they passed it back and forth without talking. There was nothing to say and no words to say it with.

They sat watching the clouds blow across the top of the arroyo, feeling the breeze coming up the draw, and taking in what it meant to be alive next to all of this death. It was quiet yet strangely peaceful.

It was the place after "harm's way," the time after "almost but not quite." Many men have approached this place, and some did not make it all the way. Today, they had. They had been here before, other times; but, each time was like the first time all over again.

They shared the bourbon. They shared the cigar. They shared each other's company without a word or glance. It was enough that they were both here and were both alive—this time. They knew next time could be different, and they knew there would be a next time.

The time passed without a word until Hank handed Doc the cigar butt for the last drag. Doc inhaled deeply and field stripped it into oblivion.

They both stood up and walked to the rock where the wallet, keys, and notebook sat. Doc picked them up. Hank leaned over and picked up the body bag, draping it over the boy's body; it seemed the appropriate thing to do.

He made no move to cover Jamie's body. But, he did look down at it and spit on the ground next to it; it too seemed the appropriate thing to do.

Doc opened the wallet finding 40 dollars in U.S. currency and a Texas driver's license bearing Jamie's picture but with the name Randy French. French or Jamie, or whoever he was, had an address listed as 2025 Barrington, Midland, Texas.

It had been issued on his birthday six months ago and would not have to be renewed for four years. They both knew Mr. French had probably rented a room at that address, just long enough to get the license, and then Mr. French disappeared to parts and places unknown with no forwarding address.

They agreed, if a man by the name of Randy French had ever existed, he was not the man laying 12 feet away. If he ever existed, he was probably dead and had probably had been killed by the scum laying 12 feet away. That was the way things went in this world.

Nothing else was in the wallet, no membership cards, and no pictures; none of the "stuff" men normally carry in their wallets. Randy French had no "stuff" because he did not exist, at least not anymore. The notebook was equally disappointing. Page after page was covered in meaningless gibberish.

"What do you suppose this is?" Doc asked Hank.

Hank studied it for a moment before answering. "Obviously, it's in code. I can't understand it yet, but I will. I can promise you that."

"Well, what do you think our next step should be?" Doc asked, although he was pretty sure he knew his friend's response.

"Nothing my friend," Hank answered. "We don't do one damn thing until we figure out what we have stepped in."

Doc nodded, he'd been right.

Chapter Fifteen

"First things first," Hank said. "Let's get a 'picture' of what we know. I want to do something with these bodies, and we still have to search the Jeep. That may or may not adjust the 'picture' we are about to create, agreed?"

"Agreed," Doc confirmed. "I doubt coming to this specific location was an accident. I suspect he has been here before; we need to look around down here too," he gestured around the gully floor.

"Yeah," Hank said nodding, "I'll backtrack to the left. You go right, and we'll meet back here in 30 minutes."

"Done," Doc agreed. "Hey," Doc said turning back and pointing to the rim of the gully 30 feet above our heads. "Remember to occasionally look up. We are at a severe tactical disadvantage here."

"Roger that," Hank said nodding and started off in one direction and Doc in the other.

Doc had traced the floor of the gully around two sharp turns when he came to it. During the rainy season, water would rush through this gully, sometimes filling it almost to the top. Run off from the high mountains would turn this into a fast flowing river whose life would be measured in hours.

Debris that had collected on the gully floor would be washed clean in those hours. As the rushing waters filled the little canyon, the force of those waters would dislodge anything that had fallen or been dropped into the gully.

Picked up by these waters, the debris would be broken, smashed, and tossed against the gully wall until it plunged into the connecting river and eventually into the Gulf of Mexico. It was like a natural power washer.

At the base of one wall, the rushing waters had been trying to cut through. A shallow cave had been cut into the canyon wall. It would eventually expand until the river cut through and changed course.

The cave was about 20 feet deep and about that high and wide. The floor was covered with animal tracks of all sizes. The remains of what had been human beings lay scattered around the cave and on the gully floor.

The bones were cracked and broken. It was obvious animals had been gnawing on them. It was also obvious that parts were missing, but there was no way to determine if they had been removed by the killers or by animals feeding on the carcasses. It would take a team of forensic pathologist weeks to sort out the pieces.

From the sheer number of bones, Doc estimated the bodies of 10 to 15 human beings had been thrown here like garbage. Doc found it interesting that, while the bones were scattered around the gully floor, they had been originally placed almost directly in front of the cave.

He looked up toward the rim of the gully and could make out scrape marks down the wall of the gully. Someone had dropped the bodies from the rim and several had impacted on the way down.

He checked his watch and saw he had a few minutes before he had to head back. He checked ahead a few more turns of the gully, found nothing, and headed back.

He and Hank arrived at about the same time; Hank had not seen anything. Doc told him about his discovery. "I want to take a look," Hank said, shaking his head wearily.

"I'm going topside," Doc told him. "We've been in this gully too long without a look around. I also want to see what is above the cave, which is where I'm sure at least some of the bodies were dropped from."

Hank agreed to wait there, and Doc started up. As Doc neared the rim, he stopped to listen for any sounds that would indicate they might have company. Hearing nothing, he cautiously peered over the rim and around the area.

He signaled "all clear" to Hank who moved out toward the cave. For a moment, he stood enjoying the breeze on his face then walked the rim toward the area above the cave.

"My God!" was Hank's only comment when he arrived at the cave.

Topside, Doc found what he expected, vehicle tracks and footprints. The vehicle tracks appeared to match the Jeep Cherokee's tread size and pattern and he suspected the footprints belonged to Jamie. Both suspicions would be confirmed later by examination and comparison. He got Hank's attention and motioned for him to come up. Hank nodded and started up.

By the time he arrived, Doc had used Jamie's keys to open the Jeep. He had found nothing in the glove box except the usual registration, proof of insurance, and some gas receipts.

Doc pocketed one of the receipts. Hank started toward the rear of the vehicle, and Doc electronically unlocked the rest of the doors. While Hank started on the cargo area, Doc searched the console and cabin of the vehicle. It was apparent that Jamie had packed for an extended trip. Two suitcases were packed with clothes and toiletries.

A briefcase revealed checkbooks from several different banks and under several different names, a foldout business card holder containing driver's licenses, credit cards, phone cards, and auto club cards with names that matched those on the checkbooks.

They were grouped together so that each page of the fold out contained all of the required documentation for a single identity. In each case, the picture ID was of Jamie. Also located there was a blank card on which credit card numbers and their matching pin numbers had been written.

There were sentences penciled in that Doc recognized as answers to questions that the bank tellers would use for identity verification. There was an Adidas gym bag on the right, front floorboard which had several large envelopes in it.

Doc opened one and found it contained an unknown amount of U.S. currency, neatly bundled and wrapped with rubber bands; they would count it later. "Here," Hank said, pulling something from the cargo area and throwing it to Doc. It was the twin of the Glock model 17 he had removed from Jamie's dead hand. "You might need this."

"Thanks," Doc said, catching the pistol. He dropped the magazine and confirmed the stick was full and one in the chamber. "Do you see any extra magazines?"

"Nope, not yet," Hank said. "Wait a minute; correction, here they are." He opened a gym bag and tossed two magazines to Doc. Both mags were full. "That gives each of us three mags."

Hank had already recovered Jamie's shoulder rig with its extra two mags. He had slipped it on over his shirt; the thought of it touching his bare skin was revolting.

Doc stuck the Glock in his belt and slid one mag into each front pant pocket. He put everything back in the briefcase and asked, "You find anything else?"

"A laptop computer, his clothes, and this gym bag," Hank answered. "He had your extra magazines and what looks to be a lot of kid pornography and sex tapes."

"Alright," Doc said. "Let's figure out how to make all of this go away. We are too visible standing here with this damn Jeep."

"I agree," Hank answered looking around. "There's not enough brush up here to cover a jackrabbit, much less a Jeep." He looked toward the mountains. "Let's see if we can find a place where we can get it into and out of the gully."

They went back to their horses, saddled up, and headed off in opposite directions to hopefully find a way to drive the Jeep into the Hermanos Arroyos.

About a mile from where they started, Hank found the perfect spot. He waved his hat until Doc saw him, and they headed back to the Jeep. Doc brought up some brush he had collected and tied it into bundles that he then tied to the rear of the vehicle, while Hank went back to the bodies.

Doc took some of the extra branches and started sweeping the sand, wiping out the horses' tracks and their footprints. By the time he had finished, Hank was coming up from the gully floor with the boy in the body bag over his shoulder.

Doc helped him out of the gully, and he gently laid the body bag on the roof of the Jeep.

"What about Jamie?" Doc asked. "Want me to get him?"

"To hell with him!" Hank snarled. "I left him inside that cave. He fed everyone else to the wolves; let them feed on him. At least no one will see him from above. I covered the blood with more sand and brushed out our prints. We were never here."

"Nuff said, I was just asking," Doc said, raising his hands in a mock surrender.

"Sorry," Hank volunteered. "Didn't mean to be short with you."

"It's okay, I understand," Doc said.

Hank secured the body to the roof rack on the Jeep, while Doc tied the bundles of brush behind it. Doc mounted his horse and, while leading Hank's, headed off in the direction of the vehicle entrance to the gully Hank had found. Hank followed slowly behind him in the Jeep.

It was working. Dragging the brush behind the Jeep this slowly did not create a dust cloud that could be seen miles away. Yet, it effectively wiped out the horse and vehicle tracks as they moved.

Thirty minutes later, the vehicle was hidden, the tracks obliterated, and Hank was digging a grave for the young boy with a shovel from the Jeep. He had found a stainless steel thermos in the Jeep and had spent several minutes emptying and cleaning both the interior and exterior with a paper towel.

Hank unzipped the body bag and took the dead boy's right hand in his own. Positioning a sheet of paper carefully around the thermos, he then wrapped the boy's hand around the thermos as though he was gripping it.

Hank changed sheets of paper, and then he repeated the process with the left hand. Satisfied, he carefully set down the thermos and re-zipped the bag. Carefully, he placed the two sheets inside the thermos, sealed it, then walked over and put it in his saddlebag.

"I doubt," Hank explained "that we will ever identify any of the people in that gully. We might have a chance with this boy if these fingerprints are any good and if he is registered anywhere." He looked directly at Doc and said, "When this is over, I want to come back for him. Dental records may help identify him. Okay?"

That meant, if something happened to Hank, he was asking Doc to make sure everything possible would be done to identify this kid.

Doc said, "If nothing else works, I'll make sure he is buried on your place next to the little creek; how's that?"

Hank stood looking at Doc for a second or two; they both understood what had been said and what had not been said. Finally, he nodded and said, "That's good, thanks." They carried the boy to the grave and set him gently down.

Hank offered a prayer, and Doc handed him the shovel. Hank had already made up his mind that burying this boy was something he was going to do. It was personal, it was private, and it was his job—Doc needed to stay out of it.

Doc went back to the Jeep to examine the stuff they had found in it. By the time Hank finished 45 minutes later, Doc was ready to report. Hank sat in the shade and sipped from his canteen. He was drenched in sweat from the burial, but he looked relaxed now. He had done everything he could for that kid; later, he would try to do more.

"Okay, what have we got here?" Hank asked. Doc pitched him a writing tablet and a Mont Blanc pen he had found in the briefcase.

"Take notes," Doc instructed. "We don't have much time. First of all, there are 13 separate identities in this card holder." He passed it to Hank.

"Each identity has a driver's license and a minimum of two credit cards plus a corresponding checkbook for a bank in the same city as the address on the driver's license."

"They cover 13 towns in eight different states: Texas, Louisiana, Mississippi, Arkansas, Florida, New Mexico, Arizona, and California. The only problem is each driver's license has Jamie's picture on it. He used a variety of disguises: different hairstyles, color of hair, glasses, colored contacts, and facial hair—the works."

"Next," Doc continued, "I have 27 bundles of $100 bills. It looks like there are about 100 bills in each bundle. That's $270,000 in cash. It doesn't appear there are any consecutive serial numbers or markings, although I can't be sure until I check more carefully."

"Drug money?" Hank ventured.

"Possibly," Doc said, "but one thing is for sure; wherever it came from, it was not made legally. It could be drugs, porn, prostitution, or probably all three."

"What else?" Hank asked.

"This notebook," Doc answered. "I have no way of knowing what it contains but it has to be important. There are 65 pages of encrypted information that was carefully recorded, by hand, in this book. It is important to someone, somewhere, and I don't believe that person was Jamie."

"Then, there is the laptop," he continued. "It seems normal enough, but we are going to have to find the password to get into the files and see what is in it. We need some computer help on this."

"Okay, give me your best take on all of this," Hank said.

"When I got my Master's Degree in police science," Doc began, "I did a report that dealt with Henry Lee Lucas. He had said that a group of mobile and organized serial killers existed in the United States. I mentioned this to you the other day if you remember."

"While there was never any hard evidence, it made sense to me. My research into serial killers discovered something that could only be explained by virtue of something akin to Lucas' group of killers."

"In the past, individual serial killers operated in a geographically limited kill zone," Doc explained.

"Rarely do serial killers have partners. As our interdepartmental and interagency communications improved, we found that, while bodies were being discovered in specific locations, they were not from those areas. Rather, a body from Palm Springs, California could show up in La Place, Louisiana. Of course, we also learned that many victims were simply never found."

"Alright, this is rough and highly speculative," Doc admitted, "but I think we have uncovered a well-financed, well-organized, and very mobile criminal activity. I believe that it operates across the southern half of the United States and into Mexico."

"From what we have seen at the castle and here, someone has developed a plot in which people are taken, used, abused, and eventually some of them are killed. I don't know; maybe all of them are killed. That way there are no witnesses."

"I don't think we are dealing with conventional criminal activity," he continued. "Call it gut feeling, hunch, or whatever. I think there is more going on here than selling dope or whores. I think they are involved, but it is more sinister than that."

"You don't find what we found in that gully when you are dealing with 'normal' criminals. Anyway, this is what my speculations are based on. We'll know if I'm right when we can decipher the notebook and the laptop's programs."

"I agree," Hank said, "but where do we go from here?"

"We go back to get our supplies and other animals," Doc replied. "First, we'll cover the Jeep with that tarp we found in back. Let's collect some more brush and tie it to the tarp and to the roof of the Jeep. That will make it harder to spot from the air. We'll come back for it later. Do me a favor, and check the fluid levels, tires, and belts while I get the brush. Let me know if we need anything."

"Done," Hank said starting off. Doc took the Crain and made several trips back to the Jeep carrying additional bundles of brush. Hank confirmed the vehicle was operational.

Apparently, everything had been topped off and checked prior to Jamie leaving the castle. The tarp, a light brown color, blended well with the surrounding gully wall, and when the brush was tied to the grommet holes, it provided more than adequate camouflage.

Since they had disguised the boy's grave, they made sure to mark it, so it could be found when they returned.

Everything went back into the Jeep, except the money, the notebook, and the laptop computer, which they divided out to fit between their saddlebags.

Doc moved the Glock's magazines to the breast pockets of his denim jacket, checked the cinches one last time, and mounted up.

Hank swung into the saddle, gazed at the grave for a moment, and said softly, "We'll be back in a few days, and then I'll try to take you home." He pulled the reins and spun his horse up the gully.

They followed the gully for about a mile before they found another place to exit. Both felt that the time lost in such an exercise would be made up should someone start to look for their trail.

It was not likely but "Plan ahead," Doc quoted John Thomas Rourke, again.

Chapter Sixteen

About a mile from the camp, Doc stopped to cut more brush and tied it into bundles. As they walked the horses and burros slowly, the bundles drug behind to sweep away any tracks.

Neither figured there was much sense in giving anyone the idea they had ever been somewhere other than the camp or leaving evidence that would indicate a direction that had been traveled on the return.

As they topped the bluff near the camp, they started to check the markers they had left around the camp. Nothing appeared disturbed, so they moved on in, unsaddled, and rubbed the horses down.

They gave them some water and feed; the burros still had feed. After extending the remuda to include the horses, Doc built a fire for supper. They had both been pretty quiet on the trip back.

"Okay," Doc said finally, "I've got an idea about what is going on. It has some holes in it I'll admit, but see what you think."

"Shoot," Hank said, settling back to listen.

"Remember, I told you that Val Richards reminded me of someone?" Doc asked. "I told you that the guy he reminds me of is a sociopath and that I suspect Richards is a psychopath." Hank nodded acknowledging he remembered.

"I'll explain the difference between psychopath and sociopath later." Doc added.

"Okay, he has power, wealth, and control all without visible or described means. Where does Val Richards come up with enough money to build and finance this castle and the kind of operation we discovered in Jamie's Jeep? Why build the castle in the first place? It's not just to live in, I'll wager."

"I'm with you so far," Hank responded.

"Remember what I said about Henry Lee Lucas telling the world there was an organized group of killers at work in the U.S.?"

"He described an underground group that was well-financed, well-organized, and mobile. While we were sitting in the arroyo, next to the Jeep, we described the same thing," Doc reminded him.

"Hank, what if we have discovered the first physical evidence that such a group exists?"

Hank pondered for a moment before asking, "What about the skeletons in the gully?"

"It is likely one of several dumping grounds, each picked for its ability to hide or destroy evidence," Doc answered. "Bodies are dumped from the rim of the gully in the same place each time. Why? The first reason is all of the animals around here. Every meat eater around now knows where the supper table is. The second reason is that cave."

Hank looked puzzled and Doc continued. "When the animals are through eating, the bones remain; right? Wolves, birds, and bugs will destroy the flesh, but the bones remain. Once every few days or weeks during the rainy season, it rains in the high mountains."

"That rain washes through the low areas, sweeping away everything in its path: brush, debris, bones. Everything is scattered, broken up, and spread over miles of harsh terrain. Some of it will even find its way into the Gulf. It is natural garbage disposal."

"I suspect people are brought to the castle, both guests and victims. The victims are collected from those elements of society that will not miss them. They may be offered money or drugs to come. Some victims are simply kidnapped by force," Doc speculated, "but once they are at the Castle, they don't leave, at least not alive."

"The guests come here to spend a weekend, a week, hell a month; I don't know," he continued, "but while they are there, they are able to indulge every perversion you can imagine and some we probably can't."

"I suspect that either there is a basement or some type of underground addition to the castle with a pathway that leads to the hidden door I found in that garden. That is where I think the victims are kept and where the worst activities probably go on."

"When they are used up, they are taken out like garbage. The guests return home, and the rest simply disappear, all very neat and clean."

"Okay," Hank said after a moment, "makes sense from what I've seen, but I have two questions. Number one, how do we prove it? Number two, what do we do about it?"

"Well," Doc said picking up the notebook and the laptop computer, "I think this is our evidence, but we have to decipher it and find out how close to the truth I am. Then, we'll know the answer to number two."

"I can't do it here," Hank said. "We have to get back to Presidio."

"I know," Doc said. "Let's grab chow, a couple of hours sleep, then we'll pack up and head back to Rancho Dela Vega. I suspect we are on a timeline that we don't know about yet, and whatever we're going to do, we are going to be doing it soon."

"You said you would explain the difference between sociopath and psychopath," Hank reminded Doc. "What is it?"

"This is not the scientific version," Doc began, "but let's say it's a matter of degrees. A sociopath is convinced that whatever he does is okay, and although sometimes it is difficult, that person can survive in society with a greater or lesser degree of success. The psychopath does not attempt to survive in society; rather, he tries to bend society to cope with him."

"I think Val is narcissistic as well as psychopathic; he is totally self-consumed. That kind of personality is self-centered and both intelligent and dangerous. Put the two personalities types together, and you have a seriously troubled man, one who is used to getting his way and will tolerate nothing short of winning."

It took about 15 minutes to prepare the Mountain House Beef Stew and even less time to consume it. They stretched out under the stars and dozed. Neither was ready to turn loose enough to sleep deeply, so every different sound pulled them back to consciousness.

Doc finally got up at daybreak, stoked the fire, and had coffee going when Hank awoke. An hour later, they had collected the gear, packed, and were headed out. They rode toward Rancho Dela Vega in silence, listening and thinking.

Shortly after 1400 hours, they arrived and approached the house cautiously. They did not expect trouble, but they both knew that when you least expect trouble is usually when you find it. "Better safe than sorry," Doc said softly.

Everything was as it should be, although the host was concerned they had cut their trip short by several days. Doc explained to him they had not been successful in their search for deposits and he was suffering from the heat.

Doc emphasized they had enjoyed the accommodations and appreciated his assistance. When Doc paid Gutierrez the full amount they had contracted for, the Señor relaxed. After all, it was not his fault they were leaving. Doc smiled after counting out the full amount and quoted, "Fair's fair."

Two hours later they had transferred the gear, taken a quick shower, and changed clothes. It felt good to be clean again. They shook hands all around, and Hank said they would try to come back next year with the wives for a vacation.

Gutierrez smiled quickly adding up what the price for that would be. As they drove off, Doc thought, *We will be back to this part of the country a lot sooner than next year.*

They drove out much faster than they had driven in. In only seven hours, they were 10 miles from the border. They stopped and hid the guns and magazines in the bag with their dirty clothes. They grabbed a Coke and headed on into Cuidad Ojinaja. As they drove through town, Doc noticed it was still active at almost midnight.

Hank pulled up to the international bridge, identifying themselves as American citizens. He advised the Customs Inspector that they had been in Mexico for five days on business and had nothing to declare.

The Inspector asked Hank if he minded that he search the vehicle. Hank smiled, stepped out of the vehicle, and said, "Heck no officer, go ahead. Do you want me to open the camper?"

The Customs Inspector smiled slowly and said, "No, that's okay; you gentlemen have a nice day," and he waved them across. Hank smiled back and said, "You too."

One hundred feet down the road, Hank said, "Whew, for a minute I thought we were cooked. I gambled that if we looked and acted like we had nothing to hide, the agent would figure we were okay."

They took a right and were now on American soil, a mile and a half from Hank and Denise's place. They had made it back; their arrival woke Hank's two dogs when they drove in, and the dogs woke Denise. She greeted them at the door, "You're back early."

Hank hugged and kissed her, then petted the dogs. "We had some problems," he said.

Doc went in the guest room to call Pam. "Hi, Baby," he said when she answered, sleepily.

"Hi, Honey. I didn't expect to hear from you for a couple of days. Everything alright?"

"Well, yes and no," he wasn't sure how to begin. "We are back at Hank's and we're okay, but I need to find out what you have planned for the weekend."

"I'm pretty open, why?"

"Can you come out to Hank's?" Doc asked.

"I can if it's that important," she said, sounding worried.

"It is. First of all, everything is okay," Doc said. "I'll explain everything to you when you get here. But, I'll need you to bring some things. Have you got a pencil and paper?"

Doc told her what he needed and where it was, threw a kiss to her through the phone, and told her to drive carefully. He opened three beers and went outside to where Hank and Denise sat.

"Is Pam coming?" Denise asked.

"Yes, she will gather some equipment and leave first thing in the morning." Doc said.

"She okay?" Hank asked.

"I didn't go into anything over the phone." Doc said turning to Denise. "How are you doing with all of this?"

"Well, not too well," she said. "I am seriously concerned about what happened, and I am scared to death of what happens next."

Doc smiled and touched her shoulder. "I know. So am I."

Chapter Seventeen

Pam hung up the phone and sat very still, looking at the phone.

Something is seriously wrong, she thought. *I don't know what happened, but there is trouble.*

They had only been married two and a half years, but they had been together almost six. She had finally learned to listen to what Doc did not say.

She had also learned that, generally, he was extremely open and communicative with her, but she realized there were times when he purposely did not tell her everything; he called it filtering.

It had taken her awhile to realize that while there might be a variety of different circumstances in which this filtering took place, there was always one common element — they could always be overheard if someone wanted to listen.

Doc called it Com Sec, a military term for communications security. It meant simply, watch what you say, who you say it too, and always be aware that "someone" could be listening.

Pam had also learned that he would eventually tell her everything but when they were alone and no one else could overhear. She knew that was what was happening now.

Recognizing there was no sense in trying to pump him for information, she quoted one of his favorite sayings dealing with something that was futile. "It's like trying to teach a bull to sing; it does not work, and it makes the bull mad."

Pam reset the alarm for 4:00 a.m., started back to sleep, and then wondered if she might need a couple of vacation days from work. *I'll wait and see,* she decided. *I can always call in if I have to stay past Sunday.*

When she awoke with the alarm, she located the equipment boxes Doc had requested, packed her bags, fed the dogs and cat, and was on the road at a quarter 'til five.

She stopped for an Egg McMuffin, coffee, and OJ, which she ate as she drove. At 8:00 a.m., she entered San Antonio on I-10, topped off the gas tank, checked the oil and water, grabbed a snack, and was on her way.

Traffic was heavy, and there were a lot of what she referred to as "stupid people" driving that day. She turned on the radio, settled back and began to eat up the miles across Texas. At a quarter to six, she pulled up at Hank and Denise's place.

Hugs and kisses went all around. Hank asked, "Do you want something to drink?"

"Yes, I do," Pam answered. "I also want to know what the hell is going on."

Doc said, "Hank, why don't you make us a couple of drinks and I'll move her bags inside. Then, she and I will walk down to the creek, and I'll explain what has happened."

"You've got it," Hank said and headed off to make four drinks. "This could take a while."

With bags unloaded and drinks in hand, Pam and Doc headed toward the back of the property. Pam noticed he had a pistol stuck in his belt at the middle of his back. She didn't recognize the handle.

They walked. He talked. She knew he would tell her what had happened. After he had finished, she almost wished he hadn't.

"What happens now?" she asked as they sat on a fallen tree trunk next to the little creek.

"First thing is we have to break the code on the notebook, and Hank has to figure out how to access the laptop," he replied. "He likes playing with codes, part of his intelligence background I guess."

"Anyway, he has an encrypting program on his computer. We've already scanned the notebook into the computer. Hopefully, we'll break the code today."

"What about the authorities?" she asked with concern evident on her face. "Well, we can't go to the authorities without evidence," he said. "I believe all of the evidence we need is in the notebook and the computer. Even if it is, I don't know if the authorities can or will act. If they do, it might be weeks or even months in the future."

"What do you mean?" she said puzzled.

"First of all, if I am right, this is the biggest news story since Jeffrey Dahmer," Doc said. "This could send the whole country into a panic. Plus, we are dealing with Mexico. That makes it international. With all of the political considerations, I simply have no way of knowing how the authorities will respond. We'll just have to wait and see. We'll know more if and when Hank is able to break the codes."

"Are you okay with Jamie's death?" she asked.

"There was no choice," Doc answered as he threw out the last of his drink in disgust. "He left us no choice. I wish it had not been necessary, but it was."

"How's Hank?" she asked as they headed back to the house.

Doc smiled. "He's okay; he did what he had to do. So did I, but that dead boy upset him more than he is showing."

As they came out of the draw, Hank spotted them and waved for them to hurry up. They started jogging across the open area he used for a firing range. Walking the last 15 feet, Doc asked, "What's up?"

"My computer broke the code," Hank answered, obviously pleased. "The notebook is a record of transactions, locations, and the passwords for the laptop computer's programs. I scanned a couple. You're not going to believe it."

Everyone went inside. Denise had already downloaded all of the laptop's information. She had already made copies of each disk. One set was for the authorities, and the other set would be a backup. They would work off the hard drive for now.

As Denise hit the print button, she said, "This is going to take a while. While it is printing, I am going to run up to the office supply store and get two more ink cartridges and some more paper."

"Want some company?" Pam asked.

"I would love some, thanks," Denise smiled.

Hank poured two more drinks and started sorting the paper from the printer. It continued to spit out paper. Hank was reading the stack in his hand.

"Dear God," he said after about 10 minutes. "Doc, you were right. Damn, you were right on the money."

Chapter Eighteen

By the time the girls got back, stacks of paper were spread across the top of the desk. On the top of each was a sticky note with one or more words; these would become the hard copy files.

Paper was added to the printer and the cartridge was changed. Denise brought a box from the garage to collect the papers.

An hour later, the last of the computer information had been printed. It was going to take some time to read all of this stuff.

Doc turned to Hank, "Will you make two more copies of each disk?"

He nodded. When he was finished, they had three copies of each disk and a box full of paper.

"Ladies," Doc said, "are you up to another trip to the office supply store? I need two copies of everything in this box. Can you handle it?"

"Sure," Denise said, "it will take a while to copy all of these two times."

"I know," I said. "Make sure you get every sheet of paper. If something screws up, get the screwed up copies also. Don't leave anything behind, and do the work yourself. I don't want anyone to see the originals. If anyone asks, it's a report for school."

"Okay," Pam said. "Have you got two more boxes like this?"

"Yes, I think so," Denise said.

"Bring them and some file folders," Pam instructed. "We'll make files for them as we are copying the information."

"Good idea," Hank said. "Here, I want you to wear these when you are handling the copies." He handed each of the girls a pair of soft white cotton gloves. "If anyone asks why you're wearing gloves, it's to prevent smudges; your teacher is very picky. Don't touch any of the copy paper bare handed, before or after it is copied. This is important; understand?"

"No, I don't," Pam said.

"Fingerprints can be retrieved from paper by exposure to variety of chemical processes," Hank explained. "We'll be sending a copy of everything we do to the authorities but we will do it anonymously. This precaution ensures we don't accidentally leave a clue to our identities."

"I want you both to have the gloves on before you open the packages of paper, and I want you to leave them on until all copies have been separated into their individual files and placed in the boxes. Understand? This is important, all copies. And while you are at it buy new boxes and put the copies only in the new boxes; wear your gloves whenever you are touching the boxes also."

They nodded with understanding, taking the gloves.

"Hank, have you still got your safe-deposit boxes?" Doc asked.

"Sure do, both of them." Hank smiled. Only one really was actually a bank safe-deposit box. The other was a special container that was buried on his property.

"Good." Doc smiled back. "One copy goes in each of them and, one copy to the authorities. As far as anyone else is concerned, the only copy we had is the one we'll turn over to the authorities. When the girls get back, purge everything out of the computer, and I mean all of the way out."

"There will be no trace," Hank promised. "I'll take this hard drive out and replace it with this one." He held up a new hard drive. "I'd been planning to do it anyway; this is a good reason. This hard drive and all of its 'memories' will simply go away."

An hour and a half later, the girls returned with three boxes of files in file folders. Doc set aside the one box that would go to the authorities.

In it, he also put a copy of the disks. He made sure the disks had been wiped carefully to remove any prints. Then, he threw a coverlet over the box. This was to prevent anything else from accidentally falling or being dropped into the box.

He set aside two more boxes and placed a disc in each of them. These were to be placed in storage in the safe-deposit boxes. Additionally, he placed the notebook and laptop in one of them.

With a snack lunch of tuna fish sandwiches, chips, and a drink, they all sat down in the living room and began reading. Each had a note tablet and pencil to make notes.

There were a total of 33 files; each person received eight files, except Hank who got his eight and the extra. For the next several hours, there was very little conversation; they simply read and took notes.

They were going to have to give reports. It was about 1715 hours when Hank stood up, stretched, and called a halt.

"I don't know about y'all, but I need a break." He looked at his watch. "Has everyone finished? Good. Let's wash up and order some pizza. I'm going out to the garage to set up some things we'll need. When the pizza gets here, let's move out to the garage, and we'll munch while we give our reports."

Denise phoned in the pizza order, Pam went to the little girl's room, and Hank and Doc went out to the garage. Doc helped Hank set up an old style blackboard that was mounted on wheels.

Hank had traded into the blackboard years ago and it was where he jotted down information and organized his thoughts when he and Doc were preparing one of their many projects.

Doc had instructed Pam to bring three portable white boards and easels when she came. He used them in training classes for his clients. They were all arranged at one end of the garage along with a blank flipchart tablet also on an easel.

"Well, what do you think about this case?" Doc asked.

"From what was in my files, we have one hell of a problem," Hank said. "We are going to do this one by the book as long as we can. My fear is that it's not going to do us any good."

"What do you mean?" Doc asked.

"Listen, I've been in the intelligence business for a long time," Hank answered after a moment of looking at the floor. "It is not always a nice business."

"Decisions are not always made on the basis of right and wrong. Seldom is anything that black and white. There is always a multitude of considerations in any type of foreign interdiction action."

"The political situation between the U.S. and Mexico should be very positive with the North American Free Trade Agreement but it isn't," he continued.

"As you know, for the last year or so, we've been involved in drug interdiction activities all along the entire southern border."

"Mexico has some of the finest police officers I have ever worked with but they have some of the worst also. Look, let's wait to get the briefings from everyone, then we'll talk some more about this."

Doc didn't like the sound of this but Hank was probably right. Hank had shifted totally into the mindset of an intelligence analyst. That worried Doc. This shouldn't be that complicated. They had already done the hard part; they had found the evidence.

In a perfect world, they would give that evidence to the authorities, and the Cavalry would come riding in at the last minute, rescue the settlers, and lock up the bad guys.

Unfortunately, both Hank and Doc realized this world was far from perfect. Somehow, Doc suspected someone had been screwing with the story line again.

Damn, Doc thought. *I hate it when that happens.* Then, he started making some notes on the pad he carried.

Chapter Nineteen

The evening was cool, no mosquitoes and the pizza was good. The beer was cold, and the dogs were happy their "people" were eating outside with them so that they could get the crumbs. After everyone had filled their plates and got their beers, Hank went up to the large blackboard.

Once everyone was settled in his or her place, he began. "We have stumbled into something we cannot walk away from. I am going to prepare a synopsis of these reports and present that package to a duly authorized representative of the Federal Government. This is my job and my duty."

He continued, "In a situation like this, it would be logical to expect a full investigation, swift action, and a definitive response to this threat; however, based on my experience, I suggest we develop our own contingency plans beginning immediately."

"I want to hear from each of you as to the gist of the files you reviewed. I'll be taking notes and making annotations on these boards and flip chart. I ask you present information that deals with the immediate future or greatest hazard first and expound from there. Who has the finance information?"

"I do," Denise said. "After a very quick review, I estimate we are dealing with the equivalent of a major American corporation in terms of revenue, organization and distribution. I believe we have examined the structure of only one part of one division of that corporation. In fact, Val Richards' operation is referred to in the files as The Corporation."

"As near as I can tell, Val Richards brings in approximately 37 million dollars a year from what appears to be five different locations: two in the States, one in Mexico, one in the Far East and one in the Middle East. As far as I can tell, not one cent has been reported to the IRS."

"There are what I believe to be covers and dummy bank accounts scattered throughout Mexico, the Bahamas, and Central America. We need to refer this package to a financial analyst with a background in criminal investigation and tax fraud."

Hank interrupted, "So, you're telling me what we found is not the whole problem."

"Not even close, you have only the tip of the iceberg," she answered.

"Do we have complete financial reports, spreadsheets, and all of that?" he asked.

"No, what we have is basically the profit and loss statements for Val Richards' operations, and these are not the originals," she added.

"What do you mean?" Doc asked.

"Well, I suspect that our boy Jamie was either giving these to someone else or going into business for himself. It's also possible he could have copied Val Richards' files for blackmail or extortion. Of course, now we will probably never know what he was doing," Denise concluded.

"If you're through," Pam said anxiously, "let me tell you what I found."

"Sure," Denise said.

"I have a file and it's nothing but list after list of city, county, state and federal officials that are receiving money from this corporation," Pam said.

"Now, it's too early to start screaming illegal, but the sheer volume of transactions leads me to believe it has to be illegal. I'm guessing bribe money is necessary to either fix problems that have arisen or to look the other way so that they never come up in the first place."

"Do you have names, addresses, dates, and amounts?" Hank asked incredulously.

"Yes I do, as well as the location of the transfers, the method of transfer and the bank account from which it was drawn," Pam responded. "From the looks of it, some of these are single transactions conducted once or maybe twice."

"Others have continued being paid for years and I have found a few that can be tracked for 10, 15 and some for even 20 years. It will take more study. We have many different jurisdictions and apparent levels of government influence involved; but, it is all right here, and it sure doesn't look good from where I'm standing. There's a lot more but that pretty well covers the gist of the files."

"I have the client file," Hank said. "These files are very well broken-down and cross-referenced by both client name and preference."

"What do you mean by preference?" Doc asked.

"Well, it's not just prostitution," Hank explained. "This is the oldest profession combined with every diabolical and perverted twist you could imagine. There is straight sex, gay sex, kinky sex, drug-laced sex, sadomasochism, better known as S&M, Bondage, and Domination, and lots of kiddy sex and porn. They have recorded both the preferences and the evolution of preferences with their clients."

"What, the hell do you mean 'evolution of preference?' " Doc asked.

"The Corporation is not just a whorehouse," Hank explained. "These places don't just provide sex; they cater to it, and they exploit it. Joe or Jenny Blow—Mr., Ms. or Mrs. Average American finds their way into one of The Corporation's resorts. That's another thing; they are referred to as resorts in all of these documents."

"Someone spends a night, a night and day, a weekend or a week. During that time, they are wined with the finest vintages and dined with the finest cuisine you can find. The visit is top drawer all the way, and expensive but extremely chic and ultimately discreet."

"Slowly, Joe or Jenny is introduced to variations," he continued. "These are fantasies we all have and wonder about. They are introduced to stimulants and stimulation never experienced before."

"Sex becomes like a drug, and these Resorts become like a closed community with its own morals, rules, and judged behavior. Each visit gets a little wilder as the client tries to recapture that first incredible exposure to this lifestyle."

"It's exclusive, by invitation only, and expensive but very, very discreet. The customer's every whim is catered to, every desire can be realized and every passion can be experienced. Nothing is restricted. Nothing is taboo. Nothing is ever reported. The Resorts protect the client at all costs, period."

"What you are describing is the equivalent of a sexual speakeasy from the Prohibition Era," Doc said.

"You got it," Hank said, "but at a level of sophistication, expense, and depravity even Capone could not imagine. The Resort is actually divided into levels that are color-coded. It is considered a badge of accomplishment and a status symbol to progress from level to level: pink, orange, red, green, purple, blue, brown, and ultimately black. They also operate like a timeshare condo. You can even go to different Resorts."

"It's marketed only to those who are very rich, very powerful, and very hungry," he added. "You will be surprised at some of the names I have already recognized and the levels they are currently at. The Corporation's doctors check the sex partners, and the clients to ensure they have no sexually transmitted diseases."

"At the lowest levels, it is simply an extremely expensive, exclusive, and ultimately discreet whorehouse that caters to men, women, straights, gays, and bisexuals. Some people can come in at a higher level. These include the S&Ms, B&Ds and the pedophiles. All are actually considered quite socially advanced at the Resorts."

"You are telling me that sadists, masochists, bondage and domination freaks, and pedophiles are considered 'quite socially advanced?' " Doc asked.

"Within this social structure, they are viewed as not only socially advanced," Hank answered said, "but emotionally and intellectually superior. Like I said, these Resorts have become worlds unto themselves."

"Well, let me really ruin your day," Doc said. "I have the last file, and we have a serious problem."

Chapter Twenty

"First of all," Doc began, "this file deals with the operational end of The Corporation's resorts. There's evidence that in addition to Val Richards, that there are several people at Val Richards' level who also operate or 'manage' Resorts. At this moment, I cannot speculate on how many managers there are, but the indication is there are several."

He continued, "These resorts are divided into several departments and these appear to be consistent throughout the operation. First is housekeeping. These people appear to be simply employees, maids, chefs, groundskeepers, etc. They are not 'players' and it is conceivable they have no idea of the true purpose and orientation of the resorts. They are usually locals who are hired in the area each resort is located in."

"The manager and his 'assistant' are 'players,' " Doc said. "They direct and oversee the 'activities' of the clients, ensure a supply of sex partners, oversee security and dispose of problems, or as we have already seen, 'trash.' Additionally, they coordinate the selection and movement of the 'partners.' "

"What do you mean, 'partners?' " Hank asked.

"Here is where it gets really strange," Doc said. "These are the people who the customers have sex with. There are types of 'partners' or what we would call 'victims.' Type One is made up of paid volunteers that contract themselves out. Some are even clients or past clients themselves. Some are high school and college kids, while some are professional and high-dollar hookers. Some are even housewives interested in making big money in return for a few days or weeks 'work.' "

"Type Ones function at the lower levels of the scale and appear to simply be into the prostitution and softer aspects of S&M, B&D, and pornography. These people 'play,' but they do not get hurt."

"Type Twos are used when things move out of the 'victimless' crime arena and start getting nasty," he continued. "Type Twos work the harder side of the streets. These 'partners' may be volunteers. Others may not be volunteers."

"They are kidnap victims. In San Francisco and other shipping centers during the Old West, there was a popular term, shanghaied. It meant someone was drugged or knocked unconscious. When they awoke, they found themselves on a ship, miles out at sea. It was a common practice at most seaports in America."

"It was difficult to obtain crews for some of these ships. Some companies actually paid the kidnap victims for their services. Following the trip, they would be released back at the original port city. Others were not so fortunate.

They had been stolen and taken into slavery. Some of them eventually escaped, but most vanished and were simply never heard from again."

"How could that have happened?" asked Pam, always curious.

Hank said. "Many died on the ships. Remember, we are talking about a little over 100 years ago. Most of the ships were headed to China and the trip there and back took months. This was free 'slave' labor, and the conditions were deplorable."

"Some folks died due to disease or accidents. Some were murdered because they would not cooperate with the ships' crews. Others had their 'slavery' continued when they reached China or whatever ports the ship actually docked in. The ship's Captain sold them just like the other goods he had carried from America. There was good money in it in those days and few repercussions."

"How can that be?" she asked. "You can't steal people and just sell them for Christ's sake."

"Number one," Hank continued, "the victims were generally from a segment of the population that no one would miss and certainly would not look for very long. When one of these people vanished, there was not even a ripple on the pond of society."

"Number two, the authorities could not and would not do very much. If no one makes a report, there is no investigation for the authorities to follow up on. Also, money often exchanged hands to ensure that, if a report was filed, the investigation was redirected or delayed. Most of the time, the ship was already at sea before the person was even missed."

"Communications weren't like today," he concluded. "In those days, you couldn't radio the ship and tell them to turn around or fly out to the ship to investigate. Radios and planes had not been invented."

Pam looked at Doc and said, "You're saying this 'shanghaiing' is back. That's where the Type Twos come from?"

"Probably some of the Type Twos and all of the Threes," Doc said nodding.

"What's the difference?" Denise asked.

"Simple, the Type Twos are generally in fairly good physical condition when they arrive. They are used at the resorts for several months and eventually traded to other resorts or sold to 'investors' for their own private pleasure."

"Type Threes are traded like cattle; they are considered 'expendables.' They are saved for 'snuff films' and the more 'advanced forms of entertainment' at the resorts. In other words, they are tortured for fun and either are killed on purpose or die from their injuries and mistreatment."

Pam exclaimed. "How can this be happening?"

"The same way it did in old San Francisco," Doc answered slowly. "First, you find someone who has a need and is willing to do anything to satisfy that need. Then you find a ready supply of 'expendables' that no one cares about or will miss. In fact, most of society would prefer there were less of them around anyway. Add to that organization, power, and money, and you have the problem we have uncovered."

Doc continued, "Type Twos and Threes are tricked, seduced, hooked on drugs, or simply kidnapped. Each resort has at least one, sometimes two 'assistant managers' who are responsible for obtaining 'partners' and keeping the client's needs satisfied. We have already met Val Richards and his assistant manager Jamie."

"There is a 'schedule of events' so to speak at each resort," Doc said as he drew on one of the white boards to depict the relationship he was describing.

"The manager and at least one assistant manager are always present during what they refer to as a 'cruise.' A cruise is when the resort is in operation and partners are required. Cruises are set for weekends and variations ranging from three to seven days."

"Between cruises, the assistant managers go out to 'audition' new partners and collect them in preparation for the next cruise. Apparently, that was where Jamie was going when we ran into him again. During the cruises, the retreat has, on average 10 to 15 clients. Extra staff people are hired to handle security issues and other client requirements. The housekeeping staff is increased slightly also."

"What does this cost the client?" Pam asked.

"Depends on what they want and how long they want the cruise to last." Doc said. "Based on what I have seen so far, it is a pretty wide spread. A Type One weekend is the cheapest cruise and goes for about a grand. It is actually not out of line for some other vacations, and for this case, it is quite reasonable."

"The full package for a complete Type Three cruise seems to average between $20,000 to $35,000 per client. Get this, there are, on average 24 cruises a year at each resort, with a lot of repeat business. It appears to be Très chic, mon cher."

"By the way," Doc said concluding his briefing. "According to this information, we have 10 days left before the next cruise starts, ten days to do whatever we are going to do."

Chapter Twenty-One

Sunday morning, Doc woke up and eased into the kitchen for coffee. He let Pam sleep. Hank was up and handed Doc a cup.

Doc looked at Hank and said, "We have a serious problem here, don't we?"

"We sure as hell do," he agreed. "I'm telling you right now the government is not going to do shit, certainly not in the next 10 days. There's no way in hell things will move that quickly on something like this."

"So what is your suggestion, old All Knowing One?" Doc asked, afraid he knew the answer.

Hank began, "We divide the problem into three phases. Phase one—I'll prepare the information we have to present to the proper authorities but by surreptitious and anonymous means. We'll hope the authorities will respond appropriately and handle this mess the way that it should be handled. After all, sometimes the system does work."

"Great," Doc said. "What's Phase Two?"

"Oh, Phases Two and Three are simple," Hank said smiling. "Since we both know Phase One is not going to work but we also know we have to try it, you develop the contingency plan."

"All YOU have to do is come up with the right plan, the right people, and the right equipment to go in and rescue the innocent, identify the bad guys, and blow the hell out of the resort; and do all of this without getting busted by either the American or Mexican governments, while not dying in the process."

Doc had known the answer; damn it, he hated being right all of the time.

When Pam got up, they had a quick breakfast, and then she and Doc left for home at daybreak. The drive back to Houston would be long, Doc let Pam lead, and he followed her. He started compiling a mental list of names for the tactical team needed for this operation. By the time they hit San Antonio, Doc had 15 names refined down from an initial list of 103. Each was someone he knew personally who had a particular talent or ability that would be needed if Phases Two and Three went operational.

Almost all were veterans and, while most were Air Force vets, he also had Army, Navy, and the Marine Corps represented. He had no doubt these folks could do the job; his only question was if they would want to.

Three hours after leaving San Antonio, they pulled off of Interstate 10; twenty minutes later they were home. After unloading the car, feeding the animals, and checking phone messages and the mail, Doc settled down at the computer.

He started a file for each person and began building a dossier on each of the 15 people he had come up with. The dossiers detailed historical biographical information on each person. These were people he knew personally, some he had served with and, some he had not.

Richard Bach, an author, is fond of saying "Like attracts like" and that was how Doc had met most of these folks. They had simply arrived at the same places at the same times and recognized "like" or at least similar characteristics in each other.

Out of the 15 names, Doc was pretty sure not everyone would be able or would want to come on a "mission" like this; but, he felt comfortable that, from this master list, he'd be able to put what would be needed into the field.

Next, he began working on the equipment that would be necessary for such a mission. He knew equipment was as important as personnel.

First, he had to figure out who he had and what was needed. Then, he'd figure out what he could actually get, followed by going back and reworking what was needed into what he actually had.

From his days in mission planning for the old Counterterrorism Team, Doc looked at a team's basic requirements first. While he had done assault entries with less than what was considered required, he never liked to have an entry team consisting of fewer than three people.

His plan was to have two active and involved entry teams with an additional one in reserve, which could act as a covering element. He was up to nine people so far. Two sniper teams would be nice, he decided; he was now up to 13.

Now, he looked at communications. He reasoned that the Single Channel Air and Ground Radio, better known as SINCGARS, were the best bet and probably the easiest to obtain.

He knew that, given the right set of circumstances, this type of equipment could be "borrowed" from a National Guard Armory; and, as long as it was returned in operating condition, no one would ever know it was gone.

He made plans to have his communications man, or comm. man, determine and report on what the effective ranges would be for backpack, vehicle-mounted, and aircraft-mounted systems. His fear was that they would need at least one relay station to link all elements of the units.

He knew there would have to be modifications done to some of the equipment, but he had confidence in his comm. man.

Transportation was the next consideration. Time and stealth were two essential elements of this mission. They would have to do this mission quickly and without being observed. They would not have the luxury of driving down in fancy all-terrain vehicles armed for bear. They would have to be dropped within range of the Castle and approach on foot without being detected. They would have an advantage because they were familiar with the grounds and castle layout thanks to the Intel and recon photos.

Night was clearly the only option for this mission. He estimated the team would have to be three to six clicks out from the target. He eliminated a parachute drop, as he knew that not everyone on his list had jumped before and there was no time for training.

It would have to be an airmobile insertion. He knew that everyone on the list had repelled before. Helicopters would be the way to do it.

Helicopters, at least two, would be needed he decided after going through some quick calculations. This meant at least a pilot and co-pilot on each plus a crew chief. That totaled 19 people so far.

Detection would not be as critical on the way out. Once they made contact with the target, the bad guys would know they were there. But, if they successfully rescued the number of victims they expected, there would be at least double that number of people involved.

Doc figured to be safe he had to plan on a total of 30 to 38 people on the way out, 40 to be on the safe side. He estimated the number of victims by the number of known rooms he had counted in the Castle. Already, the numbers were not working.

Doc knew at 120 knots a Huey gunship could travel about 240 miles and skim the ground doing it. He once asked an old time Chopper Jockey how low a Huey could fly. "As long as the skids are not sticking in the mud, they do pretty well," was the laconic reply.

The range would work about right, but even two Hueys would not carry 40 people. He had his first problem.

Doc continued down his checklist. He had to set up the Command Center and the Field Hospital, just in case they had injured who needed treatment. He also had to set up security for both.

From his own experience, he knew the people on his list would have their own armament. Each man would be expected to carry a primary long gun, preferably a .223 or 7.62x39; a primary and secondary sidearm, at least a 9mm; gas mask and cover and Load Bearing Equipment better known as LBEs. In addition, each would need to carry two canteens, a flashlight, radio, ammunition, gas and smoke grenades, and a combat knife or bayonet.

With the exception of the radio, gas, and smoke grenades, each person could supply the rest of his armament.

He started going back through the entry team's requirements. He decided on two teams, Red and Blue, with three men on each.

Entry team one would be the Red team, this team being the primary entry team. The number one man, Doc himself, would be the TAC Team Leader. In addition to his primary weapon, he would add a secondary long gun, probably a modified 12-gauge pump shotgun.

The number two man on the team would carry bolt cutters in addition to his other equipment. One .22 caliber Colt Woodsman would be temporarily modified for his use. The number three man would act as scout and rear guard for the team.

Entry team two would be the Blue team. Blue team would be a reserve team and each man would be armed with rifles and handguns. Their primary mission would be to take out communications in the Castle and back up the Red team.

Team three would be a sniper team that would provide cover for Red and Blue teams. Its designator would be Carlos. Team Carlos would carry one long-range bolt action and scoped weapon, preferably a 30.06 or .308 as well as one scoped .223 or 7.62 x 39 semi-automatic rifle. To complete their equipment, a spotter scope or high power binoculars would also be carried.

Doc knew he could scrounge enough military D.C.U.s, officially known as Desert Camouflage Uniforms, to outfit the teams. Boots would not be a problem either. Boonie Hats or other soft covers would be worn instead of Kevlar or steel helmets. These were too heavy and noisy for what he planned.

Everyone would have on gloves from the time they left transport until the mission was over. Knee and elbow pads would be mandatory for the entry teams. Once at the Castle, goggles would be added. If gas was deployed, the goggles could be easily slipped into gas mask covers when the masks were being worn. They would be using the M-17A1, and since Doc wore glasses, he had to dig out his inserts and make sure the prescription was up-to-date.

No one would carry identification of any type.

Chapter Twenty-Two

As Doc thumbed through the dossiers, each of their faces came back to him. As he read their call signs, the memories resurfaced. Some of the memories were fresh, a few months or a few years.

Others went back over 20 years; Doc knew where a few were but wondered where the rest of these men were. What were their lives like now?

Doc thumbed through the names; he still had the original dossiers for most of the men he selected. Years ago, when he had commanded a Tactical Neutralization Team for the Air Force, he had compiled most of them himself.

He took that format and added information that he knew on the few who had not been on the team. An hour later, the new dossiers were complete. This new team, the TAC Team, would consist of men and women he knew well, people he trusted.

He smiled as he pulled the first two out of the pile. Hank would handle the Command Center and coordinate the actions of the ground unit, and designate the TAC Team. Additionally, he'd handle the victim recovery site, design the M.A.S.H., and the two Black Hawk helicopters necessary for the insertion. The choppers would be designated Birdman 1 and 2.

He went back through the notes he'd started on each of the three teams making up the TAC Team.

The TAC Team would consist of two squads or fire teams—Blue Team and Red Team plus a two-man sniper team, designated Carlos. Doc would lead the Red Team himself as well as lead the entire TAC Team.

Blue Team would be led by Warlord, John Roberts, Doc's son. Doc double-checked the dossiers for Hank and Warlord:

Harry Devlin, Call Sign: Hank
Age: 52
Current location: Presidio, TX
Physicals: White, Male, 5'10" blond/blue

Military: Enlisted 10 March 1968, Basic Military Training—Lackland AFB, TX—Jun 1967, Security Police.
Awards and Decorations: Presidential Unit Citation with One Device, Joint Military Unit Award, Air Force Outstanding Unit Award with Six Devices, Air Reserve Forces Meritorious Service Medal, Air Force Good Conduct Medal with One Device, Air Force Longevity Service Award with Five Devices,

National Defense Service Medal with One Device, Small Arms Expert Marksmanship Ribbon with Device.

Background: Air Force Security Police Investigations 10 years, Air Force Reserve 10 years.

Specialties: Strong mechanical and computer background. All military personnel transports including Hum Vee, Deuce and a Half, Six-packs, sedans, etc. also licensed for motorcycle.

Weapons: Qualified expert USAF on Colt M-16 rifle and M-203 configuration, Smith-Wesson .38 caliber K-38 Combat Masterpiece pistol, Beretta 9mm M-9 semi-automatic pistol. Preferred personal weapons: Weatherby bolt action 300 Magnum Rifle with 3-9 Bushnell scope, Ruger Mini-14 .223 caliber semi-automatic rifle, Colt .357 Lawman with four-inch barrel, Colt Detective Special with 2-inch barrel, and 80 lb. PSI Compound Bow.

John Roberts, Call Sign: Warlord
Age: 27
Baton Rouge, La
Physicals: White, Male, 5'10", 155, Red/Hazel

Military: First Enlistment Louisiana Army National Guard 19 July 1989, Basic Military Training, Fort Sill OK – July 1989 Specialties – Communications (31 V) and Infantry (11B) Transportation (88M). Second Enlistment United States Army 4 Feb 1995 Basic Military Training, Fort Knox KY. Feb 1995 Specialty Tanker (19K) Third Enlistment Louisiana National Guard 31 Dec 97 Specialty Communications (31U).

Awards and Decorations: Army Commendation Medal, Army Achievement Medal, Southwest Asia Service Medal with One Device, Army Good Conduct Medal with Once Device, National Defense Medal with One Device, Army Service Medal, National Guard Achievement Medal, Infantry Cord, Small Arms Expert (pistol, rifle, M-60, M-203, M-2, .50 Caliber Machine Gun, M-240, Grenades), Armorer qualified, Expert Driver's Badge (Driver/Track-M-1A1 Abrams Tank, M-113s, Bulldozer) and the Zaire Paratrooper Medal.

Background: US Army and Louisiana National Guard – total of 8 ½ years. Upon honorable discharge held four military job specialties (MOSs): 31 Victor –Communication Specialist, 11 Bravo – Infantry Specialist, 88 Mike – transportation Specialist, 19 Kilo –'Tanker Gawd' (On one occasion reports having a M1A1 Full Track Combat Heavy Main Battle Tank with 120mm Main Gun clocked at 70 mph. On another had the Tank airborne with the tracks were five feet off the ground. Of course, he broke the track, broke the road wheel arm, stripped the tension bar, snapped two torsion bars and ripped a sprocket off).

Vehicles: Hum Vee, a Tank Transport called a H.E.T., Jeep, Deuce and a half, 5 ton, scrapper, bulldozer, front-end loader, 113s known as Armored Personnel Carriers or A.P.C.s, and the M-1 A1 120mm Main Battle Tank (Abrams).

Specialties: Can operate any type of vehicle with four wheels or tracks. Strong communications background with expertise in radio equipment modification/repair and Land Navigation. Repel and jump qualified. Black Belt in Karate and instructor qualified for several martial arts weapons, including his own non-Kendo version for combat use of the samurai sword. Combat Life Saver qualified

Weapons: Qualified expert on M-203 (a combination weapon consisting of and M-16 with a single shot 40 mm grenade launcher mounted underneath, the Ma Deuce or M-2 .50 caliber heavy machine gun, 7.62 mm M-60 machine gun and its tank mounted version the M-240, M-16 .223 caliber rifle, Beretta 9 mm M-9 piston, Model 1911 .45 caliber pistol, and a variety of shoulder and tripod mounted missiles to include the LAWs (Light Anti-tank Weapon), AT-4s, and the Dragon. Preferred personal weapons: Ruger Mini-14 .223 semi-automatic rifle with folding assault stock, 12-gauge assault pump shotgun, habitually carries a 14 shot Para Ordnance .45 caliber pistol and a customized model 1911 .45 called The Warlord. Minimally is known to carry an A.G. Russell Sting A-1, a Benchmade Combat Switchblade and either a Cold Steel Trail Master Bowie or SRK Rescue knife.

*****

Doc knew how to contact these two essential leaders, but the others would prove more difficult. The names and faces came back to him. Moving to the computer, Doc set in motion the mechanics of locating the ones over the years he had lost track of.

He had no idea if they were even still alive or what physical shape they would be in. It had been more than 20 years since he had seen some of them.

As he initiated a search, Doc reviewed his proposed plan. M.A.S.H. would be headed up by Dr. B.J. Garrett, call sign Top Eye. In-flight emergency medical care and staff nursing at the M.A.S.H. following the mission would be headed up by Jean Bracken, R.N, call sign Nightingale.

The Black Hawk Pilots would be Jean's husband, Maj. William S. Bracken, call sign Leprechaun and retired Chief Warrant Officer 4, David Dillon, call sign Cobra Innkeeper.

Red Team would consist of: Doc; Danny Bookman, call sign Bush Hog; and Donnie Three Wolves, call sign Psycho.

Blue Team would consist of: John Roberts, call sign Warlord; Derrick Perce, call sign Mongo; and Frank La Borde, call sign Jarhead. His brother David La Borde, call sign Squirrel, would act as a door gunner on one of the Black Hawk's during insertion.

Gregg Paul, call sign Reverend, would be the primary sniper with a spotter named Lynn Rogers, call sign Mountain Man.

Rich Leonard, call Sign 2nd Chance and T.K. George, call sign The Wizard, would help take care of the victims upon their return and help return them to their families and to a normal life.

These were all folks he had maintained a relationship with over the years and knew how to make contact. He hoped that he could find Jay Moore, call sign Whisper; Steve Ingles, call sign Domino; and Mike Staten, call sign the Dago.

Jay had been Doc's partner when he was on active duty in the Philippines. Jay was deadly with firearms as well as with his hands and feet, not to mention all forms of martial arts weaponry.

Domino and the Dago had both been on Doc's TNT team. This would be their chance to hook back up, if he could find them. Tomorrow, he would start making some phone calls, cautious phone calls.

He did not want to give out too much information until he was sure the person would be willing and able to go on a mission like this. First, he would check their availability for making a three to four day trip to Mexico in about a week. The initial cover story would be that he had a private hunting trip lined up and several people had canceled at the last minute. The trip was already paid for, so it came down to whether or not they could take a few days off from work and if they felt they were in good enough shape to spend several days on foot in the Mexican high desert.

If they could not get away from work or home or felt their physical condition would keep them from going, it stopped there. If they were interested and able to go, his plan was to bring them together in the next few days for a full briefing at Hank's place in Presidio, TX.

Each would receive an envelope with sufficient money to cover their expenses for coming to the meeting and for living expenses during the mission. This would be provided out of Jamie's $270,000. He would use the bad guy's own money to finance their defeat.

At the meeting in Presidio, they would then be told that, in fact, it was not a hunting trip but a private rescue mission. No further details would be discussed until he had a personal commitment from each one.

The next day he started with Danny Bookman, call sign Bush Hog. Doc felt Bookman should be handled differently from the rest because of the time and distance in traveling from Anchorage, Alaska. Doc felt he'd have to share more information with him.

He finally got him on the fourth try. Bookman had his own construction company, but at the moment, things were relatively quiet. He indicated he would be interested in the trip. Yes, he was in shape for it. Yes, he could get away for four days.

Doc gave him a phone card number and the number of a pay telephone about a mile from Doc's house. He instructed him to begin calling that number in 30 minutes and to use the phone card. Doc also told him to go to an isolated phone booth to make the call.

When Doc arrived at the pay telephone, it was in use. He went inside the convenience store and got a soft drink. As he watched, the person finally hung up, so he went back out and waited for Danny's call.

As he approached the phone, it rang, and Doc snagged the receiver on the first ring. "No names," Doc said. "Do I know who is making this call?"

"I guess you do," Bookman answered. "You told me to make it. What the hell is going on?"

"I'm going to put you on the spot," Doc said. "If you lived closer, I would handle this differently, but you are too far away."

"Okay, so put me on the spot," Bookman said.

"The time frames we discussed are accurate," Doc said, "but it's for a very different reason. All I can tell you right now is it is not a hunting trip. It is a rescue mission."

"I believe that between 10 and 15 American citizens are being held at a location in northern Mexico, against their will and without the knowledge of the Mexican government. But, for reasons I won't go into right now, I do not expect help or intervention from either the Mexican or U.S. government."

"That means, if something is not done by somebody very soon, these American citizens will be tortured and killed."

"I take it," Bookman said after a moment of silence, "we are going to be that 'somebody,' correct?"

"Correct," Doc said. "There will be more than just you and me but yeah; WE are going to be that 'somebody.' "

"Do you know what we're getting into?" Bookman asked. "Do you know how to do something like this, or are we going to join the people we are setting out to rescue?"

"Like I said," Doc stated, "it is not just you and me. Most have a military background and the experience necessary. I will not lie to you and say there's no danger. One of the bad guys has already died. I need people who are tough, who can follow orders when I give them, and who can think on their own. Some of us may not make it back, but none of the victims will if we don't try. So here's one question and I need one answer right now. Do you want in?"

"Yes," came the response after a thoughtful silence of about 30 seconds.

"Good," Doc said. "Any questions?"

"Just one," he said. "What made you think I'd say yes?"

"Like attracts Like" Doc quoted. "Bring your own boots, weapons, and personal gear. Ammo and everything else you'll need will be waiting for you."

"Got it," Bookman said.

"One more thing," Doc said, "thanks," but all he heard was the phone being quietly hung up and the connection broken. *That's one,* he thought.

Doc went back to the phone. The next call was to Major Garrett, USAFR, Top Eye. Doc explained the cover story, Garrett bought it, and yes, he could get away. Doc knew he was in shape for the trip.

Doc gave him the calling card number and the phone number where Doc was. Somewhat surprised, Garrett agreed to comply with Doc's request. He called right back.

"No names," Doc said when he answered. "Okay," he said, "but what is going on?"

Doc told Garrett the real reason for the trip, what they had found and what they expected to do while they were there.

"I have a special need for you, Major," Doc said. "I have to have security set up to cover the Command Center and the M.A.S.H. It has to run for 24 hours a day until it is broken down. It also has to be set up about 12 hours before the operation begins. I need you to be directly over the set up and operation of the M.A.S.H. Most of the medical staff will be civilians with no background in military operations or discipline."

"I'm giving you advanced notice of what is really going on because you're going to need time to gather equipment and have everything staged to go. You will be armed, and I expect you to have the M.A.S.H. and the surrounding area totally secured and ready for incoming patients and follow-up care within five hours of your arrival. Are you interested?"

The line was quiet for a minute.

"You aren't going to need me on the assault team?" Garrett asked somewhat disappointed, Doc could tell.

"Major," Doc said, "I've got people for the team, but I know we'll be bringing back some folks who have been physically abused, doped up with drugs, and probably injured in the assault. I have a limited number of folks to operate with. This is where you will be the most important and can help save some lives instead of just taking some. I know you're good with a gun, but I also know that, as a doctor, you are good with people. I must have a secure landing zone to bring these folks to. I need you at the Command Center and the M.A.S.H."

"I'll have a Chief of the Command Center, but I need someone I can trust on this to handle the M.A.S.H. and coordinate with the CC. Do you want it?" Doc asked with his fingers crossed.

For a long moment, Garrett was quiet. Then he boomed, "Alright First Sergeant, if that's where you need me, that's where I'll be." Then, he began to ask questions, about 100 all at once.

Doc was Garrett's First Sergeant at his old Medical Squadron; they went back a long way together. Doc was pleased he accepted. He knew Garrett was right for the job. Doc smiled, and shook his head, and waited for a chance to respond. It came about 10 minutes later when Garrett finally quit talking. Doc finally got to say, "Thanks Major."

While his contact at the military locator was trying to come up with last known addresses and phone numbers for the rest on his list, Doc knew that he might not be able to locate some of the missing ones and he knew that some of the others might not be able or be inclined to make either the fake "hunting trip" or the actual mission.

By evening, Doc had contacted all of the people on his list and had eliminated several for one reason or another. Generally, their schedules just were not right to be able to take several days off in the middle of the week. He had 13 confirmed takers.

He called Hank to see where his part stood. He hoped that they had been wrong and the authorities would step in and do what needed to be done, hoping they would not have to go in after all.

Chapter Twenty-Three

Hank answered the phone on the third ring. "Hello." "How are you coming on this project," Doc asked.

"Not good," Hank replied. "I've got to go to the grocery for some grub. Can you call back in 30 minutes?" They spoke in a prearranged code for communications security.

Doc translated the code in his mind before responding, *I don't trust the phones here. Refer to the third list of phone numbers I gave you and call me there in 30 minutes.*

"No, I can't," Doc said. "No big deal, I'll talk to you in a day or so." Hank translated, *I got the message, understood, and will comply.*

Thirty minutes later, a phone rang on the West Side of Presidio and was picked up on the first ring.

"Well?" Doc asked.

"The information is there, but the situation is not good," Hank said. "I accessed some files containing land titles and deeds in that state. The area was originally being held in a 7,000 acre land bank, administered by the governor. Val Richards' property sits right in the middle of that acreage, plus he owns the only road in or out of the land. No one can build anywhere around him."

"Some surreptitious name dropping confirms that Mr. Val Richards is considered a Numero Uno in that area, being personal friends with anyone who is anyone. I suspect that we would find several of these big wigs are in fact clients and customers of the Resort," he added disgustedly.

"What about our people?" Doc asked.

"Like I said before, unless the local government pushes something, do not look for involvement from Capitol Hill," Hank emphasized.

"Fine, but what about the Bureau and Wonderland," Doc said, referring to the FBI and CIA. Surely, they see the potential problem and commonly do this type of interdiction." He said, getting angry.

Hank explained, "I think the problem is that they already know about the Resort, but I suspect it has been given hands-off status. Whatever happens there happens quietly and remains there. No one gets embarrassed. No one goes public."

"I suspect they are willing to allow a 'known devil' who operates quietly outside of this country. If the suspicion is that Mexican officials are partying at the Resort, it is also possible, even probable, that we have some American officials partaking of the fare as well."

"I guess you're right," Doc admitted. "I hadn't thought about it from that angle. Better to let whatever happens happen out of the country and in a controlled setting. That way, no one is embarrassed; no one goes to the talk shows or tabloids. It is better for the image, better for the country, better for the politicians and business people that play, and better for everyone I suppose."

"It is better for everyone except the 'victims,' " Hank pointed out. "So, what do we do now?" Doc asked.

"I have done all I can do without compromising ourselves and our 'potential' mission," Hank said frowning.

"I sent a package to some folks who I believe should be able to appropriately respond to this information. I also took the time to ensure that it would not be traced back to us. I also gave specific instructions on how to contact us through the personal section of the *Dallas Morning News*. They are to place a classified ad in the automobile section of the classifieds."

"It will say, 'To Bill, you left your wallet at our store. Please call 555-3030 to identify and claim,' " Hank added, "I know that when we call there will be a trace initiated, but I have that under control."

"Also, I've confirmed that the package arrived yesterday, so the clock is officially ticking. Day after tomorrow, we'll check the *Dallas Morning News* automobile section, and one way or another, we'll have our answer. So, there is nothing we can do until then but wait. How does it look from your end?"

Doc responded, "First of all, this is the last time we will discuss operations over the phone. From today forward, we have to assume someone, somewhere, could be tracking us and tap into our phone lines."

"Now, my Sit Rep. I've compiled my initial list for the team. From the original 15 names selected, I have confirmation on two pilots, two co-pilots, two three-man assault teams, and one two-man sniper team."

"At 1900 hours next Tuesday evening, two Army National Guard Black Hawk helicopters will take off from Biggs Army Air Field in El Paso, Texas on an approved training run. Shortly thereafter, they will drop under the civilian and military radar covers, and cross the border approximately 12 miles west, northwest of El Paso."

"They will remain in periodic radio contact with their base and transmit erroneous information that coincides with the training mission parameters. In actuality, they will be ferrying our team into position approximately 4.5 kilometers west, southwest of the castle, where at approximately 2000 hours, we will exit the choppers. The choppers will continue on for another five clicks and land."

"Using standard land navigation techniques, two small squads, our entry teams, plus the sniper team will traverse on foot the 4.5 kilometers. It should take them approximately 90 minutes with arms and equipment. They will arrive at the rendezvous point at approximately 2130 hours," Doc continued.

"They will establish a defensive perimeter and listening posts at this position and hold until given the go-no-go signal at 2300 hours."

"If it's a no-go," Doc said, "they will beat feet out of there with no contact. If it is a go, they will terminate radio contact at that point and initiate the mission. They will recon the area watching for any type of detection systems or equipment and report back."

"A sniper will set up on the rise above the castle to provide 'close-in fire support' if required. One explosive charge will be placed to drop the radio tower. It and the rescue attempt will be set to go at 2400 hours sharp. There will be no recall and no way to stop this once we have terminated radio contact," Doc emphasized.

"All of the guests should be occupied by that time," he added, "as should the staff. Once entry is made, the victims are all we'll be interested in. We are getting people out, not administering judgment or enforcing morality. If everyone cooperates, we are in and out with the victims in 12 to 15 minutes from go. Everyone else from the castle will be ordered outside, told to strip and instructed to begin walking south on the road."

"We reactivate radio contact and call the choppers in. They arrive, we load up, and, by 0200 hours, we are back across the border. Victims and team members will be dropped off, choppers landed at the base with you and I drinking Black Label Jack Daniels and smoking some of Val Richards's cigars," Doc said.

"Do you really think it will be that easy?" Hank asked.

Doc paused for almost a minute before answering. "No, I don't. If we have to go in, someone is going to get hurt or dead. I just pray it's the bad guys."

"Are you sure we can we pull this off?" Hank asked.

"I really think so; there are some points in our favor," Doc said. "First of all, we are not dealing with an armed military force. At best, we are dealing with some hoodlums and, at worst, some psychopaths. Now, they can be dangerous enough; but remember, our intelligence shows us that no one has ever challenged them before. No one has tried to penetrate their security. No one has been a threat."

"As I've said before, people with Val Richards' personality type like to think of themselves as in total control," Doc added. "Now, they can be dangerous as hell, but that is when they are initiating action themselves."

"They don't respond well to what someone else is doing to them. They like to be in control. In addition to them believing that anything they do is perfectly all right, there exists a fair degree of paranoia in these people."

"My goal is to wait until they're occupied with their pleasures," Doc explained. "I want them to feel confident and comfortable that this night is just another night of pleasures and profit. Then, we'll hit them so hard and so fast that they'll be totally disoriented. We'll have snatched control away, and we simply will not let them have it back."

"Surprise will be on our side, and that's real important," Doc said. "But, we'll also have a purpose and a well-thought-out plan. We will know what we are doing and why; they'll have to figure that out before they can mount a significant resistance."

"Now what kind of resistance can we expect?" Hank asked.

"As we say in the old time military, 'kick ass and kill the bad guys business'—I believe they will be uncoordinated and weak. I don't expect more than 10 to 15 hard guys, max. By hard guys, I mean armed personnel that could and would respond to shooting. With two three-man teams inside and a sniper team outside providing cover, we should literally catch them with their pants down."

"What type of weapons do you expect to encounter?" Hank asked while taking notes.

"I'm guessing, but I would expect handguns primarily; the hard guys will have theirs on them. If they're able to get to a weapons locker, they will probably have shotguns or, maybe some small caliber submachine guns," Doc admitted.

"It's reasonable to assume fairly conventional weapons and munitions. Remember that these guys are on their own turf. These people have never had the need to prepare for any serious threat to the place or the people; that is until we come along."

"What about our people? What will they carry?" Hank wanted to know.

"Every person will provide their own weapons," Doc said. "We do not have time to train everyone on single types of primary and secondary weapons, although that would be my preference."

"A single type of primary and secondary assault weapon with matching ammo and a single type of tertiary weapon, personal and backup handguns with matching ammo, is always the way to go. I believe we'll have quite a variety. We'll have some people using .223 in at least two different types of rifles," Doc said.

"Several will be using 7.62X39, but luckily, all will be using the Russian SKS. Long-range sniper will be 7.62 NATO or .308 caliber, and all shotguns will be 12-gauge loaded with #4 shot and carrying some extra specialty rounds."

"Handguns will be .45s, .40s, 9mms, and a special subsonic .22 with a sound suppressor. The only thing I know to do is try to assign the teams on the basis of job requirements and try to match as many weapon types and ammunition requirements as we can. We have some body armor, but only three are rated for tactics such as this. We have some gas and some smoke, enough that each team has a mixture of both but there's none to spare."

"There's also a mixture of L.B.E.s." Doc continued. "Some are using their own old Y and H harnesses, some have newer equipment, and some even have the newer assault vests. One thing I am doing is providing everyone with the BlackHawk CQB/Rescue Belt to use as a replacement for their normal pistol belt."

"What is that?" Hank asked looking up.

"It's the newest and greatest" said Doc. "It's a special belt that can be worn as a trouser belt or hooked to the L.B.E. I'll fax you a specification sheet when I get back. It's sold by U.S. Cavalry. It has a swing-out parachute V-ring that can be hooked to a repelling rope with either a carabineer or a locking D ring to replace the heavier Figure 8 Descender. This is important because I expect our people will punch out of the chopper and repel to the ground."

"It'll be quick, and I think the most appropriate method to insert our personnel. They'll hit the ground and run off their ropes, replace the carabineer or D ring on their L.B.E. for later use, and keep on moving. I anticipate all eight men on the ground and moving toward the objective in less than 10 seconds. Check your fax later for the spec sheet."

"Fine, but one question. Why do you want them to repel?" Hank asked.

"As I said, it's quick and probably as quiet an entry as we can make," Doc explained to Hank. "Noise is a big factor. The way we're planning it, no one will hear the choppers flying around just a few clicks away and probably won't be able to tell anything has occurred."

"Okay," Hank said, "but let me make you aware of something. There are two major sounds with a chopper: engine noise and rotor noise. At 4.5 clicks, an untrained person is probably not going to pick up the differences in engine noise, but the rotor is a different story. The rotor makes a distinctive noise when it is providing lift, such as in a hover for a repel. I think that landing and discharging personnel is not only going to be safer but quieter also."

"Okay," Doc said. "Let me think about it, and I'll let you know. You may have a point, but I am still concerned about the speed of the insertion. Faster is going to be better in this case."

"I have enough D.C.U.s, soft covers, canteens, and equipment to go around. We'll at least look like a military unit, if you don't look too closely, and I think we can keep that from happening."

"Explosives are my only concern. I would like a little C-4 to take out the radio antenna and possibly to open some doors, if need be."

"No problem," Hank said smiling, "we'll just make our own. If we don't get the authorities to move, I'll make a run to the store and pick up the mixin's. You will have to confirm the flight ops side of this and make sure we can stage everyone at the appointed time with all required gear. Any problems from your side?"

"No, it will be tight," Doc admitted. "I'm hoping the authorities will simply do their damn jobs. That will mean we don't have to do all of this."

Hank smiled. "I'll bet you still believe in Santa Claus."

"Absolutely," Doc said with a smile, "and the Easter Bunny. Pam and I will see you late Friday night." Doc hung up; he knew in his heart what was going to happen. They both did. Both had known since this thing got started, but they had to try to do it the right and the responsible way. They had to try.

Doc had a lot to do between now and the time he'd be heading back to Hank's Friday for the big meeting.

Chapter Twenty-Four

Saturday morning, Hank's garage was in use yet again. The meeting would start promptly at 0900 hours, and although everyone was in civilian attire, the military atmosphere was obvious.

This initial meeting would be with the Team leaders and those individuals necessary for the operation to succeed. The people seated at this table represented each of the essential factors of this mission.

Their additional people would be arriving over the weekend and would be briefed.

Air Ops:
David Dillon, Call Sign: Cobra Innkeeper
Major W. S. "Sherry" Bracken, Call Sign: Leprechaun

Air Intel:
Harry Devlin, Call Sign: Hank

Mission Ops, Equipment and Logistics:
Doc Roberts, Call Sign: TAC Leader

Manning:
John Roberts, Blue Team Leader, and Doc's son, Call Sign: Warlord

Medical Logistics/Treatment:
Jean Bracken, Registered Nurse, Call Sign: Nightingale Major (Dr.) B.J. Garrett, Call Sign: Top Eye

Doc had arrived late the evening before, but alone. Pam had decided to stay in Houston and not drive in until late Sunday evening. She was taking the next week off as vacation time but had to finish some last minute sales contracts at the office.

Denise had been on the phone for three days handling what Hank was calling "Phase 1 Alpha." Doc had no idea what that was, but she was still on it. As soon as everyone had coffee and a doughnut, Doc started the meeting.

"Welcome, I appreciate the sacrifices each of you made to get here. Let me begin by telling you that we are continuing to pursue another resolution to the situation that has brought us together; however, if our attempts continue to be met with the level of success we've had so far, something will have to be done. In all honesty, I don't know who else to turn to."

"I have worked with or known each of you for a number of years," Doc continued. "I've presented my analysis of your potential contributions to this mission to Hank and have assured him I have total confidence in each of you. Right now, we need some answers. If we have to go in, we only have a couple of days before we will have to move."

"Needless to say, what is said here must remain here, except to brief your own people when they arrive. I expect each of you to present a vague mission orientation to your people based on the information you will receive today; focus on logistics and supplies only. Beans, bullets, boots on the ground, agreed?" They nodded.

"Good, if it is determined that we will launch this mission, a final briefing with all involved personnel is scheduled for 0800 hours Monday. Agreed?" They nodded.

Doc turned to Hank. "Hank is our air intelligence specialist. He is also one of the two people who uncovered this situation. I'd like for him to give you an initial briefing on what we suspect, what we know, and what has been done to date. Bear in mind, if the decision is made to go in, there will be additional briefings with everyone involved to go over again what you are hearing today and any last minute changes in the ops plan."

Hank stood and walked slowly to the blackboard. "Good Morning, I haven't met each of you, but I've heard some wonderful things. I can tell you that, if one-tenth of what Doc said about each of you is true, this mission can be pulled off successfully."

He explained how he and Doc had originally gone to Mexico to look for gold deposits and had stumbled onto the castle.

Hank continued, "I am introducing Val Richards by passing out copies of the printout that we had pulled from the National Crime Institute Computer, or as most of you know as the NCIC."

"His complete name is Juan Valentino Richards. He was the product of a short-term liaison between his mother, Emily Richards, and the family stable boy, Juan Valentino Sanchez."

"Sanchez was Puerto Rican, and Emily was pure blue blood Boston society. Needless to say, Emily's indiscretion, coupled with the fact that she had elected to name the bastard after his father and kept the child to raise herself, set the family's proper standards of behavior spinning."

"Although there had been several indications that as a juvenile Juan Valentino Richards had encountered the law, those records were sealed by court order due to his juvenile status. There had been no indictments as an adult, although there were indications he had been questioned several times by local authorities over the years."

"Checks with other agencies and data banks revealed that Val Richards had attended the finest private schools throughout his academic career. Beginning between ages of 14 and 15, his grades took a dip. He and his mother had been called in for several formal counseling sessions from school administrators; the subjects of these discussions are unknown."

Hank admitted there was insufficient material for a complete background. However, in his experience, what was present indicated that more was there. Not one to speculate, he was confident a deep search of Val Richards' past would uncover things that Mr. Richards would prefer be left alone.

Next, Hank went into as much background as he had defined on the Resorts and The Corporation. Again, apologizing for the insufficient time required for a more thorough investigation, Hank was able to present some new facts even Doc had not heard.

The Resorts were apparently all licensed through the Eros Corporation, which was actually a holding company with an unnamed Board of Directors. "Given sufficient time," Hank said, "I would be able to identify the principals involved, but that is secondary information. Interpol—the International Police Organization—has received several complaints related to missing individuals and questionable activities at several of the Resorts."

Initial investigations had not confirmed the reports, but Doc found it very interesting on two counts. First, the fact that such complaints had been made gave additional validation to their beliefs about the operation of the Resorts. Second, that a veil of secrecy could be erected over the Resort's operations with sufficient speed and credibility as to foil Interpol's investigation.

Apparently, the Resort they were preparing to enter was, in fact, the newest in the chain. It had only been in operation for about six months and constructed for a cost in excess of 12 million dollars. That was over double what Hank would have estimated for the cost of the Castle. According to Hank, that meant much of the castle could not be seen. It had to be underground. This tied nicely with the "tornado shelter" Doc had discovered in the back courtyard.

Hank continued, "We have been able to access some, but not all, of the architectural plans. What we knew as the covered corral and connected garage, we now know also contains a disguised airplane hangar. This hanger is large enough to house a twin-engine plane of fair size. Access is controlled by an electrical system that allows sections of the surrounding fence to be lowered into concrete structures set in the ground."

"Then, an entire wall swings up and out of the way, kinda' like a garage door, allowing a plane to simply drive in. The road in front of and alongside of the property doubles as the runway. Once the plane is concealed, passengers are off-loaded in privacy and taken into the castle."

"Based on the records we've examined," Hank said, "we've been able to estimate that, during an 'event' at the resort, there is an average of 12 to 15 people housed at the castle—either as individual clients or client couples."

"There's an average of five 'hard guys' brought in to handle and dispose of problems and situations that arise. With Val Richards and one—possibly two assistant managers, the opposing forces will not be evenly matched. The good news is that we are expecting the trouble; hopefully, Val's team will not. As Doc says, we should have the element of surprise."

Hank closed his portion of the briefing by identifying that a sterilized box of files and computer disks had been delivered to the authorities five days ago.

As of this moment, there had been no response or contact attempted by the authorities. However, according to Hank, this was not unexpected. Analysis of the data would have begun, but until the Feds had some idea of what was contained within the information, they would not respond.

Hank also identified that it was entirely possible no response would ever be forthcoming.

He then passed the podium to David Dillon and Major Sherry Bracken. Each stood and went to separate writing boards. While Dillon began making annotations on one board, Bracken set two model helicopters on the table in front and said, "I'm Sherry Bracken, call sign Leprechaun, and this is David Dillon, call sign Cobra Innkeeper. We'll be your bus drivers for this mission and also provide some limited air cover during the withdrawal phase of the operation."

"This is your bus," he continued, picking up a model helicopter. "The Army's UH-60 Black Hawk helicopter can carry a fully loaded combat squad and their equipment. As this is not a formal military briefing, David and I will 'skip to the chase.' These planes," he said as he picked up the other model, "will get us in without interference from either Mexican or American authorities. I cannot go into very much more information because of security classifications on the equipment and systems."

"What about the border radar?" John Roberts asked.

"When you know where it is located and what the coverage is, which we do, slipping under it or through the holes is not as difficult as one would think." Bracken explained.

Dillon took over. "The birds will start here at Fort Hood outside of Killeen, Texas. I have already walked through approved flight plans for two Black Hawks to fly to Biggs Army Air Field outside of El Paso. Flight crews will be limited to the pilot and Weapons and Electronic Systems Officer, or W.E.S.O, instead of the normal four-man crew."

Dillon continued, "Jean Bracken, call sign Nightingale, will fly as W.E.S.O. on Birdman One, Major Bracken's chopper, and will also be available to treat the wounded and injured upon extraction."

"David La Borde, call Sign Squirrel, will fly W.E.S.O. on Birdman 2, my bird, and will become the door gunner on the M-60 machine gun once we cross the border. Once we have arrived at Biggs, we will refuel and appear to participate in a joint training exercise called 'Night Watch' with selected infantry personnel, supposedly from Fort Polk, Louisiana."

"Of course, there is no such exercise, but training flights of this nature occur all the time from units all over the states. As long as the flight plans have been approved, there is no reason to expect that we'll run into any problems."

"The two choppers," Dillon continued "will depart Biggs according to our time table, each carrying one half of the assigned personnel. They will fly N.O.E. to crash the border approximately here," Dillon pointed at the map "and then fly contour to the target."

"What is N.O.E?" Doc asked, for those who might not know.

"Sorry, Nap of the Earth," Dillon said. "We'll be flying with N.V.G.s, that's Night Vision Goggles, just high enough to miss the cactus and the jack rabbits and at only about 50 knots. Once we can fly contour, which is after we have penetrated the radar, we will be higher and faster."

"The trip in should take less than an hour. Then, we'll insert the ground unit, code name TAC Team, approximately 4.5 clicks from the objective. Originally, this insertion was to be done at the hover by repelling ropes. Instead, we will do a 'combat debarkation' and deploy the Team."

"Once the TAC Team has been deployed, both choppers will fly to this designated point, which is approximately five clicks further inland. They will land and maintain Red Con Level 2."

Bracken explained this meant Readiness Condition Level 2, which meant the birds could be airborne in less than 10 minutes. He continued, "At approximately 2000 hours, radio contact will be broken with the TAC Team and remain so until 2330 hours. At that time, a final radio check will be conducted, and a go/no-go signal will be transmitted from the choppers and acknowledged by the TAC Team Commander, call sign TAC Leader."

"If the mission is a no-go, or if for any reason the ground unit finds itself unable to carry out the mission, the TAC Leader will at this time transmit the message 'ABORT—NEGATIVE—ABORT,' " the Cobra Innkeeper continued.

"The TAC Team will withdraw to this position," he said while pointing "approximately 2.3 clicks from the objective and await helicopter extraction."

"Are there any questions?" There were none.

"If the mission is a go and the TAC Team is able to initiate the mission, the TAC Leader will at this time transmit the message 'ENGAGE—POSITIVE—ENGAGE.' "

"Radio contact will then be terminated until it is time to recall the choppers. The ground unit will secure the communications equipment so that it's protected during the engagement. Exactly 15 minutes after communication is broken off, both choppers will initialize all systems and prepare for takeoff."

"Once the TAC Team transmits the retrieval message, the choppers will head for this position on the road, which is immediately adjacent to the castle. TAC Team will set up a secure perimeter, and Leprechaun will land to extract the victims and any wounded. During this time, I will be flying cover for the operation."

"Once Leprechaun is loaded, he will lift off and provide cover while I retrieve the TAC Team. At this point, all we have to do is point northeast and beat feet out of there. Again, we will fly contour until it is necessary to drop back to N.O.E. to penetrate U.S. air space."

They sat down and Jean Bracken stood up. "I'll be flying in the lead chopper. I will keep us in contact with Command Center, which will be located here," as she pointed to the map on one of the boards. "Once retrieval has been accomplished, I will try to stabilize any wounded until they can be dropped at the Command Center, which is where our M.A.S.H. will also be located. This drop site is about 50 miles from El Paso."

"All wounded will be treated here. We will be limited to only the basics, but we cannot go to hospitals with bullet wounds, not without being reported to the authorities. We will have one table, one surgeon, damn little equipment, one other nurse, and me. Field appropriate Buddy Care may be required, and each man on the TAC Team will carry a basic first aid kit. I will give a refresher class on CPR and Pressure Points before the mission."

"Dr. Garrett will be in charge of setting up the M.A.S.H., ensuring we are secure for this entire phase and ensuring coordination between those requiring medical treatment and needing transportation to different parts of the country. He and I will work closely on setting up this mission and providing pre-mission physicals on all personnel."

"Most of the team is in excess of normal age parameters for such a mission and have not maintained a strict program of physical conditioning. If either Dr. Garrett or I eliminate someone from the field operation, it is for their own good and the good of the team. We are not to be challenged; our medical rulings will be final, agreed?" All nodded.

"This place," she said pointing to the hospital, "is call sign M.A.S.H.; my call sign is Nightingale. Dr. Garrett's call sign is Top Eye. He runs the M.A.S.H.; his word is law, and it is final. He is the only team member who is to have direct contact with the civilian medical personnel I will be bringing; any questions?" There were none, and she sat down.

John Roberts took the podium. On one of the boards, he drew out two three-man teams and one two-man sniper team. He asked Doc to pass out some materials he had compiled and proceeded to draw out the castle's compound on the board.

"There will be three components to the TAC Team. These two entry teams, designated Red and Blue and this sniper team designated Carlos."

"These teams will be dropped approximately 4.5 clicks out and are to move as quickly as possible into position. Everyone will be traveling on foot, so prepare yourself and your team appropriately."

"Carlos will move out first and scout the way in. Carlos will consist of two people. First is Lynn Rogers, call sign Mountain Man. He is familiar with the general terrain and is an excellent scout and hunter. He will be the spotter."

"The second Carlos team member, the primary Sniper, will be Gregg Paul, call sign Reverend. He'll be carrying a Stoner SR-25, which is a semi-automatic .308 specialty rifle with a heavy scope."

"They will stay approximately a half click ahead of Red and Blue Teams. They should spot any problems before they themselves are spotted and before Red and Blue can be spotted."

"Once at the castle, Carlos will set up here," Roberts said, pointing at the plot table mockups. "This rise is approximately 50 feet higher than the castle's wall and about 100 meters from the main house. Red Team will move to this location, and Blue will move to this location." He pointed again at the table map. "Here, all teams will establish lookouts, while resting and recovering from the trip in."

"When the final radio communications are given, if the mission is aborted, Carlos will remain in position to cover the withdrawal of Red and Blue. If it is a go, the TAC Team will drop all of their comm. equipment in place and Carlos will provide cover fire for the movement of each element. Carlos is the only team with access to comm., and that's only to call in the choppers."

"Reverend will have a green light to take out any hostiles once the teams have reached these points. Mountain Man will act as his spotter and backup. From this position, they can control front and rear courtyards, the roofs, three sides of the castle, and the disguised hanger."

"Red Team, consisting of Doc Roberts, call sign TAC Leader; Danny Bookman call sign Bush Hog; and Donnie Three Wolves, call sign Psycho, will cross the wall here. Psycho will take out individual area lighting with a sound suppressed .22 caliber pistol. The team will then take up a position here next to the patio."

"They will then scale the walls to the roof. This will be accomplished by a combination of available structures and grappling hook with rope. Once on the roof, they will prepare to enter through the skylight in the master bedroom."

"Blue Team, consists of myself, call sign Warlord; Derrick Perce, call sign Mongo; and Frank La Borde, call sign Jarhead. We'll set explosive charges at the base of the radio antennae and adjacent to the fuel tanks of all vehicles found in the garage and hanger. Once these have been set and all is going according to our plan, Blue Team will return to this point and prepare to enter through the tornado shelter. A small charge will be used to blow the door and down we go."

"It is important that Red Team enter the castle five minutes before the Blue Team blows the door to the Tornado Shelter. That will give the team time to be in position and be ready when the explosions start because, at this point, our element of surprise is lost."

"The other charges will be on a 45-second delay to blow in sequence after the charge that blows the tornado shelter door. That should add and continue to add to the confusion as well as eliminate any escape vehicles. However, it may become necessary for some flexibility on the part of the Team Leader once the operation is in motion. Are there any questions?" he finally asked. There were none.

"Okay," Doc said as he stood, "I want to be sure we are all in agreement with this mission plan?" Everyone nodded yes.

"I want to thank each of you for your hard work; now, we have to wait and see if we are going to be forced into Phase 1 of the mission."

"We'll know Monday morning. If it's a go, the TAC Team and Command Center/M.A.S.H. Element will leave for Biggs Air Field in El Paso, TX, and Air Ops will head to Ft. Hood in Killeen, TX; all this will happen by noon on Monday."

"The airlift components will initiate Tuesday morning and we hit the ground in Mexico at 2000 hours Tuesday night."

"Any questions?" There were none. "Then, let's get out of here."

Chapter Twenty-Five

The rest of the team members arrived by Sunday afternoon and were stationed at different motels in the area. Following a barbecue for everyone Sunday evening, it was decided everyone would meet at 1030 hours Monday morning.

Monday morning, Doc looked at his wristwatch; it said 0800 hours. The garage had been cleaned out, and the chalk and white boards set up. Hank had a TV and VCR set up to watch a travel video showing the area and talking about the flora and fauna we were likely to encounter, friendly and otherwise.

He had created a plot table with a model of the castle compound to include walls and compound buildings. While it was not to scale, it wasn't far off. Doc was impressed and was sure to say so.

"No big deal," Hank said, "just some Styrofoam, spray paint, and plywood."

"Right," Doc said. He knew Hank had not come inside until almost 0230 hours this morning. Now, he knew why.

"I'm going to pick up the morning paper," Hank said as he started his truck. "Hopefully, the authorities will announce their interest by using the personal ads as we suggested. Keep your fingers crossed."

Doc crossed his fingers and held them up for Hank to see as he drove off. Doc went into the garage where Pam stood with two cups of coffee. She had arrived late last night from Houston.

"Here," she said passing one to him. "Is he going after the paper?"

"Uh huh," Doc mumbled taking a sip of hot coffee at the same time. "He should be back in about 30 minutes, and then, we'll know what the deal will be."

"Thirty minutes, huh?" she said moving closer to Doc.

"Come on, you're going to be busy later. As a matter of fact," she said smiling, "you're going to be busy now." She pulled Doc into the house and toward the guestroom. Thirty minutes later, they heard Hank's truck pull up.

"Well, I feel better," she said. "How about you?"

"Oh yeah!" Doc confirmed, as he buckled his belt and slipped on the T-shirt he had been wearing. He slipped into some flip-flops and went outside to see Hank. Hank was just standing there, looking out toward the back of his property.

"No response," Doc said.

"None," Hank replied. "I figured there would be something, some kind of response, but absolutely nothing. This is very disappointing."

"Look, you tried," Doc said. "Now, we know what we are dealing with. Let's quit worrying about what might have been and get focused on the job."

"Hoo Rah," Hank said, turning and heading for the garage.

"Hoo Rah," Doc said, and he headed to house to place a call to his son, John. "We go," Doc said when John Roberts answered the phone. "Gather your people; have them collect their gear. Check out of the motels, and be here at 1000 hours sharp."

"Damn Dad," John said. "Isn't there another way?"

"No Son, there doesn't appear to be one." Doc said and hung up.

By 0945 hours, all of the members of each section were gathered. This was the first briefing which included everyone that would be involved in the mission. Flight Ops, Command, Medical, and the Ground Unit were present and seated around the plot table Hank had constructed in his garage. Bags of gear and weapon cases were stacked just outside the garage.

Hank went to the chalkboard and began the briefing by saying, "Well ladies and gentlemen, we tried but apparently to no avail. No attempt has been made by the authorities to make contact with us. Therefore, we must assume that nothing will be done unless we do it."

"Before we go any further, I want to explain something." He looked slowly around the table at each person. "For those of you who just arrived yesterday afternoon, we purposefully kept the exact nature of this operation from you until you arrived here yesterday. Each of you will find a complete brief of what the real purpose of this 'get together' is on your chairs. Please begin reading it."

"You were not kept in the dark because of a lack of faith in any of you. It was simply operations security. In all honesty, I—we had hoped this mission would not be necessary and we would all spend some R&R time around here then head back home; but, as I said, it looks like we are going in. Anyone who wishes may be excused."

"Most of you were brought here under false pretenses, thinking this was going to be a hunting trip. Now that you know what is involved, you may not wish to or may not be able to participate for a variety of reasons. Feel free now to back out without any loss of honor and with our deep appreciation for having come to this stage."

For two long minutes, two very long minutes, he was silent. He looked into each person's eyes around the table for a sign one way or the other. All he saw was a nod from each.

"Okay then," he said and turned to Doc. "Well, you sure know your people." Turning back to the group, he began with a general overview of the initial trip into Mexico and how he and Doc had come to this point. Hank had prepared packets for each person's review. They included as much relevant information as available on Val Richards. The packets also included diagrams of the proposed routes, diagrams of the castle, call signs, team make-ups, and a recap of each person's responsibilities.

Moving to the plot table, Hank identified the drop site and loading zones for both the abort and mission completed scenarios. Doc took over and walked through the TAC Team's approaches, positions, and movements. For an hour, they dissected and refined the plan until they were satisfied that they had addressed all they could beforehand.

John Roberts moved to the front of the table. "Some of you have your own L.B.E.s and are welcome to use them. If you need gear, see me after the meeting. I see that the new D.C.U.s and Boonie hats I issued yesterday seem to fit everyone. Good, each person will also be issued one of these." He held up the BlackHawk Last Resort belt and a locking D-Ring, explaining their purpose and use.

"We had originally planned to do a repelling insertion— that has been discarded in favor of landing the choppers to discharge personnel. Each team member will still be required to wear the Last Resort and carry the D-Ring. One roll of rope will be carried by each team in case it is needed at the target. Once you are on the ground, set up a security perimeter. Doc, the TAC Leader, will confirm communications and will signal the choppers to depart. From the start of the mission, we'll being using our team call signs. Pay attention; all communications will be as follows."

"Mountain Man, you and Reverend are call signs Carlos 1 and 2." Both men acknowledged and John continued.

"TAC Leader, Bush Hog, and Psycho, you are Red 1, 2, and 3."

"I'm Blue 1; Mongo and Jarhead, you're Blue 2 and 3."

"Major Bracken in the lead chopper will be Birdman 1. Mr. Dillon in the second chopper will be Birdman 2."

"Nightingale will fly as W.E.S.O. on Birdman 1 and be available to treat wounded and injured upon extraction."

"David La Borde, call sign Squirrel, will fly as W.E.S.O. on Birdman 2 and move to door gunner on the M-60 once we cross the Mexican border."

"Hank, Denise, and Pam will be Command 1, 2, and 3. They will meet the Nightingale's medical crew at the M.A.S.H. and help establish the Command Center, and then, they wait."

"Major Garrett, Top Eye, you will assemble the support personnel as well as develop and implement a plan for security at the Command Center and M.A.S.H. That security needs to run 24 hours a day until further notice."

Garrett nodded and John continued, "During extraction, Birdman 1 will land to pick up our rescued targets and any wounded, while Birdman 2 provides cover. Once Birdman 1 is airborne, he will provide cover for the pickup of the team members. Birdman 1 and 2 will then proceed to this point, call sign M.A.S.H., to offload all rescued targets and wounded. Are there any questions?"

There were no questions, and he turned to Doc, indicating it was his turn to talk. It was time to wrap it up, and Doc said, "Ladies and gentlemen, that concludes the briefing."

Doc looked at Top Eye and said, "Top Eye, lead us in prayer please." Everyone bowed as Top Eye lead a prayer asking for God's protection over the mission and over each member as they faced evil and did what honor required of them.

When Top Eye had concluded, Doc said, "If there are no further questions, stow your gear in the assigned vehicles; we leave shortly. With the exception of vehicle operators and flight crew's personal identification, car keys and anything else you have in your pockets is to be placed in one of these envelopes, sealed and your name written on the outside."

Doc passed out the large manila envelopes. "Drop them in the box by the back door; you will get them back at the end of the mission. I take it that everyone has checked out and is ready to go?"

They nodded. "Good. Birdman 1 and 2, Nightingale, and Squirrel, you are released. Make tracks for Fort Hood; you have a long drive. Check in with Command 1 on his cell phone once you've arrived or on fly over the Command Center and M.A.S.H. Everyone throw all notes, papers, maps, and other materials that contain mission information into the burn barrel outside the door as you depart."

Birdman 1 and 2 and their crew headed off to the chopper base at Fort Hood in Killeen, Texas, which is located in central Texas. The other eight members of the TAC Team gathered in front of the garage. Their L.B.E.s, SINCGAR radios, handguns, and equipment were stuffed in B-4 bags.

Large padded gun cases carried their primary and, in some cases, their secondary weapons. These were all being loaded into the two extended cab pickup trucks they would use for the trip to El Paso.

The Command Section, Hank, Denise, and Pam, finished rigging a SINCGAR, booster, and antennae to Hank's fifth wheel camper trailer. Hank and Doc loaded a military GP medium tent and poles in the back of the F250 and connected the trailer.

Garrett, The Wizard, and 2nd Chance would follow the Command Center Team. 2nd Chance had his Chevy Suburban outfitted with everything they would need for the next several days, including extra firepower, flares and launchers, N.V.G.s, and a small refrigerator.

Hank said to Doc, "We'll be leaving at the same time you do. Denise and Pam will drive their automobiles, while I drive the F250 with the fifth wheel. Top Eye, The Wizard, and 2nd Chance will follow in a fourth vehicle. All four vehicles are equipped with CB radios, and we'll be on Channel 15 unless otherwise directed. Doc, you and the TAC Team will be in front of us; each of your vehicles will be CB equipped and also tuned to Channel 15. Command/Security will leave the main highway here," he said pointing at the map, "and continue to this spot about four miles off the road."

"By the time you arrive in El Paso we should have set up the GP medium tent, and it will appear that we are the lead elements for a family reunion camp out and barbecue. The additional medical folks should arrive about 1700 hours Tuesday afternoon, set up their equipment, and try to grab some sleep. Once the GP medium and the fifth wheel have been set up, Pam and Denise will initiate the next phase of their duties, Operation ATM."

"What exactly do you have them working on?" Doc asked.

"Oh no, my friend," Hank smiled. "Need to know basis only. Now, you sure you don't want me going with you?" he asked.

"I'm sure," Doc said. "Only two of us know what Val Richards looks like. If something happens to me, you're still out here. Besides, someone has to be the final go-no-go authority. That has to be you. You and Top Eye keep the area safe and secure. I'll be seeing you."

"Wait," Hank commanded, as he took Doc off to one side. "Doc, there is one point I didn't bring up at the briefing," Hank said in a lowered voice. "We can't do much about it anyway and maybe I'm just flinching at shadows. It is, after all, a real long shot."

Doc rolled his eyes and said, "I really hate it when you start off like that; I seldom like what follows."

Hank said, "The choppers won't have any real trouble getting under the radar coverage for the local radar but there is a fly in the ointment. There is another type of radar out in Virginia most folks have never heard of called ROTHR; it stands for Relocatable Over The Horizon Radar. This rig bounces its signal off the ionosphere and back down to earth, which allows it to see a really long way."

"Any chance it can see us?" Doc asked.

"I'm afraid so, Doc. They probably can't make out our altitude, but they will likely be able to see us if they're looking. My view is we're not going to be airborne very long; hell, the choppers will be on the ground most of the time anyway. We have a good chance of catching a break. No biggie, but I wanted you to know."

Doc thought for a minute, "Nothing we can do at this stage; we go anyway."

Hank stuck out his hand and shook Doc's. "Hey, I expect to see you early Wednesday morning, and bring me one of Val Richards' good cigars," Hank added.

Doc laughed, "I'll bring you a cigar and a bottle of his Crown Royal." They shook hands, and Doc went to tell Pam good-bye.

Neither of them said anything at first; they just held each other tightly for a long time. Doc looked into her eyes, kissed his index finger, and traced a line from her widow's peak to the bridge of her nose. "Mark against evil," Doc said. "It will protect you while I'm gone."

She tilted his head and kissed him between the eyes leaving a lipstick mark. "Mark of the Coon-Ass," she said. "That will bring you back to me."

He patted her butt, stepped back out on the porch, and hollered out to the team, "Saddle up!" He kissed her hard on the lips and took his position in the lead truck headed for the highway to El Paso.

Pam went inside, composed herself, and then made a call to check on the dogs. The neighbor advised her that the dogs, cats, and fish were happy and well. Next, she checked in with her boss and found everything was in good shape there too. He told her that two of her deals had closed and to relax and have a good vacation. She told him she would check in again tomorrow.

Part Three
The Assault

Chapter Twenty-Six

Tuesday, 0800 hours C.S.T., Fort Hood, Killeen, Texas—D-Day

Birdman 1 and 2 walked into Flight Ops at Fort Hood, signed out their respective choppers, and began the preflight inspections. At 0900 hours, the two UH-60 BlackHawk helicopters took off and, following their flight plans, headed for their refuel stop on the way to El Paso.

"Birdman 2, this is Lead." Bracken's voice cracked. "Go Lead," Birdman 2 said.

"My compliments, that went very smoothly; you had everything greased quite nicely." Bracken said.

"Well, thank you Sir; we do try to please," Birdman 2 said. "These UH-60s should handle this job nicely." He smiled and winked at his W.E.S.O. The rest of the flight was uneventful. After a refueling stop and a leisurely lunch, they again did a preflight inspection, and by 1330 hours, both birds were back in the air.

Two hours later the call came, "Lead, this is Two," Dillon's voice sounded in Bracken's headset.

"Go Two," Bracken said.

Dillon said, "We'll be over the M.A.S.H. site in 15 minutes, how 'bout a fly over?"

"Roger that," Bracken said, "let's find some landmarks that can be picked out during the night approach."

"I make that car lot in a straight line with the radio tower at two o'clock, and the M.A.S.H. should be one click further on. There it is," Birdman 2 said just before they passed over the site. "Looks like they've erected the tent and set up the antennae for the SINCGARs," he announced. "I see Hank going back inside the trailer."

Hank entered and keyed the handset to the radio. "Birdmen, this is Command 1, radio check, over."

"Command 1, this is Birdman 1, five-by-five, over."

"Command 1, this is Birdman 2, five-by-five, over."

"Birdmen, this is Command 1. You are both five-by-five; take care, and we'll leave the light on for you, over."

"Roger that Command 1; any messages for the grunts, over?" Birdman 1 inquired.

"We are still a go; tell them to be careful, over," Hank said.

"Wilco, Birdman 1 and 2 enroute to next phase, out." Both choppers banked sharply at the same instant and headed to El Paso.

"Confirmed, Command out." Hank set down the handset and ran his hand back through his hair.

"Okay, ladies," Hank said as he walked back outside where Denise and Pam waited, "things seem to be going well. That was our Chopper Jocks checking in. TAC Team will check in with us again just before liftoff. They should all be sleeping about now. They'll have a long night."

Tuesday, 1500 hours C.S.T., El Paso, Texas—D-Day

In fact, the members of the TAC Team were not sleeping but were resting. They arrived in El Paso late the night before. They checked into the first Holiday Inn they came to, which was only 30 minutes from Biggs.

After checking in, each man retired to his room and spread out his equipment, double and triple checking it.

Every round for every weapon was satisfactorily cycled through the weapon at least once. Magazine followers and floor plates were checked. Final edges were being honed on combat knives, not that it was necessary, but because it helped to deal with the waiting.

They slept in this morning but agreed to meet downstairs at 1500 hours in the private lounge for an early supper. Steaks, baked potatoes, a salad, and apple pie with ice cream were to be the menu, a fitting last meal if it turned out that way. They spent the ensuing hours alone, remembering other times in other places with other friends. Some of those friends had not come back from similar missions as this one.

While they had confidence in their abilities and faith in each other, they all knew—when your number is up, it was up. At 1500 hours, they were in place and eating what they hoped was not their last meal.

When Doc saw that all were about finished, he looked around the table and began tapping his fork on the water glass. When everyone was quiet, he stood and held his glass of Jack Daniel's out for a toast.

"To absent friends," he said.

"Here, here," they cried and everyone took a swig.

"To a worthwhile mission, a safe return, and our comrades in arms," Doc said.

"Here, here," they called again, and everyone took a swig. "To us and those like us," Doc said.

"Damn few left," they responded loudly, and everyone took a swig.

Sitting down he said, "All right, it is now 1550 hours. I want everyone back in their rooms and crashing for the next two hours. At 1900 hours, I want everyone to have shit, showered, and shaved. I want you in uniform and ready to move out at 1915 hours with all of the gear you will be carrying."

"No heroes tonight, gentlemen. We have a job to do, and people counting are on us. Those people don't even know we are coming. For them, this is a night of horror and death for which they have no possible escape. We'll encounter some bad men tonight. These people created this night of horror for their own enjoyment. That situation cannot and shall not be allowed."

"No heroes tonight, gentlemen. Work as a team, and cover each other. Do your job. We have surprise, training, experience, and commitment on our side. Work as a team. These people shall not prevail."

"No heroes tonight, gentlemen. We have a long way to go and a short time to get there; pace yourselves. Some of us are considered over-the-hill; we'll see. I'm a firm believer that 'Old age and wisdom can always defeat youth and strength.' Work together; take care of each other."

"No heroes tonight, gentlemen. We have been and are professional warriors. 'Old warriors are smart warriors, not lucky warriors,' " Doc quoted.

"You are reminded that tomorrow morning at 0900 hours your presence is required in this room for a mandatory breakfast. Are there any questions?" There were none.

"There is an old joke that says 'I'd rather be lucky than good.' Well, I know you're good, so to hell with luck. Okay, dismissed and hit the sack,"

"John, stand by for a moment will you?" Doc said.

Once everyone had left, John came up to Doc. "You ready for this?" Doc asked.

"Sure. I wished we didn't have to do it, but it has to be done. So, I guess it's up to us."

"Okay," Doc said. "Your team will plug the back door at the tornado shelter; mine will come in from the roof of the castle. We may flush some bad guys toward you; be on your toes."

"I will be; you just be careful," John said as he turned to leave.

"Hey," Doc said.

John turned and said. "I know. I love you too. Be careful; you're buying the Jack tomorrow night." Doc threw a kiss and a pickle at him then went into the private lounge next door.

He sat, alone with his thoughts, a lighted Garcia Vega cigar, and his old friend Jack Daniels. *Okay,* he thought, *I'm still struggling with the cigars; is it not better to struggle than to give in?* He went over the plan in his mind for the umpteenth time. He felt they could pull this off, but you never know until you are finished.

He remembered the old military adage: "It is absolutely imperative that a plan be developed, researched, and refined; otherwise, when the first shot is fired, you would have nothing to throw out the window."

He slugged down the bourbon and snubbed out the cigar. With any luck, in a few hours, he could be enjoying one of Val Richards' excellent cigars. He went to his room, locked the door, set the alarm on his new Timex Humvee watch, and then called the desk for a wake up in two hours. *Better safe than sorry,* he thought.

Then, he stretched out on the bed, taking a long slow breath in. By the time he exhaled that breath, he was asleep. It was a trick he had learned a long time ago. Doc was a firm believer in the saying, "Don't run when you can walk, don't walk when you can rest, don't rest when you can sleep, and when you can sleep, do it—you might not get another chance."

Tuesday, 1835 hours C.S.T. El Paso, Texas—D-Day

A few seconds before the wake-up call came, Doc arose; his mental alarm had gone off. He stood up, stretched, shut off his wrist watch alarm, and opened the window.

The sky was getting darker as the sun set lower and lower. He thanked the desk for the wake-up call and followed the advice he had given the rest of the team. He shit, showered, and shaved. Thirty minutes later, he was in uniform and ready to go.

He was wearing an older pair of combat boots, as everyone else would be. He knew that a cross-country hike was not the time to break in a new pair of boots. To keep from upsetting the locals, he kept his shoulder holster and L.B.E. harness packed in a carry bag.

The Widow Maker would be riding under his left arm in a holster that his friend Jerry Ahern made for him. On the left shoulder strap, he carried a three-inch mini Mag light and a pistol oiler. On the right shoulder strap, he carried a Benchmade Auto Opener, the Cadillac of switch blades. On the offside, he carried two extra magazines and a SOG Pentagon knife.

Over his holster would go his L.B.E. He had the Crain LSX on the left side of the Black Hawk Last Resort Belt and his Ruger 9mm P-85 in an SAS holster on the right side. He had an 18-round Ram Line inserted in the magazine well and an extra 18-round mag on the holster. He carried the A.G. Russell Sting A-1 in a special holster rigged on the outside of his left boot. On the right side of his belt and in the back, he had the AMT .45 caliber D.A.O. Back Up. In the horizontal left-handed sheath was the Randall Model 1. Two canteens would finish the load on the belt.

The pouches on the assault vest contained extra 30-round magazines for the CAR 15 .223 rifle; this would be his primary weapon. He also carried an extra mag for the Widow Maker and two extra mags for the AMT .45. There was also a compartment for the SINCGAR radio and an over-the-shoulder double holster.

This contained his sawed off pump 12-gauge with a pistol grip, loaded with seven rounds of #4 buck shot and an extra six rounds, as well as two #4s and four door busters in an attachment called a sidesaddle on the left side of the receiver. Next to the 12-gauge, his two-handed Wakizashi sword rested for a right-handed draw.

Attached to the shoulder pads were his compass, locking D-Ring and a new USMC Kabar Combat knife. Though not a very pretty knife, it was tough and battle proven. In his left breast pocket he carried an American Derringer .25 caliber Pen Gun.

This single-shot pistol was an emergency hideaway that was loaded with a 2,000 fps Glaser round. In normal form, it looked similar to an old style pocket flashlight. To fire this unique weapon, the two ends would be pulled apart slightly. This allowed a "bend" at the tube of the gun which resulted in a trigger popping out and the gun assuming a rough L shape. It was for last-ditch and strictly up-close shooting.

His fanny pack contained four extra 30-round mags for the P-85 and SWAT Knee and Elbow pads to be used for entry into the castle. It also carried the Russian Spenatz Spring Dagger and some lightweight cable. This spring-loaded knife launches a double edge blade that is capable of sticking in a man, or a block of wood at a distance of nearly 20 feet. It also has a cover for the blade that makes the missile into a blunt baton for stunning.

Doc had exchanged the knife/baton for the grappling hook version of the projectile. It could be spring launched to the top of a building or ledge. It would trail a lightweight cable that would be attached to a heavier climbing rope. This rope would be pulled by means of the lightweight cable, through the ring at the base of the projectile.

He took a moment to call Command and let Pam know they would be leaving shortly. "I love you," Doc said.

"Bring me back a serape; I love you too," she said.

They hung up. She knew better than to wish him luck. Nothing would doom a mission quicker than that.

Next, he called his daughter Madison. She answered and asked, "What's going on?"

"Oh, I'm headed for a quick trip to Mexico," Doc said. "Should be back tomorrow, but I thought I'd better check in and say good-bye. How's my grandbaby?"

"Oh, she's rotten, but luckily she's asleep," she said.

"Don't wake her; just give her a kiss from Paw Paw when she wakes." Doc had trouble seeing as the tears collected in each eye, but his voice remained steady.

"Got to go, Bear," he said calling her by her childhood nickname. "I love you."

"Bye Dad, love you too," she said, and the connection went dead. She would not be pleased when she would find out later about this little mission.

With one last look around, he hefted the bag with the L.B.E., picked up the gun case, and went outside. He wondered if he would see this room again. John was waiting by the truck.

Doc asked him if he had checked in at home. He said he had, but no one was there; they were probably at his mother-in-law's.

By 1900 hours, everyone had loaded their gear and was ready to leave. Doc had paid the Holiday Inn bill in advance so that they wouldn't have to deal with checking out when they left. He instructed everyone to leave their keys in their rooms as the hotel had instructed him to do.

They entered the gates at Biggs Army Air Field without incident about 30 minutes later. They were able to find parking spots next to the hanger where the Black Hawks were located.

Leaving the now empty carry bags, gun cases, and the driver's wallets in the vehicles, they separated the gear and weapons into two piles that were staged next to the appropriate chopper.

When the air craft commanders, better known as ACs gave the high signs, they began loading.   As they were instructed in the briefing, Red Team and Mountain Man would ride in Birdman 1. Blue Team and Reverend would be in Birdman 2.

Doc looked inside the choppers and checked out the layout of the seats. He thought about how different they were from the Huey's he had ridden on in the old days.

The team buckled on their L.B.E.s, and the AC pointed out their assigned seats and passed out headsets. Each man took his seat. The AC left the side doors open, cranked the chopper, and waited.

It looked like a normal military operation, one this airfield had seen thousands of times.

Tuesday, 2000 hours C.S.T., El Paso, Texas—D-Day, D-Hour

Fifteen minutes after the choppers were loaded, they received permission to lift off. Ten minutes later, both had dropped to N.O.E. and had penetrated the Mexican border.

After another ten minutes, they shifted to contour flying. In this mode, they increased altitude to about 25-feet above the ground and were able to increase speed from the 50 knots used in N.O.E. to about 70-75 knots.

The AC's voice rattled in Doc's earphone. "Looks like a clear night." Doc nodded and sat fiddling with his locking D ring. Ever since he had a carabineer open up on him during a building assault, he had little faith in the snap link. When given the chance, he always used locking rings. For this mission, he had the chance and made the choice for the whole team. He sat back and surveyed the rest of the team.

Psycho was armed with a Bennelli 12-gauge. It was a monster shotgun that could be fired semi or pump action at the flip of a switch. He carried a special chest-mounted ammo pack of shotgun speed loaders, two in each of six compartments. On his left shoulder strap, he had taped his Navy Mark II knife.

He had used this knife when he was a SEAL. The edge was like a razor. On his left hip, he carried a Cold Steel Recon Tanto with blackened blade; on his right was his Sig Saur .45 loaded with Carbon ammo. He knew there would be no need to double tap when using this stuff. Doc knew there was a special .22 auto with a suppressor in his fanny pack along with a box of subsonic ammo.

Bush Hog carried a Ruger Mini-14 with a 4X scope, see-through mounts, and a 30-round magazine. On his left hip, he carried a Glock model 27 .45 in a low slung SAS holster which carried two extra magazines. An Al Mar Warrior Combat Knife hung from his right side, and he had taped a Kabar to his left harness strap. Extra mags for the Mini-14 were in M-16 style mag pouches on his belt.

Mountain Man carried his scoped SKS rifle and a 15 shot Ruger P-89, the later version of Doc's own gun. He carried a monstrous Ruana Bowie knife. The Bowie had a grip in which stag inserts had been mounted, in what looked like a solid polished aluminum handle. The blade was 10 inches long, over 2 inches wide in some places, and more than a quarter inch thick.

A solid bar of brass had been inlaid along the spine of the blade. Doc recognized this as a mark that old time knife fighters from the 1800s had used. When the hardened edge of an opponent's knife would hit the soft brass, the brass would catch and hold the blade if the defender twisted hard enough and fast enough; at least, that was the theory.

Mountain Man was quiet. He sat in silence and continued to whet the blade of the Ruana on a pocket stone. He looked uncomfortable being in the helicopter.

Doc leaned forward and shouted. "You know, I've been up in choppers, but I've never landed in one. For some reason, I've always had to jump out."

"I'll tell you one thing," Mountain Man shouted back, "after tonight; you'll never see me in one of these things again."

They both laughed.

Chapter Twenty-Seven

Things were going much the same in the other chopper. They were making their last minute adjustments. Warlord, like his father Doc in the other chopper, was watching his people.

Mongo was quiet, as usual. On the floor of the chopper, he sat the butt of his modified Remington Model 1100. He was continuously wiping its metal barrel and action with a silicon impregnated cloth. Mongo had that shotgun when John, as a child, first met him, which was over 20 years ago.

It, like its owner, was still in remarkably good shape. Mongo was heavy built with dark hair and a drooping mustache. Warlord was trying to get used to the amount of gray hair Mongo now sported. He didn't let the gray deceive him though; Mongo's grip was strong, and his shoulders and arms were as massive as they had ever been.

John remembered the story of the time Mongo and Doc had busted a guy in a car for dope. The doper's partner had gotten "mouthy," as Doc described it. Mongo was not a cop and had just been riding with Doc. As story has it, Mongo reached in through the passenger window and pulled the 170 pound man through the window, using only his right arm. John would bet anyone that Mongo could still do it today.

In addition to his Model 1100, Mongo carried only a vintage 1911 Colt .45 in a flap holster and the Kabar knife Jarhead had given him. Over his L.B.E., he had a simple shooting vest crammed with extra 12-gauge shells.

John surmised that Mongo must have figured he wouldn't need much more. *I'll bet he is right,* John thought.

John checked his own gear. He had his 14 shot Para Ordnance .45 and extra magazines in a shoulder holster exactly like his father wore. These holsters were the first two of that model Jerry Ahern had made; at least, that's the story they got.

His customized Model 1911 .45, The Warlord loaded with a 10-round magazine and 2 extra mags, rode in an SAS combo holster low on his right thigh.

On his left side, he carried a Cold Steel Trail Master Bowie with a Carbon V blade. On his right side above The Warlord, he had a Cold Steel SRK, but its Carbon V blade had been blackened at the factory. At the small of his back, he had a Smith and Wesson Model 629, .44 magnum, which was loaded with jacketed hollow points. Additionally, he carried four speed loaders in his Mussete bag.

He touched his left breast pocket and felt his .25 caliber Pen Gun. He and his father carried one round in the Pen Gun and six extras in a waterproof tube.

He doubted the sense in having such a gun initially, except that it was awfully novel. But, he found with a little practice and a two-handed grip he could regularly hit a man-size target in the head at 20 feet.

"Everyone needs a little edge," he said quoting his father. *Damn, I have to stop that,* he thought.

He replaced his stainless A.G. Russell Sting A-1 into the special sheath he had sewn on his left shoulder strap.

Jarhead was taping the sling and swivels on his SKS for silent movement. He was comfortable with this rifle; it had been his for a long time. It felt like an extension of him. He didn't really aim the gun. He'd look where he wanted the bullet to go, and that's where it went. His face was already painted; he looked like a recruiting poster.

As the only Marine, Jarhead found himself the brunt of numerous attacks from the other members of the unit. While they were convinced "God made Marines for us to pick on," Jarhead was convinced "the poor devils are just jealous." So in the time honored tradition, an intense but good-natured inter-service rivalry continued.

Jarhead carried two Kabars. The one on his left hip was a "utility knife." The other was taped to his left shoulder strap. He knew when he pulled this one that someone was going to die very quickly and very quietly.

The Reverend was the only one with his primary weapon still cased, the Stoner SR-25. Its case and the attached shoulder sling were padded for more comfortable carrying.

His twin .40 caliber pistols rested in a Galco double shoulder rig that he was wearing. His magazines and extra ammo were mounted at the small of his back.

When in action, snipers spend most of their time on their stomach, which makes front-mounted equipment uncomfortable and difficult to get to. His Stoner bayonet rode on his right hip. He had given his Zeiss binoculars to Mountain Man who would be acting as his spotter.

Simultaneously, Birdman 1 and Birdman 2 advised the team leaders in each chopper when they were 15 minutes away from the drop zone. The side doors opened, and the men adjusted their goggles. Two would exit from each side of each chopper.

Squirrel secured his M-60 and moved it out of the way. It would not be needed again until the retrieval after the assault. *Hopefully, it would not even be needed then,* he thought.

Unlike a Huey, a BlackHawk has no skids, only wheels. The Team members were sitting on the deck with their feet hanging out of the choppers. To exit, the teams would simply step out and run away from the chopper to establish a security position.

The choppers landed. On signal, eight men simultaneously sprang out of their doors. Once off, each man ran about 10 meters, knelt down, and assumed a defensive posture all facing away from the landing zone.

The two choppers were airborne before the men had even established their positions. The insertion had taken less than 10 seconds, from touchdown to take off. At a distance of 4.5 clicks, it is unlikely a person would have heard the Black Hawks, but the desert night sometimes did strange things with sound. The insertion had gone so well that, even if a person had been listening, they would not have been able to tell the flight path of the choppers.

Doc, the TAC Leader, signaled for everyone to form up around him; he took a head count. Radio checks were made to confirm team status and that radios were functioning.

After a call to the choppers, Birdman 1 advised "Roger, five-by-five and I copy—all chicks are accounted for."

"Affirmative," Doc radioed back.

"Then, we are out of here and off the air until next scheduled contact." Birdman 1 replied, "Dark of the moon, TAC Leader, over."

"Roger and same to you, Leprechaun. TAC Leader out."

They were on their own. Doc motioned for Mountain Man and the Reverend to move out. They would move fast but with caution. He instructed that if they encountered anything to halt, wave their light sticks and wait for him to bring the team up to them.

The two men of Carlos Team nodded and took off at a jog. The sticks were specially modified Cyalume light sticks; both members of Carlos team carried one and had another taped to the back of their L.B.E. As they moved ahead, they could be seen at great distance by the rest of the team, just as planned. As long as the light stick was pointed away from view, nothing would be seen.

Doc checked the sky and called Warlord over, and he said, "We have a clear night with a bright moon. That will help us over the next 4.5 clicks, but I sure hope we get some cloud cover for the final approach. We won't want this much light."

He scanned the horizon and said, "We might have a chance if those clouds keep moving in the right direction. Let's get ready to move."

Doc told everyone to take a last pee break; there would be no stopping until they reached the objective.

They made the last adjustments to their gear, and like Carlos, Red Team and Blue Team moved out at a jog. The next stop would be 4.5 clicks away. They could just barely make out the lights from Carlos in the distance; they followed them.

Chapter Twenty-Eight

Four kilometers at a jog, carrying a full load of combat weapons, ammo, and gear, took the team just under an hour. At night and over three miles of unknown terrain, while watching out for bad guys, *Not bad for a bunch of old men; the two young guys didn't do too badly either,* Doc thought.

Doc called a halt, and the team set up a perimeter. He figured they would make the final 500 meters with the two teams separated by about 75 meters. With ten meters between each man, they had good spacing; Doc could still direct individual or team movement with hand signals.

He was watching the sky as they moved in toward the castle. The moon was slipping behind the clouds. *We will have the "dark of the moon" after all,* Doc smiled as he thought. Doc caught Warlord's attention and pointed skyward. He nodded with understanding and flashed a thumb up.

The two teams spread out at the base of Carlos' position. Doc went up to get a report. The Reverend and Mountain Man had their position; it afforded an excellent view of the compound, while providing good cover for them as well.

Doc moved into position between them and took the Zeiss binoculars from Mountain Man. Scanning the compound, he saw nothing or no one that would indicate a problem for them. Less than half of the lights in the house were on. Doc could see no activity through any of the windows or garden doors.

"Apparently, everyone is busy with whatever and whomever they wish to be with," he said in a whisper.

"It's been like this for the last 10 minutes," the Reverend whispered back. "That's the way I want them," Doc acknowledged.

Pulling the handset from his shoulder strap, Doc called the choppers. "Birdman 1, this is TAC Leader, over."

There was no response.

"Birdman 1, this is TAC Leader, over."

"TAC Leader, this is Birdman 2, over," Dillon said. "Go ahead 2. Where is 1, over?" Doc asked.

"Nature call, I'm on the net, over," Dillon replied.

"Roger that, contact Command Center on your cell for mission status," Doc directed.

It was interesting that, with several million dollars of military hardware at their disposal, they still had to use a cell phone to call Command Center. They were out of range of the radios but within the service area for the phones.

Two minutes later, the radio cracked. "TAC Leader, this is Birdman 1, over." It was Bracken.

"Go ahead 1, over," Doc replied.

"We have a go," Bracken announced. "I repeat, a go mission, over."

"I copy that," Doc acknowledged. "I say ENGAGE—POSITIVE—ENGAGE, over."

"I roger that; take 'em down, Birdman 1 out." Bracken killed the radio in his chopper.

"Well that's that," Doc whispered to Carlos 1 and 2. "Are you boys going to be okay up here?" Doc asked as he started shucking his radio.

"Snug as a bug in a rug," Reverend said smiling. "This is the best hide I've ever seen. Only thing missing is cable TV."

"One thing we do want to ask of you," Mountain Man said, trying to whisper but it wasn't working. "Tie us some 'tell tells' on your way in?"

"Will do," Doc promised and headed back to the teams.

Doc had not thought about "tell tells," but was sure glad that Mountain Man did. "Tell tells" were small flags that were used to indicate the wind direction. He'd seen them made of small pieces of cloth or twine tied to a feather. It would help his snipers since their bullets were affected by cross winds and could be blown off-target, particularly if that target was several hundred meters down range. Doc started thinking; *I'll let Warlord handle this one.*

"Okay, we have a go," he said to Warlord. When he got back down the slope, he asked him, "Carlos wants to have some 'tell tells.' Can you handle that?"

"Sure," he said. "I'll use the extra bandana's I brought for 'just in case.' "

Then, it was time to go. He and Doc looked around for a moment and then at each other. They reached out and shook hands, and then each promised, "See ya."

Doc looked at Warlord, his son, and said, "Be careful; remember, I'm buying." Warlord flashed a grin and said "I'm counting on it," then he and the rest of Blue Team was gone.

Doc gave them two minutes, and then Red Team moved out. Red Team was able to get within 30 feet of the wall, under cover and concealment. Each team member moved one at a time, while the others covered.

In a moment, all three were at the wall. Psycho pulled the short straw; he knew this meant he was to go first. Bush Hog and Doc leaned their backs against the wall with their knees bent. It looked like they were sitting in invisible chairs.

Psycho placed his right foot on Doc's thigh and then stepped up. His left foot went to Bush Hog's shoulder, where Bush Hog grabbed it. His right foot went to Doc's shoulder and he grabbed it. Psycho got set and gave the signal. As he sprang up off their shoulders, they lifted him high enough so that he could grab the top of the wall and pull himself up and onto the wall.

He pulled the silenced .22 caliber pistol from his fanny pack. Psycho knew the word silenced was actually a misnomer; the weapon was more correctly described as sound suppressed. Using the subsonic ammo he'd previously loaded in the pistol for this special occasion, he took out three of the lights that had illuminated the courtyard. Then, he replaced the .22 in his fanny pack, slid down the wall in a spider crawl, and assumed security for Red Team.

Doc kept his position with his back against the wall. It was Bush Hog's turn to go now. He placed his right boot on Doc's left thigh and stepped down. His left boot went to Doc's right shoulder, and Doc placed his hands under the heel to help steady him. When Bush Hog was stable, he pushed with his left leg and pulled his right foot to Doc's left shoulder. Doc put one hand under the heel of each boot and waited for Hog to settle himself.

When Hog was ready, he gave a little spring, and Doc pushed up with both arms. Bush Hog rose up alongside the wall until he was able to grasp the top edge. He pulled himself up and lay flat on top of the wall. He extended his left hand, while Doc backed off a few feet.

Doc commenced a short run toward the wall and at the last moment jumped, his hands seeking the top edge of the eight-foot wall. He caught it! Doc began pulling himself up with Hog's assistance. Hog grabbed the back of Doc's harness. Doc was over the wall in a moment.

They eased to the ground next to Psycho and moved out quietly toward the main house. They arrived at the castle and moved around to the patio area. One wall was solid adobe brick supporting a flat roof that covered the patio area.

Psycho and Bush Hog used the same procedures they used to scale the previous wall. When it was Doc's turn, Psycho dropped a line of tubular webbing 12 feet in length. Loops had been tied at both ends. One loop went around Doc's right hand, while Psycho grasped the other. Bush Hog also grasped the line.

On Doc's signal, he ran toward the wall as they pulled on the webbing and stepped back. Doc was able to literally run up the wall. It was quiet and very effective. Pyscho retrieved his tubular webbing, rolled it up, and stowed it in his fanny pack.

Doc went into his pack and pulled out the bag containing the unloaded Spenatz Spring Knife. Instead of loading the knife projectile, he substituted the grappling hook. Once the device had been cocked, the trigger was set and a safety pin installed. This would prevent an accidental launch. A lightweight line was threaded through the ring attached to the rear of the hook device.

Doc stepped back from the wall and aimed the device so that it would sail over the battlements and land on the roof. Satisfied with the trajectory, he looked around one last time and pulled the safety pin.

Aiming again, he squeezed the trigger, and the hook launched into the dark night sky. It sailed quietly between two upright sections and landed on the roof.

Pulling on the line, Doc moved the hook into position. The tines had opened automatically in flight, and two of them were pressed against the solid stone-work. Doc attached a climbing line to the lightweight line. He pulled until the climbing line had passed through the hook's ring.

He quickly rewound the lightweight line on its spool and stowed it and the launcher in his fanny pack. Adjusting the sling of his rifle, Doc began climbing the wall to the second roof. It was not a difficult climb.

When he reached the top, he peeked over and saw the roof was clear. Grasping the edges, Doc climbed over and stepped lightly on the roof. Quickly, he detached the hook from the climbing line and tied the line around one of the battlements.

Then, he stowed the hook and moved to the skylight. Bush Hog and Psycho made the climb behind him, each covering the other. They joined him at the skylight.

They left the climbing line attached to the battlement and decided to simply reposition the knot. Doc spent his time prying the cover of the skylight loose with the Crain LSX. He cautiously lifted the cover and peered into the room below. Nothing!

They dropped the rope down the opening and, one at a time, hooked their Last Resort Belts, and locking D Rings into the rope for a short repel. In less than one minute, they were in. The room was checked, and a "clear" signal was given.

They gathered at the door to begin clearing that floor. They knew one of the problems with an operation like this was the ability to secure the areas behind the team's movement. They knew it was absolutely essential that every room, corridor, nook, or cranny be checked and verified as not containing a threat.

As they moved down the top floor hallway, Bush Hog and Doc prepared for room entries, while Psycho covered their backs.

At each door, they stopped. Doc would position himself on the right side of the door prepared for a high entry. Bush Hog would prepare for a low entry from the left side of the door. Each time they were in position, they would coordinate and verify who would do what on that particular room. Doc would then hold up his left fist and with an exaggerated movement would bring up one, then two, then three fingers.

On the third finger, Bush Hog would silently turn the doorknob and push the door quietly open. Doc would step inside to cover the room, making a quick sweep of the closet, bath, and other areas. When complete, he'd make the "clear" sign, and they would move to the next room.

It took several minutes to clear the entire second floor; but once done, they knew they would have no problem from that area. They moved in the direction of the stairs that would lead to the first floor.

Psycho was stationed in the hallway. From his position, he was able to stand hidden in the doorway of one of the rooms facing the stairwell. In the darkened hallway, he presented such a small target silhouette that he'd easily have the drop on anyone coming up the stairs.

Bush Hog and Doc low crawled to either side of the landing. Using mirrors, they checked out as much of the bottom floor as they could see.

No one was visible, but Doc knew from his previous visit to the castle that there were several areas they would not be able to see from their current location. He signaled for Psycho to join them, and they moved toward the stairs.

Doc started slowly down the stairs. He began scanning the kitchen and great room areas he could see. Once down, he did a quick sweep of the kitchen and signaled "clear." Doc moved to a position where he could cover the uncleared portions of the first floor as the other two descended.

Once all three men were on the first floor, the process of searching began again. At the second closed door, Doc heard conversation. He recognized one of the voices as belonging to Maria, the housekeeper who had treated him so well on his last visit.

There was fear in her voice. The other voice, a male voice, was angry. Maria was speaking Spanish, but the male was talking in English.

"You bitch," the man said. "I told you what I wanted, and you're going to damn well give it to me." The sound of the slap was unmistakable.

Doc prepared to enter the room. Bush Hog silently turned the doorknob; it was unlocked.

Doc indicated he wanted him to enter the room and hold the door open. He would enter next, and Psycho would be the last one in. On the count of three they moved. Doc was two steps inside the room before the man lying on top of Maria was even aware the door was open. He was a Caucasian American and around his mid to late forties.

By the time he rolled off of her and turned toward Doc, Psycho was in the room, and Bush Hog was closing the door. Doc noticed the man's right hand go under his coat reaching for his piece. Doc's right fist caught the man's chin, knocking him out cold.

Doc reached out to Maria and pulled her out from under the unconscious man. She recognized Doc and started to speak, but Doc placed his fingers to her lips for silence and shook his head. She understood.

Bush Hog pulled the man's weapon loose from the shoulder holster. A quick pat down followed, while Psycho duct taped the man's legs together at the feet and knees.

They rolled him off the bed and slipped a flex cuff on his hands, pulling them together behind him. A strip of duct tape was placed over his eyes and another over his mouth. They were careful not to plug his nostrils; they wanted information from him, so they needed him alive. He stirred and went tense as he gained consciousness.

Doc leaned down and whispered in his ear. "Do not make a sound. If you do, it will be your last. Do you understand?"

The man made no response. Doc sat him up and took his knife to the cuff of the man's right sleeve and cut up toward the shoulder, repeating the process on the left side. Then, he cut horizontally across his shoulder.

Doc jerked the shirt off in two pieces and laid the knife next to the man's throat and hissed, "If I ask you a question, I require an answer. If you do not answer, I will terminate this interview."

Doc moved the edge of the knife gently across the man's throat, carefully slicing through just the top layer of his skin. "Do you understand?"

Slowly and carefully, the man nodded. A thin red line appeared beneath Doc's blade and began to ooze blood. Doc knew it was not a serious cut, but it had to sting like hell. *It must be torture to be tied up and out of control,* Doc thought. *It's about time you find out how it feels.*

Doc placed his blade behind the man's left ear and held the ear in place against the blade with his thumb. Doc gave a little tug and increased the pressure of the blade.

The message was clear. With a pull and a twist, Doc could and would mutilate him. While Doc knew the loss of an ear was not necessarily life threatening, it would definitely make it harder to find sunglasses that fit.

Doc whispered his next question. "How many of your people are here tonight?"

The man opened the fingers on both hands wide, and then he closed them and held out only two fingers.

"Twelve?" Doc asked, and the man nodded.

Doc took a chance. "Are the rest downstairs?" The trapped man jerked, obviously surprised that Doc knew about the downstairs.

"Are they all packing like you?" Doc hissed. The man nodded. "How many guests?" Doc asked. "Fifteen" the man signaled.

Forming his right hand into what is called Shuto, the knife hand, Doc chopped at the base of the man's neck, and he went unconscious again.

Doc pulled the man's elbows together behind him, and Bush Hog firmly taped them together. They slit the tape about the man's knees and feet and cut off his trousers. Naked, except for his underwear, socks, and shoes, the man did not present as intimidating a picture.

Maria laughed softly. Doc whispered in her ear, "How many workers like you are here?"

"Two more," she answered.

Doc asked, "Can you get to them and get all of you out of here without being seen?"

"Si," she said.

"If I release you, will you get them and leave now?" Doc asked.

"Si, Señor," Maria answered.

Doc looked at her seriously and said, "Then go Maria, go. This is a bad place where bad people do bad things; it must stop tonight. Get away, far away, and do not come back. There will be nothing here to come back to, do you understand?"

"Si," Maria said.

She slipped another dress on, some shoes, grabbed her purse, and looked at her face in the mirror. One eye, the left, was purple and almost closed from swelling. Her lip was puffy and still bleeding.

She walked to the unconscious man who had beaten her and who was going to rape her. She aimed a kick to his face, but Doc stopped her. "With his mouth taped like that, he could drown in his own blood from a kick to the face. We may need him for more information." Doc whispered.

She nodded. She stepped back and adjusted her point of aim. Her foot traveled as straight and sure as a professional field goal kicker trying to score from the 35-yard line. Her toes smacked into the man's unprotected crotch. Doc cringed; it hurt him just to watch it.

Psycho turned away, a groan escaped his lips. Bush Hog smiled, but Doc noticed him step back.

Maria surveyed her handiwork, looked at Doc, and nodded. "Now I'll go, Señor. He and I, we are, how you say—even."

Doc smiled and said softly, "Señorita, I think you're a little ahead."

"Wait a minute Maria," Doc said as he remembered something. He put two pieces of duct tape around her left arm. One piece was placed at the bicep and one between the elbow and wrist. This was the signal the TAC Team had agreed upon to identify released non-combatants. The duct tape on her arm would ensure a safe exit for her and anyone with her. She left and quickly slipped out the kitchen door to get the others.

Doc checked his watch. It was now less than two minutes before the first explosion would rip the night. They moved forward and made a quick sweep of the rest of the first floor.

It was clear. They now headed down the stairs to the basement. They were each getting themselves prepared for what they were about to encounter.

As Doc's hand grasped the doorknob to the basement, an explosion went off, splitting the night. *Down goes the radio antenna,* Doc thought as he smiled.

Chapter Twenty-Nine

The pound or so of homemade C-4 worked exactly as it was supposed to. Twelve inches of metal in two of the three supporting legs simply vanished in a blast of light and sound. The remaining leg twisted itself out of shape as the radio tower collapsed.

Blue 1, 2, and 3 had positioned themselves next to the "tornado shelter." They had already cleared the outbuildings and pump houses.

When the kitchen door of the castle opened, everyone froze; all guns were at the ready. A woman, obviously Hispanic, was leaving the house. Warlord caught her in the scope of his Mini-14 rifle. The two pieces of duct tape on her left arm were obvious; he lowered his rifle. Facing his team, he patted his left arm in two places, at the biceps and between the elbow and wrist, and then gave the okay sign. They nodded understanding and continued with the explosives, connecting one wire to the charger.

Warlord watched as the woman went into the covered corral and as she left with an elderly Hispanic couple a few minutes later. He scoped the three of them until they were out of the compound. Silently, the three left the compound through the back gate and went a couple hundred yards up the road, and then they sat down to watch. Warlord shook his head. *Oh, well,* he thought, *Why not?*

Inside the house, the explosion shook everything. Doc heard a shout, and the Red Team backed away from the door, unable to be seen. In an instant, it flew open, and Val Richards stood there with two of his hard men.

"What the hell was that?" Val demanded.

"I don't know Boss, but I'll find out," one hard guy shouted and headed off to investigate.

Val grabbed the other and shoved him after the first. "Go with him, damn it. I want a report, and I want it now." Val turned and slammed the door. Hard guy 2 hurried after hard guy 1.

As they went out the back door, Doc gave a 10 count and opened the door that Val Richards disappeared through. A lighted stairwell went down about 12 steps and opened into a well-lighted underground corridor.

Doc went first; Bush Hog followed and Psycho brought up the rear guard. At the foot of the stairs, they employed mirrors again to see around corners. This junction contained three arms of hallway, two short and one long. The two short arms were to the immediate left and right of the stairwell. From what Doc could tell in the mirror, there were three doors on the left and two on the right. Since it would take less time to clear that side, they began on the right.

Psycho moved to "plug the bottle," while Bush Hog and Doc began to clear the rooms. Room 1, the furthest from the junction, was an equipment room. It contained the air conditioning and ventilation equipment, nothing else.

They moved back to Room 2, and Doc listened at the door. He could hear noises, but he could not distinguish what they were or what they meant. Doc touched Psycho on the shoulder. Psycho checked the hallways and shook his head. No one was coming. Doc eased to open the door. When he looked, he saw a room that was a picture from an adolescent's wet dream.

Cavorting on the bed with what appeared to be three teenage girls, was a face off from a recent CNN news cast, the face of the Honorable L. Elmore Johnson, U.S. Congressman from Massachusetts.

After his eyes adjusted to the lighting, Doc realized that the Honorable Senator from Massachusetts was frolicking with three young long-haired boys, and it was obvious they were all under the influence of something. They all froze when the slide of the 12-gauge was racked.

Bush Hog began wrapping tape around the hands, arms, legs and mouths of the captured foursome. Doc and Psycho walked outside and silently closed the door. Doc was comfortable knowing the four individuals they left in that room presented no threat, except to themselves.

Psycho made it across the hallway and was preparing to cover his team, when Val and two more hard guys stepped into the longest of the hallways. They were apparently headed back to the stairwell to check on the two other hard guys Val sent out to investigate the explosion.

If Psycho had still been on that side of the hallway, Doc would have simply gone into the equipment room to hide out; but, Psycho had no place to go, no place to hide. There was only one thing to do, so Doc did it.

Doc stepped into the hallway covering the three men with his CAR 15. "Good evening, Val," Doc said with a slight bow. Val saw only Doc.

His men stopped in their tracks. It was obvious the thought of finding an outsider dressed in desert camouflage, festooned with guns and knives, and standing in their secret basement of pleasure had never occurred to them before.

Fully in character, Val Richards was the first to recover. "Doc! Damn, it's good to see you again. You should have called." His eyes were flashing, trying to define a way out of this.

"Well Val, I was just in the area, so I thought I'd drop in for a moment. Didn't catch you at a bad time, did I?" Doc said moving the barrel of his .223.

"No, no, not at all. The boys and I were going up to get some more beer. Join me." Val Richards said smiling just as though they'd met on the street in front of his favorite bar.

"Naw, I don't think so Val," Doc said and again shifted the .223. This time Doc let the barrel of the .223 drift toward the floor. Val's eyes registered the apparent disadvantage he thought Doc was in. It was three against on, and they had the home team advantage.

Doc assessed the situation. Hard guy #3, on Val's right, had his watch on his right wrist. That indicated he was probably left-handed. Doc saw no shoulder or belt holster, which meant his gun was probably in his back and his holster positioned in such a manner as to allow Val an unrestricted draw of the weapon.

Hard guy #4 had a Sig 226 in a shoulder rig. He was clearly right-handed. Val was in the way of his draw; this would slow him down.

So, Doc focused on Val. He would be the first to clear leather. He would be the greatest and fastest threat.

Doc remembered that, in the Western movies, they say to watch your opponent's eyes or his hands. In karate, Doc had learned this slows you down. You must first recognize a threat and then react to that threat. Doc had learned to watch the chest of the opponent; there, you can see all he or she is doing.

It allowed you to turn off your conscious mind. The conscious mind is too slow. Reaction requires identification, rationalization, and selection and the response. That process involves the brain.

Reflexes are automatic; they do not involve the brain. By becoming reflexive, Doc learned to speed up his reactions by not reacting but by acting. He cut out the middleman.

When Val made his move, Doc had already made his. The .223 caliber slug tore through Val's left kneecap, bending his leg backward in the process. Val had drawn the gun that belonged to hard guy #3; he dropped it then fell back. Hard guy #3 threw his hands up and shouted, "Don't shoot, don't shoot!"

Hard guy #4 had to try; Doc knew he would. When the slug hit Val's knee, it bent his leg in a way it was never designed to. Val flew into hard guy #4. His gun hand caught Val as he was falling, then shoved him away and moved to reach his Sig Saur.

Doc shouted, "Don't!" knowing it would do no good. Doc squeezed the CAR 15's trigger three times; all three slugs tore through hard guy #4's center mass. He catapulted backward and laid there, bleeding out through the exit wounds that Doc's slugs left in the man's back.

Val sat on the floor, holding his leg and crying like a child. Hard guy #3 kept very still and cried, "Don't shoot, for God's sake; just don't shoot."

Suddenly, from down the long hall, all hell broke loose. Doors flew open, and bad guys spilled out like marbles, shooting at everything in sight. Doc spun and dived back toward the junction. Doc heard and felt the blasts that belched from Psycho's scattergun.

Doc could feel the sting of unburned powder as it peppered the back of his neck. Doc low crawled around the corner and flopped back behind Psycho.

Bush Hog gave a ten count before extending his weapon around the corner and opening up from the other side of the hallway.

The bad guys hadn't see him until it was too late. The two that did see him could not react in time to save their lives. Slugs from Bush Hog's Mini-14 snuffed out their lives and slammed them into their partners behind them.

Their partners held them in position as human shields. They struggled to get back into the rooms, while dragging Val Richards and hard guy #3 out of the kill zone. Once in, the human shields were dropped like bags of garbage, and the doors slammed shut.

Red Team reloaded during the lull. "You guys alright?" Doc asked. He was pumped, and he could tell they were too.

"Yeah, yeah I'm okay," Psycho said sliding a speed loader into the Spaz and dumping a full load in one motion.

"Me too," Hog said, as he watched the stairwell behind them. He slammed in a full mag and unsnapped his handgun. Things were going to get tight, very quick. "You call it," Hog said to Doc.

"Hog, you're on high cover," Doc said. "Psycho and I will move to the first door and begin to clear. I'm sure that Blue Team has already taken out those first two guys that Val sent, but keep an eye out anyway. This is where we earn our money, boys."

"You mean we can have all of this fun and get paid too?" Psycho asked with a smile.

"Figure of speech," Doc said with a grin. "Let's go." He began to low crawl around the wall, his CAR 15 slung across his back and his .45 auto named Widow Maker in his right hand.

Bush Hog was standing up; his rifle and one eye were all he exposed to the fire zone. He would shoot over Doc's head if anything appeared. Psycho was six paces behind Doc on the opposite wall. He had collapsed the stock on the Spaz and flipped the switch to semi-auto.

He slid flatly along the wall with the Spaz held in front of him like an antenna, searching for a target. When they came to the first door, Doc stayed on the floor and reached up to twist the doorknob.

Shots rang out. Two rounds had come through the door itself, just about chest high. Two more had bored through the wall where the bad guys had assumed Doc would be standing.

All four hit nothing but the wall on the opposite side. Psycho pumped three rounds from the Spaz 12-gauge and replaced them with three from his chest pack. Doc rolled to the opposite side of the door and got on one knee with the Widow Maker at full extension.

Doc nodded to Psycho, closed his eyes, and turned his head from the door. Psycho triggered three DustBuster rounds at the door, two at the hinges and one at the knob itself.

The DustBuster is a 575-grain projectile of compressed lead dust used for blowing off door hinges, locks, or wood frames with a minimum ricocheting or danger of penetrating projectiles. Upon impact, the DustBuster completely disintegrates. There is a recommended safe distance of 15 feet for these rounds, and Doc and Psycho were both well within that. Both of them had taken a deep breath before Psycho fired.

The door lost its top hinge first. When the bottom hinge was blasted off, the door slumped. When the doorknob was hit next, it blew the door into the room where it slammed into the bad guy.

Doc pivoted around the door face, and Psycho pivoted back to cover the hall with #4 buck shot.

Doc had a bead on the bad guy's position. He sat on the couch with the door covering him. When the door raised off of him, Doc hollered, "Don't do it! Drop the gun!" It didn't work, again.

As he raised his automatic, appearing to be a Beretta or a Taurus, Doc capped him. The single .45 Hydro-shock entered just below the man's left eye and tore through his skull. A spray of brains, blood, and bone peppered the wall behind him.

Doc moved into the room, sweeping from side to side. There was only one other person in the room, a girl who looked about 12. She was gagged and had been stripped then tied facedown lying spread-eagled on the bed. Her back and buttocks were crisscrossed with lash marks from the small whip that lay on the floor at the foot of the bed.

Doc snagged the bad guy's pistol; it was a Taurus. As he approached the girl, her head turned toward him, and her eyes were wide with terror. Doc moved to a position where he could see the door of the room and keep his back to the wall.

"It's okay, Sweetheart," Doc said and gently kissed the top of her head. "We have come to take you home. Do you understand?" She nodded.

"I am going to untie you, but I want you to do exactly as I say. Okay?" She nodded. Doc removed the gag.

Doc drew the Randall knife and cut the ropes from her hands and feet. He pulled the soiled sheet off the bed, and she wrapped herself in it like a cocoon. He reached out to her and held her in his arms, rocking her for a few seconds. "Okay," Doc finally said, "now, I want you to do exactly what I say." She looked up at him appearing to understand.

Doc pulled the bed closer to the door and made her lay down behind it. "Do not get up or speak until either I or someone dressed like me comes for you, understand?"

She nodded again. "What is your name?" Doc asked.

"Terri."

"Terri, my name is Doc." Doc looked closely in her eyes, "I have to go finish this now. There are other people being held here like you. You will hear loud noises, gunshots, and people hollering and screaming. I want you to lay still and not make any sound. If I can, I'll come back for you myself; but if I get hurt, one of my men may have to come get you. If he's dressed like me, it's okay to go with him, okay?"

She nodded. As Doc started to move away, she grabbed his arm. Doc looked at her, and she said, "Please be careful, Mister. I want you to come get me."

Doc kissed her hand and said, "I promise I will do my best, but right now, lie down and stay down."

He moved back to the door and looked at Psycho. The former SEAL was standing like a statue with the Spaz 12-gauge leveled down the hallway. Keeping his grip on the trigger with his right hand, he signaled silently to Doc.

With two fingers, he pointed at his own eyes. *I see or I saw.* He pointed to his left ear, *I hear or I heard.* He held up one finger and pointed to a door, two doors down. *One bad guy in there.* He held up two fingers and pointed to the next door in line. *Two more in there.*

Doc nodded and signaled for Bush Hog to come to where he was. He moved quickly but quietly, keeping an eye behind him as he moved. Doc pointed out the dead bad guy and gave the thumbs down sign. *He's dead.*

He pointed behind the barricade he'd erected in the room, held up one finger, and then gave the thumbs up sign; then, he followed it with the universal "okay" sign. *One person is alive over there, it's a good guy.*

Bush Hog nodded. Doc touched him on the shoulder and pointed to the room that Psycho indicated had at least one bad guy it in, maybe more.

Then Doc pointed at him and then pointed at his own eyes. *I want you to watch that room.* Hog nodded.

Doc looked at Psycho; he had not moved. The man could have been carved from rock. He moved his head, looked in Doc's eyes, nodded, and then looked down the receiver of the Spaz. *Go ahead, I have you covered.*

Doc eased to the next door in line; then low-crawled to a point where he could reach the knob. It was locked. Doc holstered the Widow Maker and pulled the Sawed Off from its holster on his back. He had it loaded so that the first two rounds were OC Penetrators and the next was a DustBuster.

Doc had done a lot of research on this round. He knew that the OC Penetrators are used to deploy oleoresin capsicum powder or pepper spray powder on the other side of a wall. During testing of this round, it penetrated three-quarter inch plywood, multiple layers of sheet rock, and even car windows in some cases.

Doc pointed the barrel of the sawed off at the door to the room so that the OC blast would penetrate, slam into the floor and bounce up filling the room. Doc squeezed off two quick shots then pointed the sawed off at the doorknob and eliminated it with a DustBuster. The door was literally blown open. A naked man, a naked woman, and a naked boy about 10 years old all huddled in the corner, crying and writhing with pain from the OC.

OC is most effective against individuals who do not know they are being exposed to it or those people exposed to it for the first time. Doc knew this; and knew that being familiar with the feelings associated with "being gassed" lessens the shock of the experience. It still hurts, but when you know what to expect, it's easier to deal with. Doc's eyes watered and burned, but he'd felt this before.

Since there was nothing to frisk, Doc bound the adults with duct tape and left them on the floor. He wrapped the boy in a bed sheet and passed him to Bush Hog. Hog told him to get behind the chair and stay there. The boy nodded and moved behind the chair.

It was Doc's turn to cover Psycho now. The room was on his side of the hall. Doc reloaded rounds into the sawed off and holstered it on his back. He switched back to the Widow Maker and pulled a gas dispersion grenade from his vest.

Doc moved to the doorknob and pulled the pin on the grenade. Psycho and Doc had both put on their gas masks. The grenade was loaded with military CS, an extremely potent form of tear gas. While the effects could be tolerated with experience, why bother? *Besides, Doc thought, this stuff will empty our sinuses and cause snot to hang to our knees, definitely not a cool experience when you are fighting bad guys in a modern day castle.*

Doc turned the knob; it was unlocked. He released the spoon on the grenade and counted to three. Doc slammed the door open, pitched the grenade high in the air, and slammed the door back closed. Before the door shut, he heard the grenade go off and someone hollered, "Oh, Shit!" The stampede began. People were trying to rush out, "giving up" in order to get out of the gas. Doc and Psycho wouldn't let them.

Doc hollered, "Everyone get back up against the far wall and put your hands on your head."

At that moment, the rest of the bad guys decided to mount an offensive. Three other doors were jerked open at the same instant and all hell broke loose, again.

Chapter Thirty

Blue Team had set the charge around the radio tower carefully. Homemade C-4 was just as effective as the professionally produced version and just as deadly.

While Warlord provided cover, Mongo and Jarhead molded the mixture along the concrete base and around two of the three legs. Jarhead explained this would destroy the concrete base, snap the tower legs, and save on C-4. Once set, a detonation cap was inserted and wire was strung back to where Warlord stood watch.

Mongo and Jarhead moved quietly to the vehicles, stuck gobs of the homemade C-4 on each gas tank, set the detonator, and ran the wires back to Warlord's location. Fifteen minutes later, everything was wired and set.

They moved quickly and cleared each of the outside buildings and structures. When finished, they felt certain that anyone remaining on the compound was in the castle.

When Red Team began their sweep, there were only two ways for the people to go, either over the Red Team or straight at Blue Team. Warlord doubted they would get over Red Team. He then positioned his people to cover the "tornado shelter."

Picking up the charger, he connected the last wire for the radio tower and squeezed the trigger. The electrical current shot down the wire, ripping the night with light, fire, and noise.

The tower yawed and twisted on its remaining leg and crashed over on its side. Warlord thought, *No communication transmission would go out of here tonight.* Blue Team was ready. Warlord said out loud, "Okay, who's next?" The kitchen door broke open, and two hard guys charged out with guns ready; but, they saw no one and heard nothing. They were looking at a small fire the explosion had started in the brush at the base of the tower.

As they moved toward the fire, it was obvious to the Warlord that these guys were amateurs. While their guns were out, they moved without the advantage of either cover or concealment. They were both standing upright with their guns extended, holding them in only one hand.

He shook his head. These guys were using that stupid "gangster grip" with the gun turned over on its side. This grip had been popularized by the movies and TV. It looked good, but he didn't know anyone, including himself, who could hit anything when using that grip.

The two hard guys moved right past Mongo's position without seeing him. Mongo slowly rose up and covered the two with his Model 1100.

"Freeze," he said quietly, unemotionally. "Drop the guns, you live. Move, you die. Questions?"

The two men froze, but they did not drop their weapons. Their eyes were wide with excitement and drugs. They were pumped. Their eyes flashed back and forth to each other; they were working themselves up to make a move.

"I said if you drop the guns, you live. Move and I'll kill you where you stand," Mongo whispered.

They still made no move to comply. "Oh, hell," Mongo said angrily. "Now, either do something, or I'll shoot you anyway."

The two men moved, swinging in opposite directions to bring their guns online. Mongo knew the man on the left would be faster, so he took him first. Swinging the 1100 to the right, he blew the second man into the burning brush by the fallen tower.

Mongo walked to the first man he had dropped, covering him with the deadly 12-gauge. He touched the man's throat feeling for a pulse. There was none.

He watched the other man cook for a minute. *No one could lie there and take that,* he thought as the smell of burning flesh reached his nostrils. He picked up their weapons and went back to his position. He squatted, waiting. He could barely hear the muffled gunfire coming from inside the castle. The battle was on.

Chapter Thirty-One

The hallway was filled with gunfire. Bush Hog was in a room, but Psycho and Doc were caught in the hallway. Doc pushed open the door to the tear gas filled room, rolling in, reversing direction, and laying down fire with the .223.

In the same instant, Psycho took a step back and leaned against the wall behind him. In an instant, he bent his knees and drove hard against the opposite wall. Like a human tank, he slammed through the sheetrock wall and dropped to the floor inside the room. Bullets continued to whiz down the hall.

Doc and Psycho knew there's a big difference between cover and concealment. Concealment is when people cannot see you because you are behind something. Cover is when they can't shoot you through whatever you are behind. Concealment does not stop lead, and concealment is all the bad guys had.

Doc took aim with the CAR-15 and started shooting rapid semi-automatic return fire. All Doc and Psycho could see were the arms and hands of the bad guys, but they didn't shoot at the hands and arms. They shot at the walls the men were hiding behind and shooting around.

They knew the bullets would go through the wall. Psycho's body had successfully penetrated through the sheetrock wall; Doc's .223 slugs, smaller and much faster, passed through the walls as though they didn't exist.

Occasionally, he'd hit a 2 X 4 stud, but at the range he was shooting, it didn't stop the slug. It simply deformed the slug, slowed it down a little, and changed trajectory.

Doc fired out a 30-round magazine, spraying the end of the hall that he faced. Bush Hog followed Doc's lead and peppered the opposite side. By the time Doc dropped that mag and slipped another in place, the bad guys had stopped firing. Psycho remained on the floor, covering the people in the back of the room he'd charged into.

Doc pointed to Bush Hog, pointed to his own eyes then the hallway. *Hey, keep an eye on this for a minute.* Hog nodded. Doc turned to the prisoners standing against the back wall. Their hands were on their heads, tears flowing from their eyes and snot dripping from their nostrils.

Doc touched Psycho's leg, indicating for him to go handle the prisoners. He stood up and went to the prisoners.

Doc provided cover, while Psycho searched and frisked each one for weapons. He made each lie on the floor. Psycho collected and cleared the six pistols: three Glocks, two Beretta 92Fs, and a Gold Cup Colt .45.

Once they were secured, Psycho dropped the pistols and their magazines into a pillowcase he'd snatched from the bed. Then, he tied a knot at the open end of the case. He slid the knot up and under his pistol belt. Doc knew what was on Psycho's mind, *Souvenirs.*

Psycho had left a Glock that had been shattered. A .223 round had entered one side of the pistol grip and torn out the other side. It was a useless mass of twisted polymer and metal.

Its owner was one of the dead ones on the floor, and he was easily recognized. His right hand consisted of a thumb, little finger, and about half of his palm. Everything else was gone. Psycho moved to cover the other doorways. He undid the pillowcase and passed it to Doc.

Four of the people in this room were victims: three women and a man. They were naked and terrified. It took a few moments before they were convinced Doc and Psycho were the good guys.

Doc ordered the bad guys to strip their coats and pants and then gave them to the four victims to cover the nakedness.

Doc confirmed the victims were okay. He told them about the other victims and then told them to stay where they were and not too move. Psycho finished putting duct tape around the hands, feet, and mouths of the bad guys. "Keep an eye on them," Doc said to the victims, as he and Psycho moved out of the room toward the hall.

Psycho moved back to the door to cover as Doc moved down the hall. As Doc came to the first door in the hall, he looked in and saw a body. Pushing the door open wide with his gun barrel, he eased inside.

Doc looked around. Nothing lived in this room. Six bodies testified to the penetration of .223 rounds through the sheet rock.

That asshole upstairs lied, Doc thought. There were more people in the place then he'd told Doc. Of course, Doc knew better than to trust a bad guy and had prepared accordingly. The body count was now five captured, probably eighteen dead and, Val Richards was still at large.

Bush Hog's gun reduced the occupants of the next room to dead meat. "Good, all bad guys," Doc whispered. Doc looked around and thought, *Where is Val Richards?*

They had only found a few victims; fortunately, they were alive. But, Doc had expected to find at least twice as many. He knew from their studies of the castle's operations and the room count that the numbers were off where the victims were concerned.

Turning around, Doc motioned the rest of Red Team back. Bush Hog went to the children they'd rescued, while Psycho and Doc began herding up the bad guys.

Doc linked all of their hands together with the repelling rope. He would send them up first, just in case there were surprises.

Doc stopped in to say hello to Terri. "I told you I would try to come back for you," Doc said and smiled.

"I'm glad you did. Is it over?" she asked.

"Just about baby, but it's definitely over for you and the others," Doc said as he ruffled the head of the 10-year-old boy sitting by Terri. "Come on," he said and picked her up; the boy stood up by himself. Doc guided the victims out, while Psycho and Bush Hog led the group of prisoners up the stairs.

It was time to regroup. They needed to drop off the crowd of bad guys and victims they had collected. Once they made it to the first floor, Doc went into the kitchen and called for Blue Team.

Warlord and Mongo came forward, while Jarhead kept security for the compound. Carlos was still providing cover from the hilltop.

Doc passed the kids off to Blue team; Mongo took the kids with him. He was big and gruff, but the kids seemed to know instinctively that he was mush on the inside.

Warlord took the lead rope and marched the bad guys out to the rear compound. They remembered to collect the Senator and his victims as well as the bad guy from Maria's room.

There was a small fenced enclosure that contained garbage cans. Warlord went to it, set the cans outside, and then motioned the mob inside.

Once everyone was in the 10x10-foot enclosure, Warlord went back to the trash cans and pulled out five empty bottles of Scotch. He looked at the bad guys.

"Now, I can tell what you're thinking," he said calmly. "You're thinking that this four-foot fence can't hold you; am I right?" he asked. A couple of the men looked at the ground.

"Well, you know, you are absolutely correct," he said smiling. "But see, this fence is not to keep you in; it's to keep something out." There were many puzzled looks.

"Let me explain something to you," Warlord said as he walked over to one of the men. "Hold out your hands flat with the palms up." The man complied. Warlord stood one of the empty bottles up on both of the man's empty hands. Then, he stood the remaining bottles at various other spots. He adjusted the man's hands a final time and said, "Be very still, okay?"

The man nodded. Warlord took five steps out, predicting the line of fire, and then faced the hilltop. Looking back to the man with the empty bottles in his hands, Warlord raised his right hand high. "Watch this, fellas," he said and dropped his hand.

The empty scotch bottles in the man's hands exploded; the other three bottles exploded as well. It was so quick that the glass from the first explosion had not settled to the ground before the final bottle exploded.

"You see," Warlord said smiling, "at night, Mexico has these really bad mosquitoes. As long as you stay inside that fence, they won't bite you."

"Are there any questions?" There were none. He waved at the hilltop and moved back to where Red and Blue Teams stood.

"That should hold them, don't you think?" Warlord said as he winked at the TAC Leader.

"It would sure as hell hold me," Doc admitted.

"Alright," Psycho said, "I'm not counting Val Richards as one of the captured or killed."

"You're right," Doc said. "By the way, Val won't be doing much running. I put a slug in his knee cap. Also, I didn't see an exit from the basement to the 'tornado shelter.' "

Bush Hog grunted, "You're right; I didn't either."

"Okay then," Doc said as he stretched, trying to get the soreness out of his back. "We go back in, but this time both teams are going. We're going to clear the whole castle."

"Carlos will have a green light on anyone who comes out of the 'tornado shelter.' This is where that flexibility I'm always talking about comes in. We're changing the plan. Have we got all of the kids secured?"

Mongo assured Doc that Terri and the others were fine. The Senator, the naked couple, and a host of bad guys were pinned up in the trash can cage.

Doc walked to the center of the courtyard, facing the hill where Carlos team was located. He raised his right hand and gave a 10 count. He knew that the Reverend, Carlos 1, would have him in the sights of the SR-25.

Doc hand-signaled to the Reverend that both Red and Blue teams were reentering the castle. Doc wanted him, as the sniper, to focus on the "tornado shelter." He wanted Carlos 2 and Mountain Man to watch the bad guys.

Doc saw a light stick moving up and down. The Reverend got the message.

"Alright," Doc said to the Team. "Psycho, Mongo, you're rear guard. Don't let anything bite us in the ass." They nodded.

He added, "Warlord, you and I will be entry; we'll decide high or low on each entry." Warlord nodded. "That leaves Bush Hog and Jarhead for cover and security." They nodded.

"Alright, let's go find that son of a bitch and the rest of the people who should be here."

Mongo was on guard adjacent to the door to the basement. Doc and Warlord led the way quickly but carefully up the stairs and began another room-by-room clearing.

When they finished, they went down to the first floor. It was clear. The Team found nothing and encountered no one.

Val Richards had to be down in the basement area. They slowly and quietly opened the door to the stairs that lead to the basement. Bush Hog and Jarhead were in the lead; Warlord and Doc were next; Mongo and Psycho had rear guard. As they reached the foot of the stairs, Bush Hog went left and Jarhead right to set up security.

Warlord and Doc went right and cleared both rooms on that side. They moved across the hall and cleared three rooms in that area, still nothing.

Doc could hear music playing somewhere. Quietly, they began to move down the long hallway. Room after room was cleared. Each body they encountered was reconfirmed as dead, still nothing.

Doc could still hear the music playing. He noticed the earlier gunfight had left its mark on the three walls that constituted this end of the hall.

Leaning toward the end wall, Doc could hear the music better. *It was coming from behind the wall,* Doc thought. He looked at the floor, both side walls, and the ceiling, looking for some type of an opening.

There was nothing. Doc went back to the last room they had searched. *The opening had to be in here, but where?* He thought. They had already looked, but now knowing what he was looking for, Doc realized there was only one place it could be.

Doc and Psycho went into the next room and prepared the group for entry. They had searched the room and its one closet before, but they found nothing. Doc now reasoned that the back wall to the closet had to be the fake doorway to the hidden room. This hidden room was a surprise but not an unexpected one. Doc didn't know who or what was on the other side of the wall.

Doc knew Val would expect them to enter by way of the hidden portal to the room. Doc signaled to Psycho who began firing round after round into the room at a 45-degree angle toward the ceiling inside the room.

The rounds he fired weren't buckshot, powdered lead, or tear gas. Each of these rounds fired two 12-gauge rubber flats that were larger than rubber buckshot and smaller than rubber batons. They are designed to hurt yet not penetrate clothing. The flats penetrated the sheet rock wall, struck the ceiling at a lowered velocity, and then came down to strike inside the room.

The rubber buckshot bounced crazily around the room, smacking anyone in its way; it came from a variety of angles and directions.

Doc had always liked this round; he knew it had its specific purpose. This round had been developed for crowd control and home protection and, while extremely efficient at this range, was rated to be just as effective up to 150 feet with consistent body hits at as far as 100 feet.

The company's motto was "Put the hurt on someone, while you still maintain a safe distance." The bouncing buckshot literally kicked the crap out of anyone it hit but without permanent damage. Doc had chosen this non-lethal ammo on the off chance there could be innocents in the room.

From the sounds of shouts and pain inside the room, it was working. As Psycho fired the fourth round, Doc signaled the team to enter the room. It was a mess. The knot of people inside was caught flat-footed. The ricocheting rubber flats bounced off of the ceiling, hitting every wall, piece of furniture, and nearly every person in the room.

Curiously, they were all lying in a circle. Doc racked his sawed off shot gun and yelled, "Everyone freeze." It got very quiet in the room. Slowly, the circle of people started to rise as one.

Doc heard Val Richards' voice, "Well, well, my old friend, is this how you repay my hospitality?"

Finally, Doc was seeing Val's face. It was lined with pain. His eyes were red; his nose and upper lip were covered with white powder, but his voice was steady.

"Hello, Val. This?" Doc shook his head, "This is not how I'm going to repay your hospitality," Doc said, smiling. "I'm going to put this shotgun in your mouth and blow the top of your head off. That's how I'm going to repay your hospitality. It ends for you tonight, Val," Doc said, clearly not smiling.

"I don't think so, you asshole," Val snarled as he took another hit of the powdered cocaine. "You think I'm going to let you come in here, kill my people, shoot up my operation, and put me in jail, without a fight? I don't think so."

Doc could now see that Val was one of eight people tied in a circle with a rope. A ninth person stood in the middle of the circle with a gas mask on. It was obvious that Val expected to get outside, hiding in the mass of the hostages. He knew the sniper would not shoot unless he had a clear shot.

Val placed the mask on a hostage hoping that, if the Reverend took a shot, he'd be killing an innocent hostage, not Val Richards. Val was wired out of his mind on pain and cocaine but was more cunning than ever.

"How's the knee Val? Still hurt? It won't for long. It stops tonight for you Val; give it up," Doc urged.

Val looked at Doc for a minute, reaching in the baggie and coming out with more of the cocaine. He held it up to his nose, snorted it up his nostril, and said, "It's obvious you do not understand what or who you are dealing with. Let me clarify it for you."

Suddenly, out of nowhere, he raised a 12-gauge 'Street Sweeper' shotgun and blew the brains out of one of the hostages. She looked to be no more than 18 with shoulder-length blonde hair and freckles. Without expression, Val slid her body out of the rope circle. None of Doc's men could take a shot without killing a hostage.

"Now, here's what we're going to do," Val said with new force and snorting more cocaine. "We are going down the hall and up the stairs. You and your men will go ahead of me; when we get to the first floor, you will tell your people outside not to fire."

Doc realized that Val had no idea how many men Doc had with him. And, more importantly, he didn't know where they were located.

"I will take my little family here to the hanger where we will get on the plane and fly off into the morning light," Val said smiling. "Now move!"

Doc motioned his team to move back. Val moved the group toward a switch on the wall, and then he flipped it. The wall pivoted; they saw the long hallway and the stairs again. *Another secret door,* Doc thought.

"I know," Val said. "You figured on taking me out when we went back through the door in the closet. Sorry." Val's eyes were like those of a trapped wolf, red and crazy.

Doc cursed silently. Val had been right. Doc signaled the team to move out behind Val and his circle of hostages. He looked at Warlord and moved his eyes to the right. Warlord nodded and moved to the right, out of the line of sight. Doc made sure he was the last person out of the room.

When the team reached the junction at the foot of the stairs, Doc hollered, "Val, don't do this."

Val looked back at Doc and laughed. "You stupid bastard, you think you have accomplished something here? You have done nothing. I will be in one of my other Resorts tomorrow. By Friday, I will have absorbed the losses from tonight. You have no idea how big an operation this is and how much money we make." Val laughed, as he snorted more coke and limped on.

Val had made a makeshift splint out of broom handles and stopped the flow of blood from his shattered knee. "Get up here with your men and make it quick. One false move and I will start killing one of these," he said with a sneer and slapped one of the hostages.

Doc motioned the team up the stairs. Doc could only hope Val did not realize there was one less team member as they ascended the steps. When they got to the first floor, the group stopped. Val motioned for Doc to go out the back door and make an announcement to his men to "stand fast."

What he didn't know and couldn't know was that there was no one out there. Everyone, except Carlos, was inside. But, Doc wanted to make the announcement.

Doc walked out with his hands over his head and continued to loudly proclaim, "Don't shoot." When he was in position to see the hilltop, Doc stopped.

He knew that the Reverend would be scoping him at the highest power his Shepherd scope had.

Doc continued to turn in circles making his proclamation. He timed it so that each time he faced the hilltop he spoke only one word before turning away. Doc hoped the Reverend understood.

What Val heard was, "Don't do anything. He'll shoot the hostages. We must let him go. We will not be able to handle this situation any further. It's over down here."

What Doc hoped the Reverend would see as he turned and spoke only a single word before turning again was, "don't . . . shoot . . . we . . . handle . . . here."

Doc continued turning until he faced the hilltop. Doc saw the light stick go up and then down. The Reverend understood.

"The game is afoot," Doc quoted under his breath.

The TAC Team came out of the castle first. They formed a semi-circle. Val Richards, disguised as a hostage, came out with his group. Val kept his head down behind another hostage. He spoke into his hand disguising his voice.

Doc and his men knew who he was. The sniper had been called off, so this was a wasted exercise. Doc saw the door from the kitchen open and silently close. Warlord was on the move. Doc had to get Val Richards' attention.

"Val," he shouted, "you know we can't let you out of here."

"Bullshit!" Val shouted, forgetting to disguise his voice. The cocaine was using him now instead of the other way around. "I'm leaving, and if you try to stop me, I'll kill them all." Val's crazy eyes showed he meant what he said.

Doc stepped out in front of the hostage group. "Val, look, let's do this intelligently," he said. "If you go state's evidence, we can resolve this without anyone dying."

"If you think I'm going to spend the rest of my life in prison, you're crazy," Val sneered; Doc moved closer.

"Okay, you tell me what you want to do to resolve this," Doc asked stepping closer and closer. He was now eight feet from Val Richards.

"You know," Val began in a whisper, taking another hit of coke. "Do you know what I want to do? I want to kill every one of these hostages. I want your men to remember they could not stop it and that all they could do is watch, while I blew brains all over the patio," he laughed.

Doc knew Val was serious. He knew Val was going to do it and do it right now. Doc knew he couldn't use his gun; if he missed, he would definitely hit someone. If Doc hit Val Richards, the bullet might pass through him at this range and hit one of the hostages.

In an instant, Doc snatched the Crain knife from its sheath and threw himself at Val Richards. Doc's goal was simple—cut Val's head off.

Doc saw the barrel of the Street Sweeper come up. He saw the blast flare out of the barrel. Doc felt the full load of 00 buckshot as it slammed into his chest, directly over his heart. It felt like a 4x4 fence post had hit him in the heart going about 60 miles an hour.

Doc hit the ground on his back, ten feet from where he'd begun his move. Doc saw the moon come out from behind a cloud. He couldn't speak, he couldn't breathe, he couldn't move, and then he couldn't see. He mouthed a single word, "Pam," then there was nothing; he was nothing.

Then he thought, *Death ain't so bad; at least I don't hurt.*

Chapter Thirty-Two

Warlord had watched his father's eyes move and understood their unspoken message. *Go right.*

His father did not want him to come out of the basement with the rest of the group. He positioned himself on the right side of the TAC Team as they started walking toward the stairs.

When he heard his father shout, "Val, don't do this," he counted *one, two, and* three. He then stepped around the junction wall and immediately secreted himself in the first room available.

He listened at the door until he heard them all go up the stairs. Then, he began stripping gear. He would have to move quietly and strike fast. The guns have to go he decided, *Too many people are too close together. If I miss or if the slug goes through the target, someone else will get hit.*

He laid the rifle, his L.B.E., and shoulder holsters in a pile. He pulled the Cold Steel Trail Master and the Sting from their sheaths on the L.B.E. He needed the reach and the strength of the Trail Master for what he had in mind. He stuck the A.G. Russell Sting in his belt as a backup. He took off his D.C.U. blouse and T-shirt; from the waist up, he was naked like the hostages. He shucked his boots and socks next. He could not afford a sound.

His target was trapped, in tremendous pain and out of his mind on cocaine, not a good situation. In his bare feet, Warlord moved silently up the stairs, the Trail Master in his right hand.

He stopped and listened. He could hear TAC Leader shouting. He knew this was a distraction to keep Val Richards's attention focused on the courtyard in front of him. *Good work Pop—keep his attention,* Warlord thought.

He silently opened the door wide enough to watch what was happening. He saw the TAC Team move out through the kitchen door. He heard Val Richards tell the hostages, "At the first sign of a problem, I'll kill every one of you."

Not if I can help it, Warlord thought, as he gripped the Trail Master tighter. When the hostage circle began to move, he did the same. Counting on Val's attention being focused forward, Warlord stooped and ran silently to the circle. He held his left index finger to his lips, signaling the victims to be silent.

Only two people saw him. He grabbed the rope between those two people and slipped inside the circle. He turned to face outward, as they were facing, and began walking with the hostages and thinking, *I have to get closer to Val Richards if I'm going to take him out without someone else dying in the process.* He knew he had to get past the rope and close to Val.

The hostage circle stopped. He heard his father speak again. "Val, you know we cannot let you out of here."

"Bullshit!" Val shouted, forgetting to disguise his voice. "I'm leaving, and if you try to stop me, I'll kill them all." Val Richards was out of his mind with the power and pleasure of the cocaine.

Warlord turned slowly and quietly. He could see the back of Val Richards, still out of reach even with the 12-inch Trail Master's blade. He began to saw the rope slowly and quietly, making very little movement. He knew he couldn't simply go under or over the rope; Val would sense or feel the movement.

"If you think I'm going to spend the rest of my life in prison, you're crazy," Val said sneering.

"Okay, you tell me what you want to do to resolve this," said TAC Leader still trying to buy Warlord some time. Doc could not see Warlord and could only hope he'd figured out a way to intervene.

Keep it going, Dad; I'm almost there, Warlord thought, sweat running into both eyes.

"You know," Val began in a whisper taking another hit of coke. "Do you know what I want to do? I want to kill every one of these hostages. I want your men to remember they could not stop it, that all they could do is watch while I blew brains all over the patio."

My God, he is going to do it, Warlord thought. The last strand of the rope parted, and he shoved the two people away from him out of the way. He saw Val start to bring up the Street Sweeper. For an instant, he saw his father's face as he and the Crain flew through the air at Val Richards.

Then, there was a blast, and his father's face disappeared.

"NOOOOOO!" The shout tore from Warlord's throat. He hit Val hard in the back.

The hostages began screaming and running, tripping on the ropes that still bound them. Warlord gained his footing and found he was looking down the barrel of Val Richards' shotgun.

"Boy." Val said, his eyes wild on the cocaine. His voice shrieked, "Don't you know," Val shouted holding his hands to the heavens, "I am the man; I am the one, the only one."

Warlord had the A.G. Russell sting in his left hand; he dove forward and to his left, slashing at Val's mid-section in a slightly modified move from one of the brown belt katas he learned in martial arts. Before he completed his somersault, the Sting's razor edge had opened Val Richards' abdominal wall.

In a blast of shocking pain, Val dropped the Street Sweeper and wrapped both arms around his stomach, falling to his knees, trying to hold his intestines where they belonged.

Warlord stood and walked to Val Richards. The Sting dripped blood and the Trail Master thirsted for some. With cold deliberation, Warlord said, "Val, you know something?"

Val Richards looked up at the half-naked, sweating demon from hell standing over him. Val could not speak; the effects of the cocaine were washed away by the pain of the cut. His eyes framed the question, "What?"

You are partially right," Warlord's voice said in a quiet and deadly tone. "There is only one, but it ain't you!"

With one backward motion of his right hand, the silver blade of the Trail Master Bowie blazed straight through Val's neck. His head leaped from the stump; blood spurted straight up as his dying heart tried in vain to keep his body alive—it failed.

Chapter Thirty-Three

The Reverend and Mountain Man took turns watching the prisoners in the fenced cage. As the Reverend took his turn and looked through his scope, he noticed the prisoners were looking at the house.

"Heads up," he said to Mountain Man, "something is going on down there. You cover the cage; I'll scope the yard."

At that instant, Doc stepped into view. His hands were held high, and they were empty.

"This is not good," Reverend said. TAC Leader is in the backyard unarmed, and his hands are up over his head.

Mountain Man was drawing a bead on the cage. He nodded and asked, "What else?"

"He is doing something with his hands," Reverend said quietly increasing the power of his scope.

"It's sign language—R. .E. .A. .D. .L. .I. .P—Read lips," Reverend said out loud.

He moved the cross hairs of the scope to the TAC Leader's face. He caught only one word—don't. Then, TAC Leader turned away. He kept turning in a circle. The next word that he could read—shoot. The next—we. The next—handle. The last—here. "Don't shoot we handle here," Reverend said, pleased he caught Doc's message.

TAC Leader stood so that he could see the hilltop. Reverend picked up the light stick, opened the window, and moved it up and down, acknowledging TAC Leader's message.

Reverend then reduced the power of the scope. This let him see more of the scene being played out below him. He saw movement at the side of the reticule. He moved the scope and focused. "Oh, crap," he said softly. "We have a problem," he told Mountain Man.

"The bad guy has made a circle with what appears to be hostages. It looks like he's wearing a mask and is in the middle of the circle. No way I could risk a shot like that unless I get a clearer shot. I'm sure I'd hit one of the victims if I tried. Doc's right; they're going to have to handle it from there."

Reverend moved the scope so that he could watch TAC Leader. He could tell he and the bad guy were talking, but he could not tell about what. TAC Leader kept inching closer and closer to the hostages.

Keep him talking, Doc. Let's do this by the numbers, Reverend thought to himself. *Get me a clear shot, and I'll part his hair for him.* But then, the Reverend felt something was wrong. *He's facing the wrong way,* Reverend thought. *He's not looking at the bad guy in the mask. What the. . .*　　　He couldn't believe his eyes. TAC Leader's face was snarled; then instantly, he was out of the scope's view.

Before the Reverend could recover Doc in the view of the scope, there was a flash. He quickly widened the view of the scope and then saw it—TAC Leader was flying backwards.

Reverend grabbed the radio's microphone.

"Birdman, Birdman. This is Carlos 1, over." Nothing. He keyed the microphone again, "Birdman, Birdman. This is Carlos 1, over."

"Go ahead Carlos 1. This is Birdman 1, over."

"Birdman 1, you and Birdman 2 get in the air now, over," Reverend ordered.

"Roger, Carlos, stand by; I'll advise when airborne, over."

"Roger, Carlos standing by, over."

Reverend picked up his rifle and reacquired the prisoner cage in the reticule. "Mountain Man, I'm on the cage now. Take the other radio down there and see if you can help out. Keep me advised as you move down. Once you're in position, I'll shut down here and meet y'all on the road."

"Done," Mountain Man replied as he moved out with the other radio. Reverend was amazed at how quietly and quickly the big man moved.

"Carlos, this is Birdman 1, over." Bracken's voice was tense.

Bracing the rifle on a rock, Reverend keyed the microphone and spoke, never taking his eye from the scope. "Go Birdman, over."

"We're airborne and en route to your location. Can you give me a sit rep, over?"

"I don't have much of one Birdman," Reverend responded. "We are not in radio communication with the other teams. I'm not sure what has happened down there, but we have several bad guys secured in one location and several victims secured in another."

"From what I could see, TAC Leader took a shot square in the face or chest. I couldn't tell which, but from what I could see, he was definitely hit with fire from something big. Mountain Man is en route to that location now with a radio. I will be en route to the road shortly to set up for Nightingale's arrival, over."

"Carlos, this is Nightingale. Are there other injuries, over?"

"Not that I can see Nightingale, but I can't be sure at this time, over."

"Carlos, this is Birdman 1; our ETA is two minutes, Birdman out."

Through the scope, the Reverend saw Mountain Man's signal him to come on down. Mountain Man was behind the prisoner cage.

Reverend cased his SR–25 and slung it over his shoulder. He grabbed the rest of the gear and the radio and moved toward the road. He realized that he had not looked at the TAC Leader's body through the scope. He did not need to see it. *No one would survive a blast like that,* he thought.

Chapter Thirty-Four

Spence, one of the prisoners, really thought he could pull it off. He saw the big man coming down the hilltop. *So, that's where the sniper is,* he thought. He began moving slowly to the other side of the cage. *Don't get in a hurry. Take your time; no one is going anywhere, yet,* he thought as he smiled.

He observed the men in military uniforms struggling to untie the victims from the circle and move them to a safe area out of the courtyard. Two of the men were at the side of the guy that Val Richards had blown away. *Man, did you see that son of a bitch go flying. What a shot,* he thought.

Now he was in position to move. Spence unzipped his pants and reached inside his fly, fumbling. He stopped and slowly pulled his hand out. As he was bringing his arm up, something smashed into his wrist and knocked his arm back down. Before he could recover, a grip like the jaws of a bear trap clamped his wrist. His arm jerked straight up and so high that he stood on his tip toes to keep from falling.

His wrist burned like hell, but his hand was numb. Spence looked up into the eyes of a man that he now recognized as the big man coming down the hill. *How did he get here that quickly, and where did he come from?* His mind wanted to know, but his mouth would not work.

Spence realized the man was holding him in midair by his wrist; only his toes were touching the ground. The big man looked down at him.

"I'm going to tell you something," Mountain Man said. "Are you listening to me?" His voice was strangely pleasant sounding, not angry.

"I want you to use your other hand and take off your belt; do it now." Spence did as he was told.

Mountain Man took the belt with one hand and threaded it back through the buckle to form a loop.

"Now, unsnap your pants and let them drop to the ground." Spence did as he was told.

Mountain Man looked down and turned to where the TAC Team and TAC Leader were located; then shouted, "I need someone over here to strip search these sons of bitches, now. I've got at least one hideaway gun.' "

He turned back to Spence and spoke as he looked at him straight in the eyes. "I'm going to give you a chance," he said. "It's a chance to live. When I turn loose of your arm I want you to put your belt on your wrist and pull it as tightly as you can, holding it that way. Do not look at your wrist or the ground. Do you understand?"

Strange instructions but sure I can do that; I don't know why, but yeah I can do that, Spence thought, and he nodded.

"This is what my ancestors called 'The Fountain of Tyre,' " Mountain Man said to him as he turned loose of Spence's wrist. Then, he saw Spence look toward his hand, but there was no hand there. Blood was shooting straight out of his wrist.

He screwed up and didn't listen, Mountain Man thought.

His grip must have stopped the flow of blood, Spence thought, feeling strangely detached.

Spence looked at the ground; he saw his hand was laying there. He looked at Mountain Man who looked back at him and said, "I told you not to look."

Spence nodded. He sat down and fumbled with the belt, watching the end of his life spurt and bubble out of his wrist.

Mountain Man bent down and picked up the North American Arms 5-shot mini-pistol. It was still inside of Spence's severed hand. He put the little gun he just acquired in his pocket. Then, he looked at his Ruana Bowie; it was covered with blood. He wiped it on Spence's shirt before he put it back in its sheath. "I'd like to see somebody do that trick with a little knife," he mumbled, as he rushed over to where TAC Leader laid, twisting and jolting.

"Choppers have been called," Mountain Man reported to Warlord. "Okay," he replied, "let's get this show on the road."

"Mongo, you and Jarhead collect the hostages and get some blankets or something to cover them up with."

"Psycho, Bush Hog, you two strip the bad guys. Take off their shoes and socks too; I want them naked as a jaybird."

"Mountain Man, you take the house. You know what to look for and where to set your charges. Hurry, you have about eight minutes."

They all moved off doing their assigned duties.

Warlord, John Roberts, sat down next to the lifeless body of TAC Leader, the body of Doc Roberts; the body of his father. Tears were in his eyes as he spoke softly. "Well old man, we pulled it off. We killed the bad guys, caught some more, and rescued the rest. You did it and did it all without losing a man, except yourself."

He let his eyes pass over his father's chest. His D.C.U. blouse was in shreds, and blood was everywhere. "I'm taking you home Dad," was all that he could think to say.

He noticed the Crain LSX was still in his father's hand. "I did what you wanted done Dad. You tried. You almost had him; you just needed to be a few feet closer."

John reached down to remove the Crain from his dad's hand. He was prying his fingers loose from the death grip on the knife when suddenly, he felt the knife jerk.

"He's alive!" John shouted as he moved to his father's tattered chest. He cut the B.D.U. blouse off. He'd been hit with a full charge of 00 buckshot square in his chest, directly over his heart and directly on the trauma shock plate of his tactically rated vest. The plate was smashed but intact.

The force of the blast must have thrown him into shock, John thought. He saw the buckshot pellets had splattered against the shock plate. He noticed many of the pellets had skidded on into different parts of his father's body. The vest cover was ripped, but the Kevlar held in place. "It saved him," John whispered with tears in his eyes.

At that moment, he heard the choppers coming in and he looked up. Reverend was standing over him, talking into the radio. "I need Nightingale to set down in the rear courtyard. Tell her to get over here with her bag. Now!"

Chapter Thirty-Five

Mountain Man quickly searched the inside of the castle. He found a 4x4 wall safe in the basement, inside the secret room where they'd found Val and his circle of hostages.

He molded some C-4 into the cracks around the door, set the detonator, and quickly moved out of the way. As he triggered the blast, the door of the safe ripped off and flew across the room.

He walked back over to the safe and smiled. "Jackpot," he said with pleasure. He unfolded a duffel bag, then removed everything from the safe and put it in the bag. As he bagged the items, he said the name of each one out loud, "Computer disks, ledger book, and a box of ID's; fake I'm sure. And last but not least, two Uzis."

He then noticed two more bags inside the safe. He opened them and found them filled with bundles of American currency. He whistled and smiled, as he dropped them in the bag as well.

In the very back of the safe, he found more bags. As he figured, they were filled with drugs. He put all the drugs in the middle of the floor, building a huge pile of cocaine and other drugs. He thought to himself, *This pile has to be worth at least two million.*

He quickly went to the garage and carried two five-gallon cans of gasoline back to the castle. He poured one of them throughout the basement. He moved quickly upstairs to the second floor landing. As he walked back down the stairs, he poured the second can of gas onto the stairs, through the great room and out the kitchen. He dropped the bag of goodies outside and went back inside to set the charges of C-4.

He looked at his watch. *Right on time*, he thought. A few minutes later, he headed out of the castle, grabbed the bag, and moved quickly toward the chopper.

Nightingale had placed a trauma suit on Doc. It had a double wall of clear plastic and was inflated on him. The pressure from the suit helped to stabilize Doc, at least for the moment. She went to the victims to check for injuries.

She was pleased they had only scrapes and minor cuts. She began thinking and sorting through the options ahead and required necessities. *I'll have to do a complete work up on each of them when we get back to the States. In addition to C.B.C.s, I'll need to check everyone for HIV, Hepatitis, and sexually transmitted diseases. And damn it, all the girls will need a pregnancy test.*

The prisoners were stripped naked. Their hands were duct taped together, and a looped rope was used to link each of them by their necks. As ordered, they were walking south down the dirt road. Psycho grinned as he thought about the eight naked men roped together, encountering the local police officials. *I hate to miss it,* he thought.

Doc and all of the victims were loaded into the first chopper. It lifted off and headed to the M.A.S.H.

Mountain Man stood next to the other chopper. Everyone was on board except for him. "It's time to finish it," he said loud enough for only him to hear. He connected the wires to the charger, raised it in his right hand, and prepared to detonate. Then, he stopped, dropped his hand and looked at the charger. He turned and moved toward the inside of the chopper.

He leaned inside, and he held the charger out to Blue 1, Warlord, John Roberts, the TAC Leader's son. John nodded and walked out to Mountain Man. He waited until Mountain Man was in the chopper and sure that a place had been cleared for him.

He looked at the castle and nodded in satisfaction as he squeezed the trigger. He dropped the charger and jumped in the chopper. As they went airborne, the chopper pulled away from the large blast.

He looked at the explosion behind them. The effect was startling. The C-4 collapsed the structure in on itself. The structure belched a big fireball. Seconds later, the structure was gone; all that remained was a roaring flame and pile of adobe bricks.

As they flew off, he saw Maria and the old couple. She waved once, and then, they began walking down the road to the north. Three minutes later, the two choppers were in formation, flying contour at a height of 25 feet and at a speed of 80 knots.

Chapter Thirty-Six

M.A.S.H.—El Paso, TX

First Memory—

Doc heard them talking; hearing seemed to be the only sense he had that still functioned.

"Okay Nurse, what have we got?" the Doctor asked.

Nurse – "Fifty-year-old, white male, multiple bullet wounds, abrasions, and lacerations."

Doctor – "Have we typed and cross-matched?"

Nurse – "Yes."

Doctor – "Well, he got himself pretty well shot up, didn't he?"

Nurse – "Yes, but, as they say, you should have seen the other guy."

Doctor – "Okay, let's get started; put him all the way under."

'Doc' Roberts could not tell if his eyes were open or closed. He knew he was returning to the deep sleep from which he had just awakened. He knew his name, even if he could not remember it at the moment. He knew where he was, even if he could not remember it either at the moment.

The mask settled over his mouth and nose, and he decided he would take a nap and "think about it tomorrow." He was out.

Later, the doctor, still standing at the operating table, stopped and thought, *Four hours working on this guy. Man, I haven't seen a mess like this since I was an intern on the Lower East Side. I'm getting too old for this crap.*

Blood spurted onto his face shield, "More suction! Damn it, we're going to lose him if we're not careful."

While the nurse wiped away the blood the doctor thought, *Buddy, if I'm too old to do what I'm doing, you sure as hell are too old for what you've been doing. You made 50, but I'm not sure you'll see 51. It would sure help if we were in a hospital. I need a damn x-ray machine. I'm digging around in you like it's 1880 and I'm a Dodge City saw bones digging a bullet out of the town Marshall. You know fella, that's not a bad analogy. Who the hell did you think you were, Wyatt Earp?*

An hour later, Dr. Michael Fortuno told his assistant to "close him up." He had to get some coffee. His eyes hurt; the lighting was bad. His back hurt; the operating table was too low. He smelled bad; there were no air conditioners, just fans.

He stripped off the gloves, mask, and finally the surgical gown. He threw the entire bundle into the biohazard container. *The conditions might be* 1880, he thought, *but the precautions are still modern day.*

"Okay." He said, as he pulled a chair to the folding table set up in what passed as the doctor's lounge. "I dug enough lead out of that guy to sink the Bismarck."

Jean Bracken, the Nightingale, bagged her scrubs, mask, and gloves and poured a mug of what passed for coffee.

"Thank you Mike," she said. "I owe you big time and so does he," she said, as she pointed to the man they'd just worked on for nearly six hours."

"You know," Dr. Fortuno admitted, "I don't know if he's going to make it or not. These conditions are primitive. I wish we would've had a more sterile environment. This guy might croak because some bugs got in while we were digging the lead out."

"Mike," she asked in all seriousness, "did you do your best?"

"Hell girl," he said flashing a grin, "I did better than my best. I thought we lost him on the table twice. Yeah, I did my best, the best I've done in 15 years. Kinda' nice to know I still have 'it,' you know?"

"Yeah, I know," she said, as her dark eyes filled with tears. "Win, lose or draw, you have my thanks and his too."

"Jean," Fortuno said, as he leaned closer toward her, "you asked me to come and I did. You asked for my help, and I gave it; but I have some questions. Tell me more about this guy."

"Mike," she said, with both a smile and a tear, "like I said, he is a friend. His name is Marv Roberts, but everyone calls him 'Doc.' If he were conscious, the two of you would talk about what it is like to 'still have it.' "

"If he makes it, I can guarantee you one thing. He'll buy you a Jack Daniels and the best cigar you've ever smoked. If he doesn't, I'll buy it for you. You and I will get drunk, toast absent friends, and I'll cry a lot."

"Ya'll are pretty close then?" Fortuno said seriously.

"Good friends and old friends," she said. "I'll keep names out of this, but you deserve to know more about him. He spent 10 years with the Air Force as a cop and qualified expert on every weapon he shot. He ran a military counter-terrorism team for two years. He's still in the Air Force Reserve as a First Sergeant."

"He loved . . . loves," she corrected "the outdoors. He and his wife Pam have actually been camping with my family. They go rock climbing, canoeing, and SCUBA diving; actually, I can't think of anything they wouldn't do. They just got back from a six day trip in Alaska, during the dead of winter. My kids think he's magic. I think it's because he believes he is."

"He has a degree in psychology, a Master's in police science, and two Ph.D.s. He is a writer and professional speaker. He quotes Richard Bach, Buddha, James T. Kirk, someone called John Thomas Rourke, and anyone else he thinks is relevant, including himself."

"That's his son and daughter-in-law waiting by the bed. They just got here from Baton Rouge. Pam has the grandbaby at the motel. They didn't want her to see her Paw Paw like this."

"His daughter Madison and her family are flying in from Virginia tomorrow," she said, as she left the table and went to Doc's bed.

Doc's daughter-in-law turned to her and said, "Is he in much pain?"

"No, he's way under sweetie, and we're going to keep him that way for a while. He's in bad shape, and he needs rest so that he can help with his own healing. The wounds are serious, plus he's dehydrated and has lost a lot of blood."

"How long before we know?" John asked, as he watched his father.

"The next few hours are critical, but we should have a better idea by mid-morning. Come on, you two need your rest as much as I do. Someone will watch him during the night."

John gently pulled away and said, "No, not someone . . . me."

Doc stirred under the blanket. John wondered, *Is he dreaming or hurting?* John picked up his father's war harness; it was draped across the chair. He pulled the massive knife from its sheath and the silver gun, the Widow Maker, from its holster. He dropped the harness on the floor and sat in the chair.

Picking up a clean towel, he whispered, "Don't worry, Dad. This time, I'll clean your weapons for you."

Second Memory—

Doc hurt. He hurt everywhere. He was struggling to make it to the surface of this raging river he'd fallen in. He could see a light at the surface, and he fought to get there. He fought for his life with all of the strength he had.

His eyes opened. Nothing made sense. He was obviously in a hospital. He'd been hurt and his injuries apparently significant.

There were bandages across his chest. One of his arms was in a plaster cast and IVs were in the other. He couldn't talk, he couldn't move, and he couldn't speak.

He looked up and saw Pam watching him. "It's okay," she said, smiling as she leaned over and kissed his forehead.

What was okay? Doc wondered.

"You need your rest; go back to sleep," she said.

Okay. Then he thought of her, *Pam,* and then was asleep again. He should not have been able to feel her stroking his forehead, but he did.

Top Eye, Major, and Doctor B.J. Garrett put his arm around her shoulder. "Pam, he's going to be fine. It's not nearly as bad as we first thought. His heart was bruised but otherwise undamaged. Once we found and sealed all of the leaking arteries, closed the cuts, and replenished his blood volume, he's been doing very well. You know Jean would've never left if she were not totally comfortable with his progress. I'm just babysitting and watching the monitors. He'll be fine."

She hugged him. "Thanks B.J., he looks a lot better, but he still looks rough," Pam said.

"He was lucky. If he'd not had that breast plate in his vest, the blunt trauma alone would have killed him," he said.

Garrett checked Doc's pulse and adjusted the IV. All of the emergency staff had departed. He was in charge of "ward duties," and things were going well.

The other victims had medical assessments and were treated appropriately. Blood and urine samples were taken on each of them. Several were under observation and were coming down from the drugs that had been used on them. Others were just sleeping. Some could not sleep. For them, it would be a long time before they could sleep normally again.

It would be a couple of days before all the lab results were in. The more stable ones were taken to a motel in the area and were under guard.

Two men were in charge—The Wizard and 2nd Chance. They had Terri and the other kids; the adults were next door in an adjoining room. John established shifts of security for the victims at the motel and for the M.A.S.H.

Garrett felt secure as he patted the butt of his stainless 9mm semi-automatic Model 659 Smith and Wesson. *Everything is nice and quiet here*, he thought, *it had better stay that way.* It would.

Garrett watched as Pam kissed her husband's forehead. Doc's daughter Madison walked in.

She hugged Pam's shoulders and said, "Come on, he's fine. He'll be up and mean as ever tomorrow. You need some rest also. Let's give him and you a break. Besides, it's time to eat. I'm starving."

They left together, arms around each other. B.J. checked on his primary patient before beginning his other rounds.

Chapter Thirty-Seven

Thursday, 1730 hours C.S.T—Houston, Texas, D-Day plus three and a half weeks

Doc was feeling much better. His appetite was almost back, his energy level was still a little low, but otherwise he felt pretty good. He was enjoying a Jack and seven and a homemade hamburger with the neighbors, family, and friends.

It's good to be home, Doc thought.

"It's a shame about the car wreck," Vanna Altoff, a neighbor said. "Are you about over it?"

"Oh yes, I feel much better," he said. "It could've been much worse."

Doc was not fibbing when he made that statement. It was true; it could have and should have been a lot worse. He and Pam had come up with the mythical car wreck as the cover story to explain Doc's current medical condition.

"Luckily, no one but me was hurt." Though, he knew this was not completely true.

Pam called from the back door, "Doc, Dave Blaine's on the phone for you." David A. Blaine was Doc's former commanding officer from his active duty Air Force days. Doc now considered him a good friend.

"Coming," Doc said. He took the phone from her hand and said, "Hey Boss, good to hear from you." It had been 20 years since Doc worked for Blaine, but he would always be "the Boss."

"I hope you think so by the end of this call," Dave said.

"Okay, what's up?" Doc said. He knew Dave did not play games. "Doc, I was recently contacted by some government officials." Doc's blood froze.

"I am coming to Houston, day after tomorrow. You and I need to meet."

"What about?" Doc asked, hoping against hope.

"I think you know. Have you got a pencil and paper?" He asked.

"Yes, go ahead." Doc was ready.

"I want you to have some other people ready to meet as well." Dave began naming the rest of Red Team, all of Blue Team, and both members of Carlos. By the time he finished, he'd named everyone.

"Dave, how bad is it?" Doc asked.

"I'll let you decide when we talk day after tomorrow," he said and then hung up.

Doc hung up the phone and looked at it a long time before he dialed Hank's number.

"I just got a call from Dave Blaine, my old commander. I'm sure you re-member me talking about him."

"Yeah," Hank said without interest.

"He knows," Doc said. "He'll be in Houston in two days and wants to meet with everyone on the team. I want you here tomorrow. Bring all of the material; I mean everything. Bring both pre and post mission material; disks, everything."

"I'll see you tomorrow," Hank said then hung up.

Doc finished his drink and the hamburger. After their company was gone, he started making phone calls. Right or wrong, Doc did not regret what he and the rest of the team had done. Now, they were going to have to play the cards they were being dealt.

As he walked to the backyard to brief his son John, Doc thought, *I wonder who is shuffling the cards this time. And, I wonder if I'll get to cut the deck first?*

Epilogue

It was Saturday morning. David Blaine was scheduled to arrive in less than 30 minutes. Friday, Doc called a friend of his, the assistant principal at the local high school. He asked him if he could borrow one of his classrooms for a business meeting the next morning; his friend agreed. Doc had given the directions to David.

Everyone associated with the trip to Mexico was gathered in the classroom, per David's instructions. It had not been an easy task to accomplish.

The assistant principal arranged for a coffeepot and cups to be set out. The coffee was strong, and Doc was sure it would be his salvation.

He and Hank had hardly gotten any sleep. After much discussion, they agreed on one thing, something that didn't make a lot of sense to Doc.

"Look," Hank said for the tenth time, "if they were just out to bust us, why do it like this? They could've simply picked us up at any time over the last three weeks. Something else is going on here." He was convinced of it.

Reverend came up to Doc. "A black Lexus just pulled in; it looks like a renter with two people in it. They are headed this way."

"That's probably David. Everyone, please take your seats," Doc said.

The door to the classroom opened, and he walked in. Actually, he marched in. David never simply walked. With him was a man that Doc did not know.

Doc stood facing David. Though neither of them was in uniform, Doc popped him a salute. Dave looked at Doc for a moment. Doc was holding the salute; finally, Dave snapped a salute in return. Then, he reached out his hand, and they shook hands.

"You have really stepped in it this time, Ol' Buddy," Dave said with an evil grin.

"How bad is it, David?" Doc asked.

"Sit down; you are about to find out." Dave spun on his heel and marched to the front of the room. Everyone was silent. He placed his briefcase on the table behind the podium. He kept his back to the room as he rummaged through the papers. He picked up several files out of the briefcase, turned around, and then set them on the podium. The unidentified man with him stood at the back of the room. He too carried a briefcase.

"Well," he said, looking out over the crowd, "you don't look like a bunch of international terrorists."

Oh shit, Doc thought.

"Ladies and gentlemen, my name is Dave Blaine," he began. "As some of you know, I'm retired military, Air Force Security Police. When I retired in '92,

I was a full Colonel, Chief of Security Police for a numbered Air Command and former Deputy Director of Counterterrorism for the U.S. Air Force in Europe. Most of my military career was spent dealing with situations similar to what you people have been indicted on."

Indicted, oh shit, Doc thought.

"Now, let me go over what we know," he said, as he arranged his files. "We have a civilian medical doctor, two nurses, and three medical technicians. We have an Army Major and two Air Force Reserve Majors. Then, there are some Air Force Reservists and Army National Guard members. We also have a handful of straight civilians."

"These individuals reportedly mounted an armed offensive strike against property and personnel located in a foreign country. During this offensive strike, several unnamed persons were brutally killed, including one person who was decapitated. The property destroyed was valued in excess of $27,000,000." Dave shook his head in disbelief.

"Additionally, several others were subjected to threats of physical violence and potential death. They were stripped and sent naked into the Mexican desert on foot."

"Finally, an unknown number of unidentified individuals, some of them children, were forcibly removed, possibly kidnapped, from this civilian compound, flown illegally into this country, and secreted away to parts and places unknown for reasons and purposes unknown."

"And, I can't forget; there's the small matter of the unauthorized use of two UH-60 Black Hawk helicopters belonging to this country's government, along with several SINCGAR radio sets that were misappropriated from government military facilities for illegal and unauthorized activities."

Consulting his notes, he looked up again and said, "Plus, there is the little matter of an undetermined amount of monies from several bank accounts that appear to have been removed without authorization. Currently, it's estimated to be in excess of $8,000,000."

He closed his files, walked to the coffeepot, and poured himself a cup of coffee. Then, he walked back to the podium and said, "Ladies and gentlemen, you had one hell of an operation."

Doc was not sure of where Dave was going with this, but in his opinion, it did not look good.

"Ladies and gentlemen, three days ago, I received a call from some people I know in Washington. Let me make this perfectly clear," he said, as he held up a packet of envelopes. "These are sealed and signed indictments. There is one for every person sitting in this room. If one word of this operation leaks out, if anyone goes public, these indictments will be served for each and every one of you."

"I have been assured that no plea bargaining will be allowed and the Federal Prosecutor will push for the maximum penalty in each indictment. For some of you, it means 25 years to life; for others, it means that the death penalty is a probable."

"Those of you still in the military will be prosecuted under the UCMJ. If convicted, which by the way you will be, you will minimally face a dishonorable discharge, loss of all pay and privileges, and internment hard labor for an undetermined period of time at the Federal Correctional Facility, Fort Leavenworth, Kansas. Now, do I have your attention?"

Sweat was noticeably running down several cheeks and hairlines. Heads were hung low and hands were wringing.

Doc thought, *Yes, I would say you have our attention.*

Dave sat down with his coffee cup and then stood back up. "There is one more thing I have to say." He slowly raised his right hand and saluted the room, "Well done."

The room was in a shocked silence. At first, only a few stood; then finally, they were all standing and returning the salute.

Dave finally dropped his hand. "TAC Leader," he said.

Doc, still standing, said, "Sir."

"I want a full report, now and in private," Dave ordered.

"Yes, Sir," Doc stammered.

"People, I want each of you to begin putting together a report of each phase of this operation as it relates to you. No one is to leave this building until I say so. Is that clear?" Dave instructed. "By the way, I'm assuming none of you have spoken to anyone about this operation?" No one had.

Doc and Hank gathered the materials and escorted Dave into another room. The unidentified man with Dave was passing out notepads and pencils.

Doc asked Dave, "Alright Boss, what the hell is going on?"

Dave smiled and said, "You have managed to embarrass a lot of people. You've heard the expression, 'damned if you do and damned if you don't'? Well, that is exactly where you have put this government. If they don't do something about this little operation of yours and the existence of it never gets out, they are guilty of conspiracy and about a dozen violations for federal and international law."

"On the other hand, if they do something punitive, it is believed that you and your people would be in touch with every newspaper and television talk show explaining how your government did nothing to rescue innocent children and kidnap victims from the grip of this insidious threat."

Hank said, "You can count on it. We gave them every opportunity to be involved; they did nothing."

Dave smiled a hard smile. "You are mistaken my friend. They did do something. They let you accomplish this mission.

"You could have been stopped anywhere along the way. Three hours after your mysterious package arrived, we knew who you were and where you were. With some computer magic, we had phone records and credit cards identified, allowing us to identify the rest of the crew. Your people were helped and guided along the way; you just never knew it."

"The airborne command posts and Relocatable Over The Horizon Radar, as most of you know as ROTHER, monitored the entire operation. Satellite coverage watched the entire operation from drop off to lift off. We even had long distance surveillance set up on the M.A.S.H. and the trailer, should anything go wrong."

"We know also that your boys" he checked his note pad, "The Wizard and 2nd Chance, have recently been appointed co-administrators of something called The Blue Feather Foundation, apparently a non-profit organization. This foundation appears to administer trust funds and is set up to finance the physical and psychological rehabilitation of some specific sexual and physical abuse victims."

"Many of these victims will require years of treatment, all of which is being provided free of charge through the Blue Feather Foundation. We find it very interesting that the Blue Feather Foundation was created just two weeks ago and that its financial resources are already at," Dave checked his notes, "seven million dollars. That should keep the agency functioning for several years even without new 'contributions,' " he smiled.

"There is an interesting side note," he said, as he held up several black and white pictures. "These are ATM surveillance pictures recovered from some ATMs in and around the El Paso area. They show individuals pulling funds out of several accounts we've traced to your 'friend' Jamie. His real name was Carey Johnson, but he had Richard French and about 12 other names."

"Interestingly, you can't see the faces of the people making the withdrawal in any of these pictures. It seems obvious they were purposely hiding their features from the camera; interesting isn't it?"

"We also find it interesting that, five days before you started this little operation, telephone contact was made with each bank, and the daily ATM withdrawal limits were increased substantially. In each incident, the banker on the phone verified identity through a series of confidential questions."

"Beginning the morning of your operation, each account was tapped daily for the full amount allowed until each account was left with only $100.00. At that point, all transactions ceased and there have been no additional transactions recorded. The account statements show a combined withdrawal amount totaling eight million dollars."

"What puzzles me is that none of your people have made deposits in their personal accounts, in excess of their normal transactions. Now, TAC Leader," Dave said, as he settled back to listen, "tell me the rest of the story."

"Well, as you know," Doc began, "we stumbled onto this whole thing accidentally when Hank and I were on a trip in Mexico. During that trip, the man you call Carey Johnson tried to kill Hank; obviously, he was unsuccessful. He tried to kill Hank because we interrupted him while in the process of raping and disposing of the body of an unidentified boy." Dave shook his head in disgust.

Hank presented a stainless thermos bottle to Dave. "In here are papers with fingerprints I took from that boy. Have the lab bring them up with Ninhydrin; they should be readable. Maybe we can get ID on him."

Hank laid out a map with an X drawn in red. "The boy's body and a Jeep Cherokee are in an arroyo right here. I'd like to bring him back."

"Will the Jeep run?" Dave asked.

"Probably, it'll probably need a battery charge, but outside of that, yeah, it should run," Hank replied.

"Alright, I'll get these to the lab, and we'll get the boy back on this side of the border," Dave said with authority.

"When we hit the castle, several hard guys 'bought the farm,' " Doc said. "None of them had IDs. We left the bodies there. We put all of them in the garage, except for one of them. The manager of the castle, Val Richards, is the one who got so excited that he 'lost his head,' if you know what I mean. He's the asshole who shot me; we left him where he dropped."

Dave nodded and said, "Val Richards was under observation for some time, but apparently there was insufficient Intel to correctly handle the problem."

"The dead ones are dead, and I don't think they'll be missed. The ones you turned loose were a very interesting group. They sparked quite a bit of discussion."

"We rescued 16 people from the castle, 7 of them children under the age of 18," Doc stated. "Some were runaways, and some kidnapped. Those who could be returned to their families have been. Some of them came from the same type of abuse we rescued them from; we didn't return those. They are being helped through the Blue Feather Foundation."

"Hank, Pam, and Denise set up the account withdrawals using information we found in Jamie's briefcase. While the TAC Team was preparing to hit the castle and for several days after our return, Pam and Denise removed the money that would be needed to care for the people we brought back."

"We created the Blue Feather Foundation to get them started on a new life. The ones who needed counseling are getting the best that's available, and it won't bankrupt their families in the process."

"We took the money from the bad guys to help care for the good guys," Doc explained. "Those who could not be returned to a family are going through counseling and training to learn the life skills they'll need to begin a new life, with a new identity. It's totally confidential and hopefully untraceable."

"Give me everything you have on the people," Dave said. "Tell your folks to coordinate everything through me. I'll set up the same security programs for them that we use for witness protection programs. No one will find them. How much money is left?" Dave asked.

"After setting up the Blue Feather Foundation, there's about a million left," Doc answered. Doc handed him the papers which showed the figures. "We gave each adult victim an envelope with $35,000. Hopefully, they'll use it to get a new start," Doc said.

"Each TAC Team member was to receive the same amount," Doc said, holding up envelopes. "But, they don't know that yet. We were going to mail them the envelopes with instructions. The instructions were going to advise them not to deposit the money until they received specific instructions to do so. The instructions would also specify only certain accounts the money could be deposited to. I suppose you'll want to confiscate these funds?"

Dave nodded. He collected the envelopes and put them in a bag he'd removed from his inside coat pocket. He tied the top of the bag and laid it on the table. "Very clean and very neat," Dave said, nodding in appreciation. "But, I have a question. Why? Why did you guys do this?"

"I don't believe there is just one answer," Hank said, after a moment of thought. "For every person involved, there might be a different answer, maybe more than one."

"I guess the simplest answer is that it was necessary," Doc interjected. "Each individual involved contributed something. They were there because it was the right thing to do. They didn't expect any financial reward, and no one has asked for one. Simply put Dave, it was what honor required of us," Doc said with conviction.

"We all saw something that was wrong and decided to do something to try to fix it. We weren't too old, too fat, or too anything else. We were at that place in time, and we did what we believed needed to be done. I remember someone asking once, 'What do you call someone who when faced with a fearful situation does nothing?' The answer was 'civilized.' "

"Well damn it, we've become too civilized if that's true," Hank said.

"I understand," Dave said, "but I am here to tell you—NO MORE. You pulled it off this time, but it's the last time, agreed?" He looked at them; they looked at each other. Hank and Doc nodded.

"Then, it's over," Dave said.

The three men went back into the first classroom where the rest of the team was still located. "Is everyone finished?" Dave asked. They nodded.

"Good. Mr. Smith, would you please collect all tablets, scrap paper, and notes?" Smith, the unidentified individual who accompanied Dave, collected everything as instructed.

"Ladies and gentlemen, from the moment I walk out of this room, this subject is closed. It will not be discussed between yourselves or with anyone else. No mention of it will be made in writing or in any other medium, including audio or videotaping."

"Please understand, Mr. Smith or one of his associates may at any time legally search your home, business, or safe deposit boxes with a Federal court order."

"If any one of you violates these instructions, all of you will suffer because of it. Do you understand?" he asked. Everyone nodded.

"This incident never occurred, agreed?" They nodded.

"It did not happen, you were not a part of it, and you have no knowledge or opinion on any phases of it, agreed?" They nodded.

"Some of you have taken human life," Dave continued. "Some of you violated laws and oaths you were sworn to uphold. All of you are guilty of violating various laws of both this country and Mexico."

He looked around the table into the eyes of each person there. "It is noted that there was significance to your motivation. Additionally, these were serious crimes against humanity that you chose to intervene in and stop. Lastly, since this operation was conducted successfully and based on your willingness to cooperate, all records of this incident will be sealed and all charges placed in abeyance."

"This arrangement is conditional on this incident simply going away. If it comes out, the deal is off. I do not want to see anyone on Oprah or CNN. Agreed?" They nodded.

"As you exit, please pick up a packet from Mr. Smith. Read the instructions inside carefully and comply with them exactly. Are there any further questions?" There were none.

"Then ladies and gentlemen, let me ask you to return to your normal lives now. I congratulate you on a successful mission, and I compliment you. But, it never happened, and it is never to be discussed again."

Slowly, they began to file out of the room. Each stopped to shake hands with Hank and Doc. Several hugs were exchanged and a few simply said, "See ya."

Then as each passed Mr. Smith, they were handed a thick envelope and went out the door, back to their normal lives.

When they were all gone, except for Doc, Warlord, and Hank, Dave looked at Smith and nodded his head. Smith collected the rest of the material and went to the car where he waited for Dave.

"You know," Dave said, as he untied the knot of his tie and sat down, "you were lucky."

"No," Hank said. "We were not lucky; we were used. We were used by this government to do what they couldn't or wouldn't do—what they simply didn't have the balls to do."

Dave looked at Hank for a long moment and said, "So, would you do it again?"

Doc looked up, but Dave was still focused on Hank. "Major, would you do it again?"

"David," Doc said, "cut the bullshit and get to the point."

"That is the point, damn it," he said leaning forward. "Would you do it again?"

Doc looked at him sternly and said, "Presented with the same situation and the same options, yes. I believe we all would. I don't think we could live with ourselves if we didn't."

Dave smiled and sat back. "I thought so." Then, he stood up and went to the chalkboard. He drew some boxes and interconnecting lines and then turned to face them.

"Gentlemen, we are not having this conversation and it never occurred, agreed?" They nodded.

"Your operation was a good one, but the scope was too limited and your mission too restricted," he began. "This government has been aware of this specific threat for some time. Unfortunately, there is no conventional tool they could use to counteract it. We can become that tool."

"What do you mean, WE?" Hank asked. Doc thought he knew the answer.

"We means, we. You, some specific members of your team, and me," Dave said. "We have some similar operations already identified. They are missions designed to recover individuals taken and held against their will. Operations designed to target and cripple or destroy a specific threat. We want to recycle resources from that threat into the ongoing battle to destroy that threat. Interested?"

Doc smirked; he was right.

"Why should we be?" Hank asked sullenly.

"Because, you already have been," Dave snapped. "Look, you did something unique. You took a bunch of old farts that had been out of the picture for a long time and made it work. You proved that guys like you and me can still perform. You proved that sometimes the best person for the job is the one who is least obvious."

"Your people are anonymous," Dave continued. "You guys are not Mr. and Mrs. America; you're just common folks. You're grandpas, moms, and dads. You are not super heroes, but you are caring human beings. You are willing to say 'Enough is enough—It stops here, and I'm stopping it.' "

"You're ordinary people who did something extraordinary," Dave said with meaning. "In a minimum amount of time and with damn few resources, you located personnel as well as developed and executed a complex and multi-faceted mission plan that involved high risk and short duration. You did it successfully and without drawing attention to yourselves or the government. What do you think you could you do with some help? Now, are you interested?" he said, smiling.

Doc looked at Warlord and smiled. Hank, however, wasn't smiling.

Dave went back to the board and pointed. "This is me; this is you. I am a shadow, and you don't exist. None of our names will be listed on any documents or found in any computer. I am the liaison, the only point of contact to you. All information dealing with this last operation is not just sealed; it has been collected and will be destroyed."

"I doubt that it's necessary, but I have taken the precaution of preparing foolproof cover stories. They are complete with witnesses who will swear to the fact each and every one of your people was located a thousand miles away from the El Paso area during the timeframes involved in this operation. If they do go to the press, we'll discredit them immediately."

"By the way, this is for you," Dave said as he pitched the sack containing the money envelopes Doc and Hank had given him. By my figures, there's approximately $560,000 in there. The envelopes that Smith gave your people each contained $100,000, plus instructions to invest in a special mutual fund called Mari-time Mutual. We control it; it's performing very well, and the dividends are not taxable."

"I know you well enough," he said, looking directly at Doc, "to know you have some money rat-holed from this operation and probably some contraband too. Don't bother to deny it."

Doc started to protest but then shut up.

"Keep it for operating expenses; if you need more, let me know," Dave said smiling. "Boys, are we in business?"

Doc looked at Warlord and they smiled.

Hank shook his head. "I'm not. Look, we did what we needed to do. I'm not inclined to become part of some government operation, been there—done that. I'm sorry, but consider me out of it. Doc, you guys do your thing; I'll wait outside." With that, Hank picked up his gear and started out the door.

"Hold on Hank," Doc said. "Won't you even think about it?"

"Doc, I'm done. You and Warlord have my blessing; watch your back Bubba." The two men hugged, and then Hank walked out and closed the door behind him.

"Well, I didn't see that coming," Blaine said. "This changes some things."

"It doesn't have to," Doc said. "Hank doesn't want to play anymore. Okay that's his call, but it doesn't mean we can't. He'll be sorely missed, but we can make this work. You collect the intelligence and keep us covered. I pick the team, and I run the operations. We plan the missions and approve them. We don't become a strike force for spooks and bureaucrats."

"Agreed," Dave said as they all shook hands. "You're on vacation the next three weeks. On the first of the month, I want the two of you in my office in Palm Springs." Dave said, as he pulled two envelopes from his pocket. "Here are the tickets; there will be a limousine waiting for you outside the airport.

"By the way, these are also yours," he said, as he handed each of them a large envelope. The envelopes contained certificates of investments in Maritime Mutual, in each of their names, in the amount of $100,000 and bank deposit books with each of Doc's grandchildren's names, each with a balance listed at $25,000. I have one for Hank too; I'll give it to him on the way out."

"Should anything go wrong, your families are taken care of," Dave said with a slow smile. "There will be a life insurance policy for four million dollars payable in full should you get whacked on an operation and complete medical insurance to cover any injuries for everyone on an op."

"David," Doc said, "for once in my life, I don't know what to say."

"For right now, don't say anything. Take time off, recover, and relax. Be in my office in Palm Springs on the first of February. Oh here," Dave said, almost as an afterthought, "Take the girls away for the weekend."

He pitched each of them another envelope, a larger one this time. Inside were plane tickets to Cozumel, hotel reservations which were marked pre-paid and what looked to be $10,000 in cash. "Marcia and I are flying down there too; we need to relax ourselves—see ya Saturday. We'll stay a couple of days and then get out of your hair." Dave saluted and left without another word. Doc returned the salute and watched him leave.

Doc erased the board, turned off the coffeepot, and locked the doors on the way out. Hank was waiting. Never one for many words he said simply, "Keep your powder dry;" as they shook hands and then he left. Doc rode back with Warlord. He liked the idea of working with Dave again. He was the best leader Doc ever worked for, military or civilian.

Doc turned to Warlord and said, "What do you think about this?"

Warlord thought for a moment before responding. "What do I think about it? Well, I think that we stomped the hell out of some bad guys. We rescued some innocent good guys. We identified some screwed up, confused guys. You and your guys ran 4.5 clicks through the Mexican desert and got shot at for free. Now, our people have been given something they've earned."

"We have a chance to do something we believe in. We know our families are taken care of and money will never again be a problem for either of us. We leave for Cozumel tomorrow on a vacation we both need with our wives. Not only is it paid for, but we have $10,000 in spending money. What a deal."

Doc could always count on Warlord to give a perspective; sometimes, it was even the right one. Doc leaned back and pulled one of Val Richards' cigars from his jacket pocket.

"Pull over," he said to Warlord. They walked to the edge of a little lake, no more than three acres in size. Doc unwrapped the cigar, bit off the tip, and spit it on the ground. He struck a match and got the cigar going well. Doc passed it to his son. They sat down and watched the sunset reflect on the water. Doc pulled his flask from his coat and quoted a toast.

"To us and those like us," Doc said.

"Damn few left," Warlord responded.

They each took a swig in turn. Warlord handed Doc the cigar. Doc took a puff on the cigar, smiled, and then quietly said, "Hoo Rah."

Team Dossiers

Harry Devlin, Call Sign: Hank
Age: 52
Current location: Presidio, TX
Physicals: White, Male, 5'10" blond/blue

Military: Enlisted 10 March 1968, Basic Military Training—Lackland AFB, TX—Jun 1967, Security Police.

Awards and Decorations: Presidential Unit Citation with One Device, Joint Military Unit Award, Air Force Outstanding Unit Award with Six Devices, Air Reserve Forces Meritorious Service Medal, Air Force Good Conduct Medal with One Device, Air Force Longevity Service Award with Five Devices, National Defense Service Medal with One Device, Small Arms Expert Marksmanship Ribbon with Device.

Background: Air Force Security Police Investigations 10 years, Air Force Reserve 10 years.

Specialties: Strong mechanical and computer background. All military personnel transports including Hum Vee, Deuce and a Half, Six-packs, sedans, etc. also licensed for motorcycle.

Weapons: Qualified expert USAF on Colt M-16 rifle and M-203 configuration, Smith-Wesson .38 caliber K-38 Combat Masterpiece pistol, Beretta 9mm M-9 semi-automatic pistol. Preferred personal weapons: Weatherby bolt action 300 Magnum Rifle with 3-9 Bushnell scope, Ruger Mini-14 .223 caliber semi-automatic rifle, Colt .357 Lawman with four inch barrel, Colt Detective Special with 2 inch barrel and 80 lb. PSI Compound Bow.

STATUS: ACTIVE (Intelligence/Chief of the Command Center)

*****

John Roberts, Call Sign: Warlord
Age: 28
Current location: Baton Rouge, LA
Physicals: White, Male, 5'10", Red/hazel

Military: First Enlistment Louisiana Army National Guard 19 July 1989, Basic Military Training, Fort Sill OK – July 1989 Specialties – Communications (31V) and Infantry (11B) Transportation (88M). Second Enlistment United States Army 4 Feb 1995 Basic Military Training, Fort Knox KY. Feb 1995 Specialty Tanker (19K) Third Enlistment Louisiana National Guard 31 Dec 97 Specialty Communications (31U).

Awards and Decorations: Army Commendation Medal, Army Achievement Medal, Southwest Asia Service Medal with One Device, Army Good Conduct Medal with Once Device, National Defense Medal with One Device, Army Service Medal, National Guard Achievement Medal, Infantry Cord, Small Arms Expert (pistol, rifle, M-60, M-203, M-2, .50 Caliber Machine Gun, M-240, Grenades), Armorer qualified, Expert Driver's Badge (Driver/Track-M-1A1 Abrams Tank, M-113s, Bulldozer) and the Zaire Paratrooper Medal.

Background: US Army and Louisiana National Guard—total of 8 ½ years. Upon honorable discharge held four military job specialties (MOSs): 31 Victor—Communication Specialist, 11 Bravo—Infantry Specialist, 88 Mike—transportation Specialist, 19 Kilo—'Tanker Gawd' (On one occasion reports having a M1A1 Full Track Combat Heavy Main Battle Tank with 120mm Main Gun clocked at 70 mph. On another had the Tank airborne with the tracks were five feet off the ground. Of course, he broke the track, broke the road wheel arm, stripped the tension bar, snapped two torsion bars and ripped a sprocket off.)

Vehicles: Hum Vee, a Tank Transport called a H.E.T., Jeep, Deuce and a half, 5 ton, scrapper, bulldozer, front-end loader, 113s known as Armored Personnel Carriers or A.P.C.s, and the M-1 A1 Full Track Combat Heavy 120mm Main Battle Tank (Abrams).

Specialties: Can operate any type of vehicle with four wheels or tracks. Strong communications background with expertise in radio equipment modification/repair and Land Navigation. Repel and jump qualified. Black Belt in Karate and instructor qualified for several martial arts weapons, including his own non-Kendo version for combat use of the samurai sword. Combat Life Saver qualified.

Weapons: Qualified expert on M-203 (a combination weapon consisting of and M-16 with a single shot 40 mm grenade launcher mounted underneath, the Ma Deuce or M-2 .50 caliber heavy machine gun, 7.62 mm M-60 machine gun and its tank mounted version the M-240, M-16 .223 caliber rifle, Beretta 9 mm M-9 piston, Model 1911 .45 caliber pistol, and a variety of shoulder and tripod mounted missiles to include the LAWs (Light Anti-tank Weapon), AT-4s, and the Dragon. Preferred personal weapons: Ruger Mini-14 .223 semi-automatic rifle with folding assault stock, 12-gauge assault pump shotgun, habitually carries a 14 shot Para Ordnance .45 caliber pistol and a customized model 1911

.45 called *The Warlord*. Minimally he's known to carry an A.G. Russell Sting A-1, a Benchmade Combat Switchblade and either a Cold Steel Trail Master Bowie or SRK Rescue knife.

STATUS: ACTIVE (Blue Team Leader)

*****

Derrick Perce, Call Sign: Mongo
Age: 50
Current location: Baton Rouge, LA
Physicals: White, Male, 5' 10, Brown/Brown

Military: USAF veteran, primary hostage negotiator for only USAF Security Police Tactical Neutralization Team to have a negotiation component of non-security police personnel. These negotiators were cross-trained in repelling, squad movement and tactics.

Weapons: Qualified expert on M-16, K-38 and M-12 shotgun. Personal preferred weapons: Favors a modified Model 1100 Remington Shotgun and a Colt Gold Cup National Match, Model 1911 .45 caliber pistol.

STATUS: ACTIVE (Blue Team Member)

*****

Jay Moore, Call Sign: Whisper
Age: 51
Current location: unknown
Physicals: Black, Male, 6'1", Black/Brown

Military: Former USAF Security Policeman following highly decorated tours of duty in Vietnam and Clark Air Base, Republic of the Philippines; was selected for special duty at the Pentagon.

Specialties: Martial arts, stealth and Hand-to-Hand Combat. This was the man that introduced me to Karate while I was stationed in the Philippines. At that time, he was single and had devoted himself to the studies of different styles of martial arts. He held multiple black belts and was qualified to instruct in several styles. He and I had developed the concept of foot patrols in the cantonment area at Clark. Our missions were primarily anti-theft and drug interdiction. We carried no communications and were, for all intents and purposes, autonomous once we were posted.

Weapons: Qualified expert on all personnel weapons in the Security Police inventory. Preferred personal weapons: favored a .22 caliber Ruger Mark II with internal silencer, a Randall Model 1 fighting knife, nunchucka and escrima sticks (used by Philippine stick fighters).

STATUS: INACTIVE

*****

Danny Bookman, Call Sign: Bush Hog
Age: 33
Current location: Anchorage, AK
Physicals: Hispanic, Male, 5'10", Brown/ Brown

Military: None
Background: Martial arts instructor in Aikido and Tae Kwon Do. Tournament class fighter. Outdoors man, avid hunter and big game guide in the North Country. Cold weather survival expert.
Weapons: Favors a modified Ruger Mini-14 Rifle with scope and see-through mounts and a Model 92 F, 9mm Beretta.

STATUS: ACTIVE (Red Team Member)

*****

Donnie Three Wolves, Call Sign: Psycho
Age: 35
Current location: Baton Rouge, LA
Physicals: American Indian, Male, 6', Black/Brown

Military: Former Navy Seal involved in repeated insertions in hostile environments for specialized Counterterrorist Team actions (termed by the government as Low Intensity Assignments), formerly assigned to the Special Warfare Group.
Awards and Decorations: Due to the fact that the majority of his career was spent in covert operations conducted with the territorial limits of other countries, his awards and decorations are classified.
Specialties: Communications, explosives, jungle operations and Land Navigation.

Weapons: Qualified expert with all weapons as required by Department of the Navy. Favors a Bennelli 12-gauge shotgun and a Sig Saur .45-caliber pistol loaded with Carbon ammunition.

STATUS: ACTIVE (Red Team Member)

*****

B.J. Garrett, Call Sign: Top Eye
Age: 57
Current location: Houston, TX
Physicals: White, Male, 6', Red/Brown

Military: Although coming from a military oriented family, he did not enlist until 30 Nov 1991. As a new member of the USAF Reserve he attended Officer Training School – Lackland AFB, TX as a Medical Officer, in the Biomedical Services Corps. Selected to attend the Air Force Top Eye Competition at Kingsley Field Klamath Falls Oregon – Mar 1995. During this assignment, flew as the back seater of an F-16 (a specially modified trainer) in that competition. In 1995 served as a backup doctor for the Space Shuttle Endeavor's launch. He has completed the following Professional Military Education Courses: Junior Officer Leadership Training, Squadron Officer's School and Air Command and Staff College.

Background: Currently a Major in the USAF Reserve assigned to the 917 Medical Squadron. Holds the Air Force Achievement Medal, National Defense Medal, Small Arms Expert with Device, Air Force Longevity Medal, and Outstanding Unit Citation. In civilian life was appointed to the Texas Optometry Board by the Governor of Texas (there are only six members representing over 3,000 Optometrists) held every office (including president) of the Pasadena School Board of Trustees, South Belt Chamber of Commerce, and Optimist Club and officer in the Harris County Optometric Society. Bachelors in Pharmacy from the University of Texas-1964 and Doctor of Optometry from the University of Houston in 1973. In high school was a triple letterman and maintains a commitment to physical health.

Specialties: CPR, Combat Medical Readiness Training 2, Buddy Care (a variety of medically oriented field expedient emergency procedures) and Desert Survival. Serious hunter and tracker.

Weapons: Qualified expert on M-16 rifle and M-9 pistol. Preferred personal weapons: Favors a Colt AR-15 the semi-automatic civilian version of M-16 rifle and Smith & Wesson Model 659 9mm pistol.

Notation: An unusual man with strong religious convictions and equally strong sense of duty. Perfectly capable of sending subordinates into harm's way, but would prefer to lead them himself. Possesses the training and abilities to purposely and with forethought engage, and/or kill an enemy if directed by proper authorities and lawful orders or if required by circumstances. However, does not possess the personal orientation to "cuss out" that same enemy. He's a good man, a good leader, and an excellent officer, a combination that is some-times difficult to find in today's military. He leads by example and operates under the philosophy "Take care of your people and the people will take care of the mission."

STATUS: ACTIVE (Chief of the M.A.S.H.)

$$*****$$

Gregg Paul, Call Sign: Reverend
Age: 50
Current location: Houston, TX
Physicals: White, Male, 6', Gray/Blue

Military: Enlisted USAF 1965 served active duty for eight and ½ years as a Communication Specialist, S.S.I.R. Top Secret Clearance with Cryptographic clearance. Joined USAFR in 1987. Served initially as Air Cargo Specialist, transferred to Reserve Recruiting Service in 1988, 1989 became NCOIC of Chaplain Services.

Specialties: Executive Protection and long range Sniper and Counter Sniper Interdiction. Skilled in rock climbing, repelling and photography.

Weapons: Qualified expert on the USAF's M-16 .223 caliber rifle, and the 9mm M-9 pistol. Preferred personal combat weapons: his pride and joy is a Stoner SR –25 Stoner .308, semi auto Counter Sniper Rifle fitted with Shepherd Rangefinder 6 X 14 scope. Scope had different adjustments and is specifically calibrated to the .308 round. At 100 yards there was almost same hole accuracy. He also likes the .50 caliber Barrett Counter Sniper Weapon. Carries two .40 caliber laser sighted handguns, one a duty size S&W Sigma and the other a Para Ordnance P12. Carried the Stoner bayonet and Benchmade AFCK (folder) with partial seriated edge.

STATUS: ACTIVE (Sniper Team Leader)

Lynn Rogers, Call Sign: Mountain Man
Age: 46
Current location: Shreveport, LA
Physicals: White Male, 6'2 ¾", Brown/Brown

Military: None
Background: While having no military experience, Rogers is a part time hunter and guide. Hunted and provided guide services to groups of hunters in this area and possesses extensive knowledge of land and people in south Texas and the northern Mexico area.

Specialties: Lineman for local power company, he has experience in dealing with high voltage electricity to include shutdowns and repairs of lines carrying high voltage. Exceptionally familiar with terrain, wildlife, and survival techniques for this area. Etc..

Weapons: Competent with variety of primitive and modern weapons to include: bow, sling, throwing tomahawk, black powder as well as conventional rifles, hand and shotguns. Preferred personal combat weapons: Favors Russian 7.62x39mm SKS rifle with a 30-round magazine and Ruger Model 89, 9mm pistol also with a30-round magazine. Habitually carries massive Ruana Fighting Bowie Knife that matches his 6-foot two-inch 260-pound frame.

STATUS: ACTIVE (Sniper Spotter)

*****

David Dillon, Call Sign: Cobra Innkeeper
Age: 49
Current location: Killeen, TX
Physicals: White, Male, 5'9", Brown/Blue

Military: 23 years as an Army Aviator, retired as a Chief Warrant Officer 4, Master Army Aviator. Qualified in the UH-1 C/M, UH-60, AH-1 G, S Mod/Prod, AH-64A, OH-58A/C, just over 4,000 hours of total flight time. (1,500 hours of night flight operations using the ANVIS-6 NVG and/or the AH-64 PNVS (pilot night vision system) 1,000 hours combat and 1,000 hours in the AH-64A). Specialist in planning and executing night deep attack missions. Also is qualified in the German Army BO-105 and PH-1.

Awards and Decorations: Master Army Aviator and Aviation Safety Officer, Four Meritorious Service Medals, Fifteen Air Medals w/V device for Valor, Army Commendation Medal, Army Achievement Medal and various service ribbons and additional medals.

Background: Assigned to 129th Assault Helicopter, Republic of Vietnam as a Gun Platoon Pilot and Aircraft Commander –1971. Assigned to A Troop, 7th Squadron, 17th Cavalry, Fort Hood, TX as Aircraft Commander and Unit Safety Officer–1977. Assigned to B Co, 3rd Aviation Battalion Combat, 3rd Infantry Division, Federal Republic of Germany as Aircraft Commander, Assistant Operations Officer, and Aviation Life Support Officer –1979. Assigned to Aviation Prepotency Office, Fort Rucker, AL as the Aviation Warrant Officer Systems Manager – 1981. Assigned to 6th Aviation Brigade Air Combat, Fort Hood, TX as Brigade Safety Officer and Aircraft Commander – 1986. Assigned to Aviation Brigade 5th Infantry Division, Fort Polk – 1990. Retired US Army Warrant Officer 4 1993. Flew UH-1C/M Gunships, AH-1 G/S Cobras, AH-64A Apache Attack Helicopter, and UH-60 Black Hawks involved in the creation, development and implementation of the Attack Helicopter Concept. Special notation also qualified in BO-105 and PH-1 German Attack Helicopters.

Special Notation: I have known Dave for 2 years and have worked with him on several projects. He is extremely security minded and mission oriented. If anyone can plan the airside of this operation, he can.

Weapons: Qualified on all Army Aerial Weapons systems to include: the UH- C/M, Cobra, Apache, and Ph-1. Preferred personal combat weapons: Favors short version of the M-16 known, as the GAU will accept civilian semi-automatic version the CAR 15 and Glock 9mm. He carries the Marine Corps Kabar knife attached to his survival vest, a Buck Folding Hunter in his flight suit; a second Kabar strapped to his right leg.

STATUS: ACTIVE (Helicopter Pilot)

*****

William S. Bracken, Call Sign: Leprechaun
Age: 35
Current location: Abita Springs, LA
Physicals: White, Male, 5' 10" Black/Blue

Military: He enlisted in the U.S. Navy in 1982, serving in Anti-Submarine Warfare. In 1984, he transferred to the U.S. Army with a full scholarship as an R.0.T.C. cadet. He graduated in 1987 and received his commission. He attended

Basic Aviation Training at Ft. Rucker, AL., and tracked into piloting the UH – 1 Huey and OH-58 Scout. Attended Advanced Aviation Officer Course during Desert Storm. Transferred to the Louisiana National Guard in 1992 and transitioned to UH-60, Blackhawk in 1997.

Currently is S-3 Training Officer for the State Aviation Command stationed at Jackson Barracks, New Orleans and is responsible for all joint command and service exercises. Currently the longest serving Aviation Command Officer in the Louisiana National Guard.

Awards and Decorations: Army Achievement Medal with 1 device, Army Commendation with 1 device, Meritorious Service, Humanitarian Service Medal.

Weapons: Qualified on all required flight officer weapons and systems for Black Hawks. Preferred personal combat weapons: favors Russian 7.62 X 39 SKS rifle and M-9 Beretta 9mm pistol.

STATUS: ACTIVE (Helicopter Pilot)

*****

Jean Bracken, Call Sign: Nightingale
Age 34
Current location: Abita Springs, La
Physicals: White, Female, 5'3" Brown/Green

Military: Army ROTC Cadet Officer. Served with honors and decorated for service.

Specialties: Registered Nurse with Master prepared. Certified trauma nurse and instructing member of the nursing faculty at one of Louisiana's leading universities.

STATUS: ACTIVE (Nurse and primary backup for Top Eye and second in command of the M.A.S.H.)

*****

Steve Ingles, Call Sign: Domino
Age: 45
Current location: unknown
Physicals: White, Male, 6', Brown/Blue

Background/ Military: USAF Security Police Specialist. Member of one of the earliest Tactical Neutralization Teams. Served with Doc from 1977-79.

Specialties: Scout and point man. Stealth entry and sentry removal. Studied martial arts during our tour together, excellent student. Repel qualified, totally fearless.

Weapons: Qualified expert with all required Security Police weapons. Preferred personal combat weapons: GAU or CAR 15 .223 caliber rifle, 9mm or .40 caliber high-capacity handgun, and USMC Kabar Combat Knife.

STATUS: INACTIVE

*****

Rich Leonard, Call Sign: 2nd Chance
Age 55
Current location: Shreveport, LA
Physicals: White, Male, 5'8" Brown/Brown

Military: Enlisted USAF in 1968 and served as a Combat Illustrator until medically retired.

Background: USAF and USAFR medically retired communications veteran with top-secret clearance. Had heart transplant almost three years ago and is in better shape at 55 than he was at 45.

Awards and Decorations: Normal unit and individual citations, qualified expert in small arms.

Specialties: Communications, photography, repelling and martial arts. Notation: Outstanding sketch artist.

Weapons: Qualified expert on both M-16 .223 caliber rifle and 9mm M-9 pistol.

Preferred personal combat weapons: Favors a sawed-off and modified 12-gauge pump shotgun as primary weapon and Sig Saur Model P226, 9mm handgun. Carries Benchmade butterfly knife with 6-inch blade and USMC Kabar.

STATUS: ACTIVE (Blue Feather Foundation)

*****

<u>T.K. George</u>, Call Sign: The Wizard
Age 68
Current location: Haughton, LA
Physicals: White, Male, Gray/Blue

Military: Enlisted in the Air Force in 1948. He served as a Logistics Specialist and in the Recruiting Service, retiring as a Senior Master Sergeant. Upon completion of military service, he returned to Centenary College and in just two years held a BA in Business. Subsequently he worked as sales manager for an electronics firm before forming his own company supplying environmental services for industries. In better physical condition that most men 20 years younger, he runs an average of four miles a day, averages at least a couple of half marathons a year, in addition to being an accomplished snow skier, martial arts instructor, and a volunteer Reserve Parish Deputy Sheriff.

Awards and Decorations: Simply put, if the Air Force could award it, The Wizard earned it.

Specialties: E.M.T. qualified, criminal investigations and rape trauma experience for both military and civilian police agencies.

Weapons: Qualified expert on all USAF required weapons at the time. Preferred personal combat weapons: Favors modified 12-gauge pump shot gun as primary weapon with 9mm high-capacity handgun and a .38 caliber snub-nosed back-up revolver.

STATUS: ACTIVE (Blue Feather Foundation)

*****

<u>Frank La Borde</u>, Call Sign: Jarhead
Age: 38
Current location: Shreveport, LA
Physicals: White, Male, 5'8", Brown/Brown

Military: Enlisted U.S.M.C. – 1976 completed basic training at San Diego, CA.

Completed additional training Fire Direction Control, Ft. Sill, OK; Field Artillery and Fire Command, Camp Jejune, NC; Field Artillery, Okinawa, Japan; Recruiter Training, San Diego, CA. Served as Operations Chief, Okinawa, Japan; Fire Direction Officer, Quantico, VA; Survey Specialist, Ft. Sill, OK; Recruiter, Joplin MO, Texarkana, TX; Battery Operations Chief, Camp Pendleton, CA; Platoon Sgt., Camp Pendleton, CA; Platoon Sergeant, Baton Rouge,

LA; NCOIC Recruiting, Alexandria, LA, Shreveport, LA and Career Retraining, Leesburg, VA.

Awards and Decorations: Navy Achievement Medal, Navy Unit Commendation with one device, Meritorious Unit Commendation with three devices, Good Conduct Medal with five devices, National Defense Medal with one device, Overseas Ribbon, Overseas Deployment Ribbon with one device, Certificate of Commendation with six devices, Meritorious Medal with six devices.

Specialties: Long Range Recon Patrol

Weapons: Qualified on all squad weapons as required by Corps. Preferred personal combat weapons: Russian 7.62x39 SKS rifle and 9mm Ruger P85 pistol coupled with Marine Corps Kabar knife.

STATUS: ACTIVE (Blue Team Member)

*****

David La Borde, Call Sign: Squirrel
Age: 36
Current location: Marksville, LA
Physicals: White Male, 5'8", Brown/Brown

Military: Enlisted U.S. Army 10 Oct 1978, served as Engineer Equipment Mechanic and Senior Mechanic. Ordered to Active Military Service during Desert Storm. Service with Company B 527th Engineering Battalion (Combat Heavy) Southwest Asia. Returned to Fort Polk, LA at the end of hostilities. Currently assigned Company B 769 Engineering Battalion (Combat Heavy) Louisiana Army National Guard. Served during the Defense of Saudi Arabia and Liberation and Defense of Kuwait campaigns.

Awards and Decorations: National Defense Service Medal with one device, Army Achievement Medal, ARCTOR, Army AAM, ARCAM, NCO Professional Development Ribbon, Southwest Asia Service Medal, BSS with two devices, ALB, Kuwait Liberation medal, Humanitarian Service Medal, AAM with three devices, Army Superior Unit Award, Louisiana State Awards – LA General Excellence Medal, LA Longevity Medal, 1st Fluor Deles LA General Excellence Award, LA Emergency Service Ribbon, LA Commendation Medal, LA War Cross.

Specialties: Infantry Squad Tactics and Scout, Land Navigation, Camouflage and Mechanized Vehicle Maintenance and Repair. Avid hunter and expert tracker.

Weapons: Qualified expert with M-60 Machine Gun, M-16 .223 rifle and M-9 Beretta 9mm pistol. Preferred personal combat weapons: Russian 7.62x 39 SKS rifle, .45 caliber pistol and M-9 bayonet.

STATUS: ACTIVE (Door Gunner)

*****

Mike Staten, Call Sign: The Dago
Age 40
Current location: Unknown
Physicals: White, Male, 5' 9" Brown/Brown

Military: Enlisted USAF Security Police- After spending time in Security Police rolled over to QC and was assigned duties with Mongo.

Specialties: Qualified in repelling, Hostage Negotiations (member of the only Hostage Negotiator Team with total integration with Tactical Neutralization Team. Martial Arts Assistant Instructor and Brown Belt in Okinawan Karate.

Weapons: 4in. Ruger .357 magnum, 6.5 Carcano "known as the Dago Derringer," specialty weapon he describes as "Exhibit A," Japanese 7.65 Rifle. Here again, was a brother that had been lost to time. Lost but remembered, lost but to be found one day.

STATUS: INACTIVE

*****

Doc Roberts, Call Sign: TAC Leader
Age: 50
Current location: Houston, TX
Physicals: White, Male, 5'10", Red/Brown

Military: Enlisted 28 May 1969, United States Air Force, Basic Military Training – Lackland AFB TX- Jun 1969, Security Police Tech School – Lackland AFB TX – July 1969 (Honor Graduate), Special Weapons and Tactics Training, North Memphis, TN Police Department – 1978, Air Force Tactical Neutralization Training – Camp Bullis, TX – 1979. Enlisted 24 May 1984, USAF Reserve Security Police Force, 1986 reassigned to USAFR Office of Social Actions –NCOIC Drugs & Alcohol, 1992 reassigned to First Sergeant

Career Field. Current grade, Master Sergeant. Current assignment First Sergeant AFSC 8F000.

Awards and Decorations: Meritorious Service Medal with One Device, Armed Forces Meritorious Service Medal with Three Devices, Air Force Commendation Medal, Presidential Unit Citation, Air Force Outstanding Unit Award with Two Devices, Air Force Longevity Service Award with Five Devices, National Defense Service Medal with One Device, Small Arms Expert Marksmanship Ribbon with Device. Outstanding Security Policeman-Law Enforcement Specialist for Clark AB, Philippines, 13th Air Force, and Pacific Air Command (PACAF) 1975. Outstanding Security Policeman-Law Enforcement Specialist for Blytheville AFB, AR and 2nd Air Force 1977. Winner: Col. John Martin Award – Daughters of the American Colonist, Department of Defense Thomas Jefferson Award.

Background: Air Force Security Policeman with security and law enforcement experience. Worked as Desk Sergeant and Comm. Plotter, Base Patrolman, Security Response Team member and Leader, Security Police Investigations, Crime Prevention Specialist, Commander of Tactical Neutralization Team (Counterterrorism Team).

Specialties: Martial Arts Instructor with over twenty-three years of teaching experience. Hand-to-hand combat instructor for military and civilian police agency. Proficient with Sai, chucks, Bo staff, longbow and sword. SCUBA certified Instructor, Repelling Master Instructor – only person known to have repelled from a hot air balloon. Special Weapons and Tactics Instructor, assisted in development, training and outfitted of several such teams for military and civilian police agencies. Notation: Has significant experience in printing, photography and darkroom techniques, rock climbing, parachuting, canoeing, cross-country and downhill skiing, camping and wilderness survival.

Weapons: Qualified expert with M-1 Grande 30.06 caliber rifle, M-16 .223 rifle, M-203 (M-16 and 40mm grenade launcher combination weapon), 12-gauge riot gun, K-38 Smith & Wesson .38 caliber pistol, M-9 Beretta 9mm pistol, Model 1911 .45 caliber pistol, Model 70 Winchester Heavy Barreled .308 caliber Sniper/Counter Sniper Weapon, and 37mm Z Gun (Tear Gas Deployment Weapon). Preferred personal combat weapons: Assault Rifle – favors a GAU, CAR 15 or Ruger Mini-14 .223 caliber rifles. Shotgun – favors modified Mossberg Model 590 12-gauge shotgun for tactical operations or modified and sawed off 12-gauge pump with pistol grip for entry procedures. Handgun – habitually carries custom .45 caliber, 14 shot pistol called "The Widow Maker," with either modified Colt Model 1911 .45 caliber or Ruger Model P-85 9mm with 15 and 30-round magazines or Browning .40 caliber High Power for back up. Also carries one of several AMT Back Up pistols (.45 or .380 caliber) in belt or ankle holster. Prefers the Crain Life Support System X as main combat knife however also known to use a variety of others including the Randall Model –1, the Al Mar Warrior, as well as Benchmade Combat Auto Opener. Carries Japanese style Wakizashi Sword with two-handed grip in over-the-shoulder holster attached to L.B.E.

STATUS: ACTIVE (TAC Leader)

List of Contributors

Editing and continuity

Pamela D. Anderson, M.Ed.—Pam has a Master's Degree in Counselor Education and a Bachelor's Degree in Christian Education. She works full time with her husband Bob Anderson, and oversees the publishing and marketing for their company Back to Basics for Success, LLC.

Kim Kuri—A new friend and an extremely valuable resource who has worked graciously and diligently for Doc and the Team.

Technical guidance concerning intelligence operations and mission planning and editing assistance

David Day—CW4, U.S. Army (Ret). He retired as a Chief Warrant Officer 4, Master Army Aviator after 23 years. Qualified in the UH-1 C/M, UH-60, AH-1 G, S Mod/Prod, AH-64A, OH-58A/C, just over 4,000 hours of total flight time, 1,500 hours of night flight operations, 1,000 hours combat and 1,000 hours in the AH-64A. A specialist in planning and executing night deep attack missions.

William S. Brannan, Col., U.S. Army National Guard, (Ret) and Michael D. Fortune, Col., AV, ARNG

Assistance in developing Team Dossiers

John R.S. Anderson, Roger Anderson, William S. Brannan, Jana Gautreaux, Denny Bascom, David Day, David Desselle, Frank Desselle, Dr. B.J. Garner, Paul Gregg, George King, Donny Morgan, Leonard Richards and Mike Stadelmaier.

About the Author

Bob Anderson
Author, Speaker, Trainer

Bob retired as a Chief Master Sergeant from the United States Air Force Reserve with over 32 years of service. His last military assignment was in Iraq for Operation Iraqi Freedom. He served as the Security Force Manager of the 732d Expeditionary Security Force Squadron, responsible for a 221 person squadron located throughout Iraq, which included two law enforcement detachments and 24 military working dog teams.

Previously, he served as the Command Chief Master Sergeant of the 147th Fighter Wing at Ellington Field, Texas Air National Guard. As a Reservist at Barksdale AFB, he served as the Security Force Manager of the 917th Security Force Squadron and as First Sergeant for both the 917th Security Force Squadron and 917th Medical Squadrons.

Earlier in Bob's Air Force career, he served 10 years on active duty. During that time he was a team commander (or TAC Leader) for one of the first Security Police Tactical Neutralization Teams. The threat of terrorism both domestic and abroad forced the USAF to deal with the increasing of "high risk" situations including anti-hijack operations, dangerous felons, and the protection of nuclear weapons, which could have included recapture and recovery operations. His team was the only one at that time that contained organic hostage negotiators.

He is a member of the Air Force Security Forces Association, Air Force Sergeants Association, Air Force Association, American Legion and Veterans of Foreign Wars.

Bob is a qualified rappel master and holds a 2nd degree black belt in karate. He and his wife Pamela reside in rural southern Missouri.

Bob speaks on various topics including survival, leadership, and military specific training. To inquire about having Bob speak at your next event, please visit www.BTB4Success.com.

Contact Bob Anderson to learn more about the
TAC Leader series or other books written by him at
www.BooksByBobAnderson.com.